AFTERWALKERS

TOM BECKER WON THE WATERSTONES
CHIDREN'S BOOK PRIZE FOR HIS FIRST
NOVEL, *DARKSIDE*, AGED 25. BORN
AND BROUGHT UP IN WEST LANCASHIRE,
HE NOW LIVES IN LONDON.

AFTERWALKERS

SCHOLASTIC

TOM BECKER

First published in the UK in 2014 by Scholastic Children's Books
An imprint of Scholastic Ltd
Euston House, 24 Eversholt Street
London, NW1 1DB, UK
Registered office: Westfield Road, Southam, Warwickshire, CV47 0RA
SCHOLASTIC and associated logos are trademarks and/or
registered trademarks of Scholastic Inc.

Text © Tom Becker, 2014

The right of Tom Becker to be identified as the author
of this work has been asserted by him.

ISBN 978 1 4071 0954 1

A CIP catalogue record for this book
is available from the British Library.

Printed and bound by CPI Group (UK) Ltd, Croydon, CR0 4YY
Papers used by Scholastic Children's Books are made
from wood grown in sustainable forests.

1 3 5 7 9 10 8 6 4 2

This is a work of fiction. Names, characters, places,
incidents and dialogues are products of the author's imagination
or are used fictitiously. Any resemblance to actual people, living
or dead, events or locals is entirely coincidental.

www.scholastic.co.uk/zone

For Jacob

". . .suddenly, he saw

a joyless woods leaning over

turbid and bloody water"

Beowulf

THE RESURRECTION MEN

On a bright and bitter winter morning in 1821, the village of Alderston came together to bury an angel. The mourners gathered on the sloping hillside behind the church, a flock of blackbirds fluttering in and around the gravestones. The women wore crepe dresses, black veils and jewellery fashioned from jet; the men sober mourning suits and top hats adorned with midnight-coloured ribbons. They were present to witness the burial of sixteen-year-old Kitty Hawkins, whose body had been found, bloated and blue-lipped, at the bottom of the pond in the woods nearby.

Tom McNally stood on the edge of the crowd, hat in hand, his large fingers toying nervously with the brim. He had known Kitty since childhood, had sat near her during lessons in the schoolhouse. Yet at that moment he felt awkward and uncomfortable, as though he was trespassing on other people's grief. Six feet tall and flame-haired, with shoulders broadened by hours working with shovel and pick on the family farm, Tom found it hard to blend into the background. When he was little his mother used to tell him that Viking blood ran through his veins – hot and bright, like molten iron. But today called for veins of ice, not fire.

News of Kitty's death had plunged Alderston into a cold pool of grief. Kitty had always been a kind girl with a ready smile, without a trace of malice or poison in her soul. All the families felt, to some degree, that they had lost a child. Now, as her coffin was lowered into the ground, the silence was pockmarked with choked sobs, rustling crepe and the flutter of ribbons in the wind. Kitty's father, John Hawkins, stood motionless by the graveside like a pale statue. Barely a year had passed since his wife, Laura, had died of consumption, and now he was sending his daughter to lie by her side. There were uncharitable whispers that he was cursed. As if he was not suffering enough without gossip rubbing salt in the wound.

When the gravedigger shuffled forward to fill the grave, Tom whispered a quick prayer under his breath. As shovelfuls of soil thudded down on to the coffin lid, the mourners began to melt away, keen to escape the cruel cold. Leaning upon one another, they headed for somewhere they could thaw their frozen hands and warm the chill from their bones.

Tom was turning to follow when he saw something that stopped him in his tracks. At the bottom of the hillside, beyond the graveyard wall, a man was leaning over the front gate of his house, coolly watching the proceedings. Even at this distance, Tom could sense malice and disdain rising off the man like steam. The rest of Alderston may have turned out for Kitty's funeral, but George Rathbone would not have been welcome. George Rathbone wasn't welcome anywhere.

"Cold day for it."

Startled, Tom looked round to find Kitty's father standing by his side. Although John Hawkins's face was haggard, his eyes were dry and his voice was steady. A proud, strong man, he would not allow himself to cry in public.

"That it is," Tom agreed. "Only going to get colder, too."

"In more ways than one. I need your help with something, Tom."

"Name it."

"I need you to protect my little girl."

Tom looked over towards the grave, which was now almost filled with fresh earth. "Kitty's dead, John," he said softly.

"Aye, I know. I watched them put her in the ground. And that's where I want her to stay." He was looking beyond Tom, his gaze fixed on the house at the bottom of the hill. "You've heard the same rumours I have. About the Resurrection Men."

Everyone had heard the rumours: wicked men stealing forth in the dead of night, cloaked in gin and armed with wooden shovels. They crept into cemeteries and dug up the coffins, stealing the bodies within to sell to medical schools desperate for fresh cadavers to work

3

on. A fortnight ago a tailor's grave in nearby Caxton had been dug up, its occupant vanishing into thin air. It was whispered that a gang of grave robbers had started work in the area. The Resurrection Men, some called them – and when they were abroad, not even the dead were safe.

Tom followed Hawkins's gaze down the hillside. "You must be joking!" he exclaimed. "Rathbone's a bad seed all right, but even he wouldn't stoop to grave-robbing."

"Nothing is beyond that man," Hawkins said grimly. "He is the devil in human form. I have urgent business with my lawyer in Manchester today – if I wait even one day, then I risk losing my home on top of my daughter. I will return tomorrow evening, but tonight I cannot watch over Kitty's grave. Will you stand in my place?"

Tom nodded. "Of course. No harm will come to Kitty whilst I have breath in my body. I promise."

"God bless you."

John Hawkins's voice cracked, threatening to betray him. He shook Tom's hand firmly and quickly walked away. An hour later a carriage rattled out of Alderston, a grim-faced Hawkins sitting in the back. Tom returned to his farm, where he spent the rest of the day pacing along the boundary of his family's land, restless for nightfall. Unwittingly his footsteps led him to the wood on the edge of the Moss. The skeletal trees were thronged with crows, who studied him with beady eyes as he strode along the hard, rutted earth. A bad odour hung in the air inside that wood – especially around the pond, with its dark history. Which made it all the more strange that Kitty had decided to walk there that Friday past, leaving her house and heading across the fields towards the dark blur of trees.

Later that night, when she still hadn't returned home, Tom had been part of the search party who had traced Kitty's footprints through the wood. The muddy ground at the pond's edge had preserved the terrible moment Kitty had slipped and fallen into the water, the smeared tracks of her stumbling pirouette. The icy pond would have ripped the breath from her chest, the tangle of her dress amongst the weeds wickedly pulling her down. No one would have been there to rescue her; nothing but shadows and timid animals to hear her splashes and cries for help. Such a dark, lonely place to die.

Tom shook his head. The vast sky above him was turning a deepening shade of blue. It was time to go. Leaving the wood behind him, he returned to the farmhouse and washed and changed his clothes, slipping a heavy cudgel inside his waistband before wishing his mother goodnight and leaving for town.

He headed for the Royal Oak first, wanting a drink before his long night's vigil. The pub sign creaked in the wind as he entered the crowded back bar. Kitty's death had lent the atmosphere a feverish edge – judging by the red faces and the spilled beer, some of the mourners had been drinking since the funeral. Tom plotted an awkward path through the throng towards the bar.

It was then, through the smoky fog, that he saw them.

George Rathbone, Lucas Forshaw and Silas Porter: a trio of villains with dirty fingernails and scabbed knuckles, who spent their days drinking and cursing, thieving and fighting. The three men sat apart from the others, as always, their heads bowed together as they supped on their bitter and spoke in low, conspiratorial tones. As Tom watched, George Rathbone looked up and caught his eye. He was a good-looking man, local girls admitted with a slight tremble in their voices, even if he was bad to the bone. There had only been one girl in Alderston with the nerve or naivety to smile at George Rathbone in the street, and brightly wish him a good day – but then Kitty Hawkins had slipped and fallen into the pond, and wouldn't be smiling at anyone any more.

Breaking away from Rathbone's steady gaze, Tom bought himself a half of beer and joined in conversation with the butcher and his lad. They chatted about the cold winter in prospect, and Tom allowed the butcher to buy him another half. It was tempting to stay in the drowsy warm, but the clock on the wall had ticked past nine and Tom knew it was time to go. He put his empty glass down on the bar.

"Leaving already?" George Rathbone's voice. He had cut silently through the crowded room like an icy draught and was leaning against the bar beside Tom, a pint glass gripped in his hand.

6

"Aye."

"It's blacker than tar and colder than a grave out," said Rathbone. "Why don't you stay in here, in the warm? I'll buy you another beer to keep your whistle wet."

"I don't need your money, George Rathbone," said Tom, careful to keep his voice steady. "Or your words of advice."

"That so?" Rathbone looked down at his hand, thoughtfully examining a scar on the back of his knuckle. "I saw you talking all hush hush with John Hawkins after the funeral today. Felt my ears burning a mile off."

"Nothing to do with you. John just wanted to make sure his girl stayed safe, that's all."

"Ever the protective father," said Rathbone, with bitter amusement. "Hawkins damn near exploded any time I raised my hat to Kitty in the street. Now she's dead it's the same. I'm not even allowed to come to the funeral and pay my respects."

"You made your own reputation," Tom said firmly. "No use blaming anyone else."

To Tom's surprise, Rathbone nodded. "Aye, perhaps you're right." He lifted his pint to his mouth and took a deep swig. "I heard it was you who found her in the pond. No way for a young girl to die. No way at all."

"It's a tragedy, all right," agreed Tom. "So the family don't need anything else upsetting them, George Rathbone. You stay out of that churchyard."

"Perhaps I will and perhaps I won't," said Rathbone. "Who knows where the night might lead me? John Hawkins might not think me fit to be around his girl, but then again, John Hawkins isn't here tonight, is he?"

Tom's cheeks flushed with anger. He could feel the molten iron in his veins begin to bubble.

"You listen to me," he said hotly. "Stay away from Kitty's grave, or so help me God. . . !"

Rathbone eyed him with cool amusement. "God won't help you. Not here. Take my advice: stay indoors tonight."

Tom strode out of the pub without a backwards glance, heading off into the night as the door closed behind him, sealing the warmth and the light and the laughter inside the building. He took several deep breaths before setting out up the hill towards the vast shadow of Alderston Church. The walk in the cold air soothed his boiling blood, and by the time he had reached the churchyard Tom was feeling calmer. He cut a path through the solemn forest of gravestones until he came to Kitty's. Her headstone was gleaming in the moonlight, her name freshly etched into the smooth marble.

As he looked down towards the road at the bottom of the hill, Tom heard a dog barking in the village. He found the noise strangely comforting. It had been easy to sound brave in the middle of a busy pub, surrounded by familiar faces. It was a different story out here, alone among the huddled gravestones and the whip and whistle of the wind. Something about Kitty's death was bothering Tom; an unsettling detail he had kept from her father. It had been Tom who had pulled Kitty's lifeless body from the pond and laid her down upon the bank. As the rest of the search party had gathered around them, the glow from their lanterns had played mischievously upon a silver band around the dead girl's finger. It was common knowledge that several men had been vying for Kitty's affections, though as far as Tom knew she had politely rejected all proposals of marriage. Except one, it now appeared. At the thought of another man holding Kitty in his arms, Tom was overcome by a guilty flush of jealousy. They had known each other since they were knee-high, and besides, everybody in Alderston loved Kitty Hawkins. . .

The distant barking stopped, the dog falling into an abrupt silence. Tom glanced around the cemetery. Lost in thought, he had strayed from Kitty's grave. The headstones around him were crumbling and covered in moss, reminders of long-forgotten townsfolk who had met their end centuries earlier. Above one grave a stone angel clasped his hands together in prayer, his eyes closed in rapturous bliss.

Somewhere in the darkness, a twig snapped.

"Who's there?" Tom called out. "Show yourself!"

He pulled the cudgel out from his belt, reassured by its hefty weight in his hand. There would be three of them creeping through the graveyard, he knew – George Rathbone wouldn't work alone. Tom didn't care that he was outnumbered. No matter how many

Resurrection Men came, they wouldn't get past him. He had promised John Hawkins.

Backing up the slope in the direction of Kitty's grave, Tom scanned the shadows for danger. The silence enveloped him so completely that he began to wonder whether he had imagined the twig snapping. A few nerves were understandable, given that he was surrounded by the dead. Stumbling backwards into something, Tom whirled round and raised his cudgel, only to find himself staring at another headstone. Tom's shoulders sagged with relief. He smiled.

It was then that a heavy weight smashed into the back of his head. Tom collapsed to his knees, the cudgel flying from his grasp as his world turned sickening cartwheels. Touching the back of his head, he saw through blurred eyes that his fingers were dark and sticky with blood. Dimly he realized that he had been hit with something flat and heavy. A shovel?

Footsteps padded up behind him; a pair of strong hands fastened around his neck like an iron collar and began to squeeze. Even as he fought for breath, Tom was consumed by the bitter realization that he was not going to be able to keep his promise to John Hawkins, and that Kitty would not rest easily that night – or ever again. Looking up towards the heavens as his assailant's fingers mercilessly wrenched the life from his lungs, Tom McNally saw the stars began to dim and fade before his eyes, and silently he cursed the name of George Rathbone as he died.

PART ONE

DIGGING

CHAPTER ONE

REMOVALS

Jamie awoke from a bad dream to find the world washing away before his eyes. Through the rain-smeared windscreen he could see a grey dawn unfolding ahead of him, the tail lights of the other vehicles dancing in and out of the gloom like red will-o'-the-wisps as they flew along the empty motorway. Jamie knew he had just escaped from a nightmare, even if he couldn't remember the exact contents of the dream; the taste of fear lingered on his tongue like sour mouthwash. He shivered.

"What's the matter, son? Someone stepped on your grave?"

A firm hand clapped Jamie's shoulder, and a bark of laughter rang around the front seat of the removal van. Sarge was in the driver's seat, tapping the steering wheel with his fingerless gloves as he guided the van along the slow lane. In the dawn's half-darkness Jamie's dad was little more than a silhouette with a shaven head and sandpaper cheeks. His bright blue eyes were always on the move, flicking up towards the rear-view mirror to check the motorway behind them. Sarge was a short man, barely taller than Jamie, but wiry and strong – like a lock pick, or a garrote.

Rain drummed impatient fingers on the van's roof as Jamie unfolded his limbs from their cramped sleeping position and sat up. As he stretched and rubbed his eyes, his elder brother Liam nudged him and offered him a half-empty can of Coke. Liam was sitting to Jamie's left, clad in a light blue tracksuit and trainers with a grey woollen hat pulled down over his head. He watched with amusement as Jamie thirstily drained his can.

"No, go on, finish it," Liam said. "I didn't want any more anyway."

"Thanks," said Jamie, wiping his mouth and handing his brother back the empty can.

A lorry thundered past them in the middle lane, giant wheels churning through the spray. The removal van hiccuped over a bump in the road, bringing a rattle of protest from the goods in the back. The family had been up late working; Sarge must have driven through the night. Jamie had wanted to stay awake with him, but all the carrying and loading had worn him out and his eyelids had quickly become too heavy to keep open. He liked the motorway best at night, when the lanes were quiet and the streetlamps flooded the van with regular bands of orange light. It was just them, long-distance truckers and deliverymen, horsemen with humming engines galloping through the darkness.

Jamie looked up at Liam. "Did you get any sleep?"

"What, with you snoring away like a chainsaw?" Liam grinned. "No chance."

"Hey!" protested Jamie. "I don't snore!"

"Yeah, right!"

Usually this kind of exchange would trigger a prolonged argument, but Sarge intervened before they could get going, nudging the van off down a slip road and pulling up on to a petrol station forecourt.

"Need to fill up the tank," he reported. "Want anything from the shop?"

"Get us a coffee, will you?" asked Liam. "And better get the lumberjack here another Coke."

As Sarge opened his door and stepped down on to the rainy forecourt, a gust of icy wind carried the sickly tang of petrol fumes inside the van. Jamie coughed thickly.

"Thought you said you'd got over that cold of yours," said Liam, his eyes narrowing.

"I did."

"Yeah, it sounds like it. Reckon we might need someone to take a look at that."

"Leave it out, Liam," Jamie said grumpily. "I'm all right."

Liam grinned. "Sure you are. My little brother, the twelve-year-old tough guy."

Years of living with his brother meant Jamie knew what was coming, but as usual, he wasn't quick enough or strong enough to stop Liam wrapping an arm around

15

his neck in a headlock and ruffling his hair. The two of them were still wrestling when Sarge reappeared in the shop doorway carrying a brown paper bag, muttering darkly to himself as he crossed the forecourt. With a final, taunting flick of Jamie's ear, Liam pushed his brother away. Sarge climbed up into the driver's seat, handing Liam the brown paper bag and slamming the door shut.

"Problem?" Liam asked innocently.

Sarge frowned as he examined his receipt. "The price these companies charge working men and women to fill up their petrol tanks," he complained. "It's more than a disgrace. It's robbery."

"Write to your MP about it," suggested Liam, lifting the lid off his coffee and blowing on the steaming liquid.

"What, a politician?" Sarge crowed with laughter. "They're the worst crooks of the lot!"

He turned the key in the ignition and drove the van off the forecourt. The outline of a city appeared on the horizon; motorway lanes swelled with early-morning commuters on their way to work. Even with the three of them up front in the van there was a chill in the air, and Jamie was grateful for the stale, sticky breath of the heater on his face. The speedometer shivered around the 40mph mark on the dashboard. Sarge observed speed limits religiously, rarely venturing out of the slow lane of the motorway. He always complained that Liam drove too fast, and rarely let him behind the wheel. For Sarge speed limits were like red lights, and the boundaries of his own temper. There were some lines you just didn't cross, not unless you were looking for an accident.

The rain intensified as the van turned off the motorway and plunged into the heart of the city, following a winding path across roundabouts and down backstreets, through railway arches and the shadow of tower blocks, until Jamie was utterly lost. Eventually the van cut through a bleak housing estate and came out beside a scrapyard ringed by high fences topped with CCTV cameras and spiteful coils of barbed wire. Liam jumped down at the front gate and pushed it open, waving the van inside the yard.

Mathers's Scrapyard was a metal cemetery filled with mangled, rusty corpses. Iron mausoleums rose into the sky, flanked by towering walls of black tyres. Washing machines lay on their sides, their round mouths open with surprise. Tall yellow cranes stood idly in the rain, their magnets switched off and their steel claws at rest. Over by the far wall a dark green 4×4 was parked in front of a Portakabin. Unlike the rest of the vehicles in the yard, the 4×4 was gleaming and new.

As the removal van came to a stop in a muddy puddle, a man in grey overalls and a yellow high-vis vest appeared in the doorway of the Portakabin. He was the same age as Sarge but a full head taller: a giant of a man, with a thick beard and thinning, sandy hair. His mouth was twisted into a constant smirk, as though he'd heard a nasty rumour but wasn't going to share it.

"Morning, Sarge," he called out in a deep voice. "I see you brought the weather with you."

"It's always raining here, Mathers," replied Sarge, stepping down into the mud. "Can't blame me for that."

They nodded coolly at each other. As Jamie followed his dad out of the van he could feel Mathers inspecting him, mentally weighing and valuing him as though he were another heap of scrap. It was only when he saw Liam that Mathers's face broke into a grin.

"Good to see you again, lad," he said. "You keeping well?"

"Can't complain," Liam replied nonchalantly.

"Bet you do though, don't you? You still training, champ?"

"When I can."

"Looks like it, too," said Mathers, admiringly. "I could set you up with a fight or two. Make some good money out of it."

"Won't be necessary," Sarge said sharply. "When this boy puts boxing gloves on it's to step into a proper ring, not get involved in some back-alley brawl."

"Fair's fair," Mathers replied, unaffected. "No harm in asking though, eh? It's all business. Let's see what you've brought me, then."

At a nod from his father, Jamie slid open the bolt on the removal van doors and opened them up. There was no furniture inside, no taped-up cardboard boxes filled with clothing and books and DVDs, only a dark tangle of copper wiring tied together in large rings.

Sarge was a removal man of a very particular kind: he removed people's possessions without their permission and sold them to other people. Other people might have called this theft, but to Sarge it was just a way of earning a living. He saw thieves and criminals everywhere he looked except in the mirror. Recently he had specialized in stealing iron and other metals – from skips and sculptures to church bells and copper wire; from plaques and statues to street signs and hot and cold taps. Whether it was steel or nickel, lead or aluminium, all metal was precious as far as Sarge was concerned. Together with Liam and Jamie he criss-crossed the country, filling up the van's ravenous belly as they went: like treasure hunters, Wild West prospectors sifting for gold.

The previous night they had descended upon a disused railway siding, Jamie left to watch through the mesh of a wire fence as his father and brother scrambled down the grass embankment and scurried along the tracks. He hated it when they stole from the railways. It wasn't just the ominous rumble of the trains, or the ever-present threat of the police. To unearth the valuable copper cable from the side of the tracks Sarge and Liam had to dig it up, risking electrocution with every swing of the pickaxe. Jamie trembled in the cold, waiting for an explosion of sparks to light up the railway line, the signal that something had gone terribly wrong. Thankfully this time the night remained silent, and Jamie's shoulders sagged with relief when he saw his dad and his brother clambering back up the embankment. They were struggling to drag up the strips of copper behind them, but there were broad smiles on their faces. It had been a bumper haul.

Mathers let out a low whistle as he examined the copper, and smiled at Sarge. "Jackpot," he said. "Where did you find this?"

"We found it," replied Sarge, straight-faced.

"Just as long as you didn't 'find' it on the railway like the last lot I sold for you," Mathers told him. "There are some serious characters in the scrap metal business these days, and they're getting territorial – word is the railways are now off-limits."

"Serious characters?" said Sarge. "Do you see me smiling?"

"Very rarely."

"Then stop worrying and let's get on with this, eh?"

They set about unloading their treasure, putting on thick gloves and hauling the heavy coils down from the van and across the yard to a skip inside a warehouse. It was tough work in the cold and the rain, and Jamie was soon lagging behind the others. He wished that Sarge hadn't lied to Mathers – of course they had found the wire on the railway, where else could they have stolen such a large amount? Sometimes it felt as though his dad couldn't do even the smallest and simplest things honestly.

When they were done Mathers took Sarge into the Portakabin to settle up payment, leaving Jamie and Liam waiting in the rain outside.

"This place is a dump," muttered Liam, zipping up his tracksuit top. "Don't know why Sarge makes us come here."

"Isn't Mathers his friend?" asked Jamie.

Liam nodded. "Best friend in the world." He snorted. "And he can't stand the sight of him, neither."

A gust of wind careered across the yard, hurling handfuls of rain into their faces. With a pained glance up at the sky, Liam retreated back inside the removal van. Jamie pulled up the hood on his sweatshirt and wandered away across the puddle-strewn earth. He didn't care that it was raining – he wasn't going to return to the van until he absolutely had to.

In front of him a car was lying prone in the grip of a crane's claw, its windows shattered and chassis buckled. Closing his eyes, Jamie had a quick, guilty vision of his family's van in its place, its tyres punctured and rotten and its engine frozen with rust. If the van stopped working maybe Sarge wouldn't have the money to buy a new one; maybe they'd have to stop travelling. It was the only way it would happen – there was more chance of Jamie winning the lottery than there was of Sarge settling down and getting a legitimate job. Jamie could daydream all he liked about a normal life with school and friends and a place to live, but his dad ran a family business and that was that. There would never be a "last job" for Sarge, not until he died or the police caught up with him. And he was adamant that the latter would never happen.

A low growl brought Jamie sharply back to the

scrapyard. He wheeled round to find a large black dog glaring at him. It barked savagely, revealing a set of sharp, yellow teeth. Jamie backed away. In the distance he heard the van door slam and Liam call out his name. The dog's muscles tensed, preparing to spring. Jamie turned to run, only to catch his foot in a trailing cable and go sprawling into the mud. He threw up his arms as the dog lunged at him, saliva spraying from its jaws.

As Jamie let out a terrified shriek, a pair of strong hands grabbed him and dragged him away through the mud.

"Calm down, Jamie!" Liam shouted. "It's OK! It's on a chain!"

Jamie scrambled to his feet. His brother was right: the dog was tethered to an iron post by a short chain attached to its collar. But it was too late now. Behind them the door to the Portakabin flew open and Sarge came stalking across the yard, Mathers at his shoulder.

"Down, Smiler!" the scrap dealer bellowed. "Easy, boy!"

The dog ignored him, straining at its chain as it snarled at Jamie. Sarge looked almost as angry.

"Can I not leave you for five minutes?" he snapped at Jamie. "We're trying to do some business here!"

"It's all right, Sarge," Mathers said, with a hint of amusement. "It's my fault; I should have warned the boy about Smiler. He's a brute when you cross him but as long as he's tied up it's all bark. A bit like your old man, eh?"

He searched Jamie's features in vain for a response.

"Hello?" Mathers pretended to knock on Jamie's head. "Anyone in?"

Jamie stared mutely at him.

"Nope," sighed Mathers. "No one home."

"Leave him alone."

Liam stepped in the gap between Jamie and Mathers, staring up at the giant scrap dealer.

"Take a breath, son," Mathers said, in a tone that was still friendly – just. "I'm only joking with the lad."

"He's not laughing," said Liam. "Can't be that funny."

"Jesus! The lad's got no mother but two fathers." Mathers smirked. "Very modern arrangement."

"Hey! What's that supposed to mean?" demanded Sarge.

Mathers held up his hands quickly. "At ease, gentlemen!" he laughed. "We've done good business here. Let's not spoil it." His voice dropped pointedly. "You wouldn't be wanting me to take Smiler off his chain now, would you?"

All of a sudden the dog was the only thing moving in the scrapyard, save the constant drizzle of the rain. Everybody else was dangerously still.

"All right," said Sarge finally. "It's been a late night and a long drive. We'll say no more about it."

He took Liam by the shoulder and steered him firmly back towards the van. Jamie followed close behind, eager to put as much distance between himself and Smiler as possible. He had settled into the front seat when a knock at the window made him jump. Mathers was standing by the driver's window. He gestured at Sarge to wind it down.

"Forgot to mention," he said. "Someone's been asking for you."

Sarge raised a craggy eyebrow. "That a fact?"

"Aye. Roxanne, it was."

"The Spider-Woman herself! What does she want?"

Mathers shrugged. "How should I know? It was you she wanted, not me. I told her I'd pass the message on anyway."

"I'm sure she'll be grateful," said Sarge. "See you around."

"You know where to find me."

Mathers stepped back as Sarge turned the key in the ignition. As the van backed up and turned around, Jamie caught a glimpse of the scrap dealer in the wing mirror. He had unchained Smiler and was standing by the side of his green 4×4. For the first time that morning the smirk had vanished from Mathers's face, and he watched them leave with a stony expression.

CHAPTER TWO

THE MOSS

They left the rain in the city behind them, the removal van creeping through a fuming tangle of motorway traffic as it headed north-west. Grey clouds gave way to a stark white sky as they neared the coast. The roads became steadily quieter and narrower. By early afternoon the van was plotting a solitary path through the countryside, surrounded by miles of barren fields. The flatness of the landscape made Jamie feel strangely vulnerable, and he found himself wishing they had stayed in the damp bustle and roar of the city.

Sarge drove the route from memory, not bothering to consult any maps. Years of navigating back roads late at night had left him with an unerring sense of direction, and he boasted that he knew the fastest route between any two towns in the country. To Sarge road signs were written in their own special language, and he carefully went about deciphering their jumble of letters and numbers like a wartime code breaker, as though the A342 and B2401 spelled out some special message just for him. He was always keeping half an ear out for traffic reports on the radio – news of a tailback or an accident at a certain junction would instantly see him mapping out a new course in his mind.

They were making for a town called Alderston, where apparently the mysterious Spider-Woman would be waiting for them. Sarge refused to say any more than that, replying to Jamie's questions with a grunt. With the copper wire sold and money in his back pocket Sarge should have been pleased, but the tense exchange with Mathers had taken the shine off his mood. Not that he was ever really happy. Sarge seemed to steal out of habit more than anything else. Even after a success like last night's, he barely made enough money to cover the petrol costs. He never bought anything for himself, staying in the same clothes for weeks on end.

All of their lives were stuck in the same slow gear. They never settled in one place long enough to interest the local police, so they never got comfortable. Jamie hadn't been to school for longer than a term since he was a little boy, but if there were social workers looking for him they never caught up with them. The family kept moving, like a shark swimming through the ocean, careful to keep one step ahead of that early-morning knock at the door, the outline of a blue uniform in the window. Every day they climbed up into the van and carried further along a bleak, endless circuit of industrial estates, warehouses and railway sidings.

Sarge glanced testily over at Liam, who was hunched over his mobile, scrolling down the screen. Liam was the only one of them who had a phone – their dad didn't approve of them, and Jamie had never bothered to ask for one. The only people he ever spoke to were sitting next to him in the van.

"Give that thing a rest, will you?" said Sarge.

"What?" Liam shot back, without looking up. "I'm checking the United score from last night."

"You kids and your bloody phones," complained Sarge. "You're so busy texting and tweeting the first thing that comes into your head that you don't stop to think about the consequences. Mark my words, there are people out there who are watching everywhere you go and everything you say. It's easier for a copper to track you on that thing than it is to follow this van."

"You know what you sound like?" said Liam. "One of them conspiracy theory nutjobs who thinks aliens caused 9/11. Where's your tinfoil hat?"

"Don't push it, son."

Liam sighed. "I've lost the signal now, any road," he said, slipping his phone back into his tracksuit pocket. "Satisfied?"

Sarge grunted, and the van fell into a moody silence. Jamie knew it was his fault his dad was angry. Why had he let Mathers's dog scare him like that? Why couldn't he have seen it was on the chain? Jamie wanted to help Sarge like Liam did, but he always seemed to mess it up. He'd drop a roll of cable brushing a spider from his glove, or his mind would wander whilst he was on lookout and he'd miss the signal to head back to the van. Every time something like that happened Sarge would shake his head and mutter about Jamie being "his mother's son". Jamie's mum had died from cancer when he was a baby, and the little things he knew about her he'd had to get from Liam – whenever the topic came up Sarge's mouth slammed shut like a safe door. But Jamie knew enough to see that in the twilight world where they lived, it was better to be like Liam was: strong, tough, brave. Not a coward, or a daydreamer, or a mother's son.

As Jamie stared glumly out of the window he saw that the road had narrowed to a single car's width. Where the tarmac ended either side of the van, the land sloped down sharply into two narrow gullies. Looking ahead, Jamie saw that the snaking road bulged out at regular intervals, forming little islands where cars could pass one another or wait until the next stretch of road was clear.

"We're on the Moss," Sarge told him, with quiet satisfaction. "Nearly there now."

A low, late-autumn sun nudged its way through the white clouds overhead, offering a wan glare but little warmth. A small wood appeared on the horizon, guiding the road into its heart. Something about the bare, spindly branches reaching up into the pale sky made Jamie shiver.

Sarge eyed him suspiciously. "What's up with you?"

"Nothing," Jamie said quickly.

"It's all this open space, Sarge," said Liam. "Gets you down if you're not used to it."

"There's an atmosphere out here, all right," murmured Sarge. "You might think everything's quaint and sleepy but country ways are *old* ways. There are all sorts of strange carryings on in the countryside: midnight rituals, sheep mutilations. . ."

". . .demon farmers. . ." added Liam.

"Demon farmers," agreed Sarge, with a straight face.

"Leave it out," Jamie said sulkily. "You're not funny."

"I'm not joking!" said Liam, his laughing eyes betraying him. "Haven't you heard about the Deadly Demon Farmer that haunts these parts?"

"Watch out, boy!" Sarge chuckled. "He's coming to get you!"

"Oooooahhhh!" drawled Liam in a yokel accent, waggling his hands menacingly in front of Jamie's face. "I'm gurna run yer ovurr in my trarcterrr. . .!"

There was a shockingly loud bang as something flew into the van's windscreen, spreading a cobweb of cracks out across the glass. Sarge swerved, yelling with surprise, and had to wrestle with the steering wheel to stop the van from nose-diving into a ditch.

"What the—?" he snarled, slamming on the brakes.

The van came to a skidding halt on the edge of the raised road. Liam had opened his door before they'd stopped moving; now he jumped out and began sprinting across the field towards the trees to their left.

"Stay here!" Sarge barked at Jamie, unbuckling his seat belt.

Jamie watched dutifully as his dad's wiry frame hared

across the field after Liam, shouting violent threats at their unseen assailant hiding in the trees. When the pair of them had melted into the wood, Jamie slid down from his seat and stepped on to the road. The echoes of breaking glass and squealing brakes rang in his ears. There was an acrid smell of burnt rubber, black scars on the tarmac where Sarge had battled to keep the van's tyres on the road. At that moment, standing alone on the raised road running through the Moss, Jamie could have been the only person left in the world.

Padding round to the front of the van, Jamie traced his finger along the windscreen's jagged wounds. He found the rock that had caused all the damage lying by the side of the road, dusted in shards of glass. It felt murderously heavy in his hand. Whoever had thrown it had not only been a dead-eyed shot, but incredibly strong to boot.

There was still no sign of Liam or Sarge. As Jamie watched, a flock of birds rose from the wood amid a flurry of wings and climbed into the sky. The wind played on the back of his neck, causing the hairs to tingle and stand on their ends. Jamie dropped the rock where he had found it and stood up. Shielding his eyes from the low sun, he scanned the fields behind him. The breath caught in his throat.

A girl was hurrying along the rutted earth towards the wood, her loosely braided blonde hair fanning out behind her as she went. She was dressed in a long skirt that reached down to her ankles and a buttoned-up white blouse beneath a black shawl. As the girl walked on, Jamie waved at her, but she didn't seem to notice either him or the van, her attention fixed on the wood in front of her. She slowed as the shadow of the trees fell over her, and Jamie felt a sudden, inexplicable urge to warn her away.

There was no need. Suddenly she was standing right in front of him. But this was no longer the bright vision he had seen hurrying through the fields. This girl's hair was tangled with weeds and her clothes were wet through, water cascading from her skirt and shawl on to the road where it formed a puddle on the tarmac. The girl's face was puffy and her skin had turned blue, as though she was covered from head to toe in terrible bruises. Staring at Jamie through sullen, lifeless eyes, she slowly raised her arm and pointed at him.

"Jamie!"

He turned, his heart thundering in his chest, to see Liam re-emerging from the trees. The girl had vanished at the sound of his brother's voice. As Liam jumped over the ditch and climbed up on to the road Sarge appeared behind him, red-faced and blowing hard. There was a murderous look in his eyes.

"Did you find them?" Jamie called out.

Liam shook his head. "Whoever chucked it scarpered."

"Lucky for them they did," Sarge said ominously. "If I'd got my hands on them they'd have got a few sharp words in their shell-like. That rock could have killed us."

Liam frowned, looking back towards the woods. "Hell of a shot, like. Don't reckon I could have thrown it half that distance. Who were they, Superman?"

"Maybe it was an accident," Jamie suggested.

"An accident?" Sarge's voice rang with incredulity. "And how d'you figure that, son?"

"I don't know," Jamie said defensively. "Things fall out of the sky all the time, don't they? Meteors and asteroids, stuff like that. Maybe that's what this was."

"Aye, and maybe one of them landed on your head when you were a baby," Sarge snorted. "It might explain a lot. Meteors and asteroids."

"You all right, little bro?" asked Liam. "You look a bit spooked."

As much as Jamie was desperate to tell his brother what he had seen, a single glance at Sarge told him that now was not the time to be talking about strange girls appearing out of nowhere. *Strong, tough and brave. Not a coward or a daydreamer, or a mother's son. . .*

"I'm fine," he said.

"Glad to hear it," said Sarge. "Now let's get on to Alderston. This place is starting to give me the creeps."

They scrambled back inside the vehicle, Sarge peering around the crater in the windscreen as he turned the key in the ignition. As the van pulled away, its tyres rolled through a shallow film of water on the tarmac, a glinting pool of tears in the weak sunlight.

CHAPTER THREE

COBWEBS

There was no sign saying Alderston welcomed careful drivers. There was no welcome at all; just a sharp breeze whipping in off the Irish Sea and across the surrounding fields. Terraced houses sheltered in a dip by the side of a steep hill, linked by a burrowing network of cobbled streets. A church hewn from dark stone slabs kept a brooding vigil over the town from the top of the hill.

Haunted by his vision of the girl on the Moss, Jamie sat quietly in the front seat as they drove past the church and headed down the hill towards the town centre. Beneath a clock tower in the main square an outdoor market was closing down for the day, traders packing away their stalls and wheeling trolleys of clothes back towards their vans. Sarge drove on, taking a sharp right down a side street where the picturesque facade of the village began to peel away like an old coat of paint. The shopfronts became more run-down, turning into hollow spaces or walls of metal shutters. Two men were arguing outside a betting shop beside a pub with boarded-up windows.

It was typical Sarge. Drop him off in the centre of any town and within an hour he'd be guaranteed to have found the shadiest business or the roughest pub, where he'd be laughing and slapping everyone on the back like they were old friends. Jamie rarely felt comfortable around Sarge's various acquaintances and associates. Even their jokes were weapons of a sort; their laughter came in harsh barks and never reached their eyes. In order to protect himself Jamie tried to hide in Sarge or Liam's shadow, vanishing into the background.

The van slowed as it passed a shabby-looking building with the sign "Roxanne's Cabs" above the door, Sarge peering in through the grilled window. He parked the van on the other side of the street and turned off the engine.

"We're here," he said.

"So who's this woman we're going to meet, then?" Liam demanded. "And don't give me any more rubbish about spiders."

Sarge stabbed a finger in the direction of the cab firm. "It might not look like much from the outside, my boys, but from inside this building Roxanne spins a web that stretches out across the entire country. She knows everyone who's worth knowing – and a few others who you're better off not knowing."

"All right," Liam said crisply. "So what does she want with us?"

"That, my lad, is the reason we are here."

Sarge opened the door and hopped smartly down

from the van, seemingly unaffected by a night and day's long drive. Jamie and Liam followed him as he crossed the street and marched inside the taxi firm. They found themselves in a cramped waiting room that smelled of sweaty armpits and chip-shop wrappers. In a glass booth an overweight man in a short-sleeved shirt sat at a raised counter, flicking through a newspaper.

"Where you headed?" he asked, without looking up.

"Through that door behind you," Sarge replied. "Don't think we'll need a cab for it, though."

"It's private back here," the man said shortly. "If you don't want a cab you can hop it."

"Now, now," chided Sarge. "Let's not start off on the wrong foot. Why don't you lift yourself off your seat, go through there and tell Roxanne that Sarge and his boys are here to see her, just like she asked."

The man stared at Sarge through heavy-lidded eyes. Then he closed his newspaper with a deep sigh.

"Wait here."

He disappeared through the door behind him, reappearing after a minute or so to press a switch underneath the counter. There was a loud buzz, and then the door leading into the glass booth clicked open. Sarge went first, nodding at the man behind the desk before heading down the corridor.

"Jobsworth," he muttered.

In his head Jamie had imagined the lair of the Spider-Woman to be some kind of draughty cave draped in deadly, intricate patterns of silken strands. Instead he found himself in a shabby office with threadbare carpet and a thick smell of floral air freshener. Roxanne, a large woman with tightly curled blonde hair and several double chins, was sitting at a desk talking on a mobile phone – one of four laid out in front of her, neatly arranged either side of a sleek laptop. The rest of the desk was covered in smiling family photographs. Behind Roxanne a daytime show was playing on mute on the television, whilst a net curtain had been drawn across the window, obscuring the view of the car park behind the building.

"All right, keep your hair on!" she said down the phone, her northern accent rich with exasperation. "I'm sending Greg round now. Yes, ten cases of whiskey. Yes, he knows to take it round the back. He has done this before, you know – which means he knows how much you owe him for it, so you'd better have the money in full or you won't get anything at all."

She had barely rung off when another phone began buzzing on her desk. Roxanne raised her hand apologetically and answered it.

"Hello, love," she said. "Everything all right? I'm at work, aren't I! It's all right . . . Keeley did what? You're kidding me! She's a regular Black Maggie, that one, and no mistake. Listen, Donna, I'll have to call you back in a minute. Ta ra."

She put down the phone. "Sorry about that, Sarge," she said. "That was my daughter."

"Understand completely," Sarge said gallantly.

"One parent to another. It's good to see you again, Roxanne."

"Likewise. Been a while. How's business?"

"Busy."

"Tell me about it." Roxanne gestured at the phones in front of her. "I spend so much time talking on these bloody things that there are days I'm afraid my tongue's going to drop off."

"You should be careful," Sarge said. "Heard using those things can give you cancer."

"If you believe what you read in the papers, *everything* can give you cancer," Roxanne replied evenly. "I'll take my chances."

Outside an engine roared as a vehicle entered the car park at speed, coming to a stop outside the window of Roxanne's office in a squeal of brakes. Through the net curtain Jamie could see the lurid red gleam of a car's chassis.

"Greg!" Roxanne exclaimed, relieved. "About bloody time, too!"

The back door to the office opened and a teenager sauntered inside. He was older than Jamie, dressed in tracksuit bottoms, white trainers, and a red polo shirt with the collar turned up. Instinctively, Jamie shrank back and looked down at his feet. Boys like Greg always seemed to zero in on him, safe in the knowledge he was too scared to answer back.

"All right, Roxanne?" Greg asked nonchalantly.

"No, I am not bloody all right!" she shot back.

"I've had Raj in my ear wanting to know when you were going to show up. Where've you been?"

Greg shrugged. "Nowhere."

"Nowhere, my foot. You've been seeing my Donna again, haven't you?"

"What if I have? Isn't a law against it, is there?"

"When it comes to you, Greg Metcalfe, there should be," Roxanne told him. "I know how many girls you've been out with. We'll talk about this later. Take the cab over to Raj's – the cases are already in the back seat."

"No sweat," Greg replied. "I'll take it round now. Tell Raj I'll be there in ten minutes."

"Yeah, I know how you drive: like a bleeding maniac! You take care with that stuff or there'll be hell to pay! And stay away from my daughter!"

Greg smirked knowingly at Jamie, and headed out towards the waiting room.

"Right then," said Roxanne, sitting back in her chair with a sigh. "Where were we?"

"I can see you're busy, so we'll take up no more of your time than we have to," Sarge told her. "I came to speak to you in person because I'd heard you were trying to get hold of me."

"Ah, that's right," Roxanne replied. "I had a gentleman enquiring whether you were looking for work. He asked for you by name."

"A gentleman?" Sarge raised an eyebrow. "There's none too many of those about these days. What's this gentleman's name?"

"He'd prefer to remain anonymous for now," said Roxanne. "Until he knows whether you're interested or not."

Sarge scratched at the stubble on his cheek – a sure sign that he was unhappy, Jamie knew. "Right. Any details as to the manner of work he was offering?"

"Far as I know, it's a local job," Roxanne replied. "In your usual line of work – removals. You can stay in the Lodge by the churchyard while you wait for him to get in touch."

"He's offering to put us up?" asked Liam.

"Keys were delivered here today," Roxanne replied.

"So we get a place to stay, but no client or job," said Sarge.

"I thought you might be grateful for a bit of R and R in between jobs," Roxanne replied.

"R and R?" Sarge chuckled thinly. "Not really my style, Roxanne. Tell your mystery man thanks but no thanks. I like to look a man in the eye and shake him by the hand before doing business. I'm old-fashioned like that."

A phone lit up on Roxanne's desk. She switched it off without checking the caller.

"Take my advice, Sarge," she said quietly. "From someone who's known you a long time: don't turn this one down."

"What's this, an offer I can't refuse?"

"Let's just say this is someone you want to keep on the right side of."

"So am I, Roxanne," said Sarge, leaning over the edge of her desk. "And I don't like being threatened."

It was as if the office had been plunged into a bucket of ice. Jamie had seen some hard-bitten men back down when Sarge got in their face but Roxanne stared calmly back at him, without a trace of fear in her eyes.

"Hang on," said Liam, placing a hand on his dad's arm. "Sarge, can I have a word?"

Liam drew Sarge out into the corridor, leaving Jamie alone with Roxanne in the back office. She immediately started texting on one of her phones while Jamie waited awkwardly, his ears just able to pick up the sound of his brother's whisper from the corridor.

". . .and have you heard the state of Jamie's cough?" Liam was saying. "He's coming down with something and more rattling around in the van isn't going to do him any favours. Where's the harm in at least checking out this house? If it doesn't look on the level we'll get in the van and drive off. But let's at least look, eh?"

Jamie's face reddened. He hated it when his family talked about him like he was a baby. Yet at the same time, he was praying that Liam could talk Sarge round. Even if it was for one night – just one night in a warm house and a proper bed, one night free of the stale prison of the van.

Sarge muttered something under his breath that Jamie couldn't catch, and there was a long pause before they came back into the room. But when they did, Sarge nodded at Roxanne.

"On second thought, no harm in having a gander at the place," he said. "Got those keys?"

Roxanne pulled open a drawer and rummaged around inside. Pulling out a set of keys, she handed them over to Sarge. "The Lodge is the last house at the bottom of Church Hill," she said. "You can't miss it."

"Right you are." Pocketing the keys, Sarge paused. "Listen, on the way up here we had a little incident in the woods at the edge of the Moss. You know of any local jokers who like to hang out round there?"

"The woods?" Roxanne gave him a curious look. "No one goes there unless they have to, not even the kids. Why, what happened to you?"

A phone flashed into life before Sarge could reply.

"What is it now, Raj?" Roxanne said wearily. "Well of course Greg isn't there yet – he's quick, but he's not Lewis Hamilton! Look, if he's not there by half-past give me a call, but until then give it a rest, will you?"

Sarge rolled his eyes and left the office through the back door.

Out in the car park, the light was already fading. Liam gave Greg's car an admiring glance as they walked past it, tracing a finger along the bonnet. They returned to the van and headed back to the town centre, steering around a herd of teenagers in school uniform spilling into the road as they walked home. Following Roxanne's directions, Sarge took a right at the junction at the bottom of the hill, passing through the deepening shadow of the crumbling stone wall around the graveyard. Above their heads, streetlights blinked orange as they awoke.

As Roxanne had told them, the Lodge was the last house on the row, a large detached house set against miles of rutted fields.

Liam gave Jamie a nudge. "Not too shabby, eh?"

Jamie nodded doubtfully. Usually they stayed with acquaintances of Sarge's, sleeping on floors and sofas in cramped, sullen houses. The Lodge was certainly grander than that, but as he stared at it Jamie felt a prickle of unease on the back of his neck. Maybe it was the late-afternoon gloom, or the barren backdrop of the fields, but there was a forbidding atmosphere about the building, the vague, distant shadow of a murder of crows on an otherwise empty horizon.

They locked the van and walked up the driveway to the house, losing themselves in the shadow of the porch as Sarge selected a key from the bunch with professional expertise and slid it into the lock. The door opened grudgingly, revealing a pitch-black hallway.

"Here we are then, lads," said Sarge, as he stepped into the gloom. "Home sweet home."

CHAPTER FOUR

THE WATCH HOUSE

They explored the house together, flicking on light switches to chase away the gloom and banishing the silence with their clumping footfalls. Judging by the stale damp in the air and the cairn of letters on the hallway floor, the Lodge had been vacant for a while. Wherever the previous occupants had gone, they had left in a hurry. The house was still filled with their possessions: the beds were made; clothes still hung in the wardrobes; coffee cups were stacked neatly on the draining board. Sarge picked up a vase in the living room, examining it with the professional eye of an auctioneer. Jamie felt like a burglar, creeping through strange rooms filled with other people's possessions and the mysteries of their unknown lives.

"It's bloody Baltic in here," Liam complained, rubbing his hands together. "Get the heating on, eh?"

It took them a few minutes to locate the boiler inside a cupboard beneath the stairs. When Sarge turned it on there was a series of loud clunks and rattles but the needle on the pressure gauge stayed rooted at zero and the radiators remained icy to the touch.

"Great," said Liam sarcastically.

"I'll have a look at it later," Sarge told him. "It's not like we're going to be here long anyway."

Jamie found a Chinese takeaway menu amongst the junk mail in the hallway and Liam ordered them some food on his mobile. But by the time the food had arrived, even the delicious aroma wafting up from the cartons on the kitchen table couldn't make Jamie feel hungry. Perhaps it was the cold house, but he couldn't stop shivering, and his hacking cough had returned. Eventually he gave up, pushing away his portion of chicken chow mein.

"You not having that?" Liam enquired, pointing at the chicken with his fork.

Jamie shook his head. "Don't feel well," he said.

"Early night. Eight hours' sleep," Sarge said crisply. "You'll feel like a new man in the morning."

Jamie nodded obediently, left the kitchen and climbed the staircase. During their initial recce of the house Sarge had volunteered to sleep on the sofa downstairs, leaving his sons to choose between the master bedroom and the adjoining box room. Liam had let Jamie take the bigger room, pushing him inside with a "Go 'ead" and a playful shove. The window offered a sweeping view of Alderston's rows of terraced houses as they melted into the twilight. Directly in front of him the graveyard behind the church sloped down the hill towards the Lodge. Jamie closed the door behind him, revelling in the fact that he had a room all to himself. For one night, at least, he would sleep in a bed, not crumpled up in the van's front seat like a discarded crisp wrapper. He didn't care about the cold seeping up through the floorboards, wrapping his feet in its icy clutches. Closing his eyes, he listened to the trees murmur in the wind.

Gradually he became aware of another noise, voices rising up from a grating in the skirting board. Jamie crouched down beside it, felt the ironwork's cool kiss upon his cheek. Through the grating he could hear Sarge and Liam talking to each other in the kitchen. A glimmer of a smile appeared on Jamie's face. He had learned from a young age that if he wanted to find out what was *really* going on in his family, he had to listen in on his dad's and his brother's conversations. Over time Jamie had developed into a skilled eavesdropper – a thief in his own right, a shadow with soft feet and sharp ears who stole snatches of other people's conversations.

". . .don't know what all this fuss is about," Sarge was saying tetchily. "I moved around all the time when I was a young 'un. That was what you did when your old man was in the army. We went from one barrack town to another, barely had enough time to unpack. I didn't stamp my feet and whine. I just got on with it."

"Yeah, so you've told us before," Liam replied. "But we're not talking about you, we're talking about Jamie."

"So the lad's got a cough! He'll be right as rain in a day or so."

"Maybe he should see a doctor."

Sarge snorted. "Might as well send him to a psychic,

all the good that'll do him," he said. "Your *doctors* weren't any use when your mum got sick, were they? All soft voices and sympathy. They're conmen, plain and simple."

"This is your fault," said Liam. "You shouldn't have made Jamie go on that railway job. You knew he wasn't well, and it was freezing out."

"I made him wrap up warm, didn't I? Someone had to keep lookout. Jamie's not a little kid, he's twelve years old! I tell you one thing – I was doing a damn sight more than just keeping watch at his age, and so were you."

"Yeah? But what if Jamie's not like me and you, Sarge? What then?"

"Then he'd better learn," Sarge said ominously. "And fast."

Chair legs scraped across the linoleum as someone got up, followed by an angry clatter of plates and water gushing into the sink. Jamie pulled away from the grate and climbed into bed fully dressed. There were times, he thought glumly, when being a conversation thief was like trying to steal barbed wire. Unless you were careful, all you ended up doing was hurting yourself. He shivered beneath the duvet, curling up into a ball as he tried to warm the cold bed. Maybe it was because of the long day, or the fact he wasn't feeling well, but Jamie's mind began to drift with surprising speed down through the levels of his consciousness, towards the deep basement where sleep waited to claim him. In his mind's eye the basement door yawned open, and he stepped inside.

For a while he drifted through his unconscious, his dreams one blank after another. Then, without warning, Jamie found himself confronted by a brilliant tapestry of stars, twinkling against the velvet folds of the night sky. He was lying flat on his back, with high walls rising up around him in a deep rectangle. Reaching out, he touched the nearest wall and felt soft, crumbling earth beneath his fingertips. He was lying in a hole in the ground. Before Jamie could get to his feet there was a scraping sound on the surface, and he was showered with earth. He tried to shout out, but when he opened his mouth more soil rained down upon him, filling his mouth and choking his cries. There was a movement at the top of the hole and a face appeared, blocking out the stars. It was Sarge, a shovel in his hands and a thin smile on his face. . .

Jamie sat bolt upright in bed, his heart pounding. Panic gripped him as he looked round at his unfamiliar surroundings. Then he slumped back on his pillow in remembrance. His forehead was burning up and his skin was damp with sweat. It felt as though there were still foggy clouds left over from his dreams inside his head, that he wasn't fully awake. As he pulled back the covers and climbed out of bed he saw that he had forgotten to close the curtains. Looking out through the window, Jamie saw a light flitting around the shadowy jumble of the graveyard.

Slowly, as though he were still dreaming, Jamie walked over to the door and left the bedroom. On the landing he pressed his ear against Liam's door, and heard the sound of deep, regular breaths. Jamie crept down the stairs and past the living room door, where he caught a glimpse of Sarge stretched out beneath a blanket on the sofa, his shoes arranged neatly on the floor by his feet. Sarge's mouth was wide open, and his throat made a harsh gargling sound as he slept. In the hall Jamie slipped on his trainers, eased open the front door and stepped out into the night.

On the other side of the road, part of the drystone wall at the back of the graveyard had toppled down, offering a narrow opening inside. Jamie pulled himself up through the gap, brushing the earth from his hands as he clambered to his feet. Headstones reared up before him, their edges gnawed by years of wind and rain, flagstones jutting out of the earth at awkward angles. Jamie carried on up the hillside towards the outline of the church. There was no sign of any light bobbing amongst the gravestones now – no light at all, save for the dim orange glow of streetlamps in the road below him. The cold air was starting to shift the fog in Jamie's head, and the first nagging doubts had sidled into his head. What was he doing out here?

He was about to turn back for home when he noticed a small stone building sheltering in the shadow of an oak tree by the east wall. It was a squat octagonal tower with a narrow spire. Two stone slabs led up to the doorway, which was secured with a heavy padlock. A rusted metal grille was set into the window recess on the ground floor, and above that there was a narrow slit. Jamie walked over to the tower and peered in through the grille. It was pitch-black inside, a cauldron of pure midnight.

Then, far above Jamie's head, the moon came out from behind a cloud, and there was an answering metallic gleam from inside the tower. Straining his eyes through the darkness, Jamie saw that a phalanx of large iron cages, bigger than a man, had been stacked against the wall.

"Looking for something?"

Jamie whirled around. A girl with tied-back dark hair stared back at him. She was dressed from head to toe in black: long-sleeved T-shirt, skirt, tights and boots, with matching black lipstick. A backpack was over her shoulders and there was a torch in her hand. Her mouth was set in an expression of defiant scorn.

"I saw a light from my window," Jamie said uncertainly, pointing back towards the Lodge. "I don't know why, I thought I'd..."

"...take a trip to the graveyard and see what was going on?" The girl snorted. "And *I'm* supposed to be the weird one."

"I'm Jamie. I'm not from around here. I didn't mean to scare you," he added feebly, aware that if anyone looked scared at that moment it was him. He rubbed his hot forehead. He really didn't feel well.

A mocking laugh escaped from the girl's mouth. "That's very good of you, Jamie-Not-From-Around-

Here, but if you ask about you'll find Keeley Marshall doesn't scare that easily."

At the mention of her name Jamie found himself back in the sour fog of the taxi firm, Roxanne's voice echoing around the back office: "*She's a regular Black Maggie, that one. . .*"

"In fact," Keeley continued triumphantly, "*I* was the one checking on *you*. I heard you trampling around like an elephant and I thought I'd check you weren't trying to break into the watch house."

"Watch house?" echoed Jamie. He looked back over the octagonal tower, frowning. "What's it watching for?"

"Bad people," said Keeley with a hint of smile. "Thieves and criminals. The kind of people who break into graveyards in the dead of night."

"I wasn't breaking in," Jamie said quickly. "I just wanted to know what you were doing, that's all."

"Whatever I want to do," Keeley retorted. "There isn't anyone here to tell me different. If they want to call me a witch, then that's what I'll be."

"Like Black Maggie, you mean?"

A shadow passed over Keeley's face. "Guess you're not so new in town after all."

Jamie looked up towards the church at the top of the hill. "You sure it's OK to hang out here?" he said dubiously. "No one ever tells you to get out or calls the police?"

"The police?" Keeley laughed. "The nearest police station's over in Caxton, and they know better than to bother coming round here anyway. Alderston folk don't like strangers coming round asking questions. They take care of things on their own. Why else d'you think Roxanne and her lot stay here?"

"I don't know anything about that," Jamie said weakly.

"No, maybe you don't." Keeley eyed him critically. "You don't look like the kind who would. In fact, you look like death warmed up. What's up with you?"

"Nothing."

"Doesn't look like nothing."

"You a doctor?"

"No. But my mum's a nurse, and I bet she'd say you weren't well either."

Jamie looked down at his feet. "I'm fine," he said. "But I'd better go. It's late, and if my dad finds out I've been out. . ."

"See you later, Jamie-Not-From-Around-Here. Take care in that place," said Keeley, nodding in the direction of the Lodge. "It's got a *bad* history – the only people who move in there are outsiders, and they don't ever last long. If I were you, I'd sleep with one eye open."

Jamie nodded uncertainly. All he could think about now was getting back to the warm refuge of his bed. He hurried away through the gravestones, his eyes focused on his bedroom window. His head was dizzy and it felt as though his limbs were on fire. As he climbed down through the gap in the wall at the bottom of the hillside, Jamie slipped, nearly falling on to the pavement below.

He had to concentrate so hard on crossing the road that he didn't register the fact that the lights were on in the front room of the house. As he fumbled with the gate the front door flew open, and Sarge's angry silhouette filled the doorway.

"Where the hell have you been?" he demanded.

"I saw a light. . ." Jamie stammered. "I thought . . . I don't know. . ."

"A light? In the graveyard? What are you rabbiting on about? Get inside!"

As Sarge reached out to drag Jamie inside the house, the world took a sickening revolution around him, and suddenly everything went black.

CHAPTER FIVE

LOCAL HISTORY

Jamie spent the rest of the week in bed, his body wracked with fever. Every muscle, every joint, ached. His lungs became bubbling volcanoes, every eruption of hacking coughs searing his chest. Shaking with cold, Jamie burrowed deeper and deeper beneath the covers in search of warmth, only to find his skin burning and damp with sweat minutes later. He slept in fitful snatches, haunted by dreams of empty graves and the soft whisper of shovelled earth.

With Jamie ill, his family had to stay in Alderston – whether they wanted to or not. Liam seemed pleased, his mood buoyed by the discovery of a boxing gym in the nearby town of Caxton. He brought down an old TV set from the attic and propped it up on a chair so Jamie could watch it in bed. As Jamie stared dully at daytime cookery shows he could hear the rapid shuffle of his brother's feet from the next bedroom as he shadow-boxed in front of the mirror.

Sarge was a different matter. Once a day, at eleven

o'clock sharp, he stuck his head through the bedroom door to check on Jamie's progress. The rest of the time he spent propping up the back bar of the Royal Oak, getting to know the locals. He never came home drunk – Sarge didn't drink – but he was short-tempered and sullen, and to Jamie it was obvious that his dad blamed him for the fact that they weren't back on the road. The first thing Sarge had done in Alderston was take the van to the garage to have the broken windscreen replaced, but now it just sat in the driveway. It was as though Sarge had looked down to find his feet had been wheel-clamped.

Just when it seemed as though he would never get well, Jamie's fever finally broke, and he woke one morning to find that his forehead had cooled and the aches in his limbs had melted blissfully away. He climbed out of bed and went across the landing to the bathroom, his bare feet hopping on the icy tiles as he turned on the shower. Thankfully the Lodge's shower worked on a separate system to the boiler, and didn't rely on it for hot water. Jamie washed and dressed, and went downstairs to find the house empty. He poured the last of the milk into a bowl of cereal and ate it at the kitchen table, aware of the sound of food crunching in his mouth. When he had finished he put his bowl in the sink and went into the hallway to put on his coat. Jamie had no idea where Sarge and Liam had gone or when they would be back, and the last thing he wanted to do was spend another day in the house on his own. Stepping outside, he closed the front door behind him.

He followed the road along by the cemetery wall, heading towards the town centre. The sky was filled with grey clouds, and there was a bite to the chill air. Jamie turned up the collar on his coat and thrust his hands into his pockets. Maybe if he asked Sarge, he could get the money to buy a pair of gloves. The streets were eerily quiet as he headed down the winding cobbled road towards the village square. No cars drove past, and there were no customers outside the terrace of shops on the other side of the road. Jamie realized he had no idea what time or even what day it was. From the moment they had entered Alderston it felt as though time had taken on a less certain meaning – though whether that was due to his illness or the atmosphere of the town itself, Jamie couldn't say.

Something hit him, hard, on the back of the head.

"Ow!"

He whirled round. The street was under attack from a barrage of hailstones, white pellets thudding down from the sky on to the cobbles. Another stone bit into Jamie's cheek, stinging his skin. He ran blindly towards the nearest shop and ducked inside, a bell above the door tinkling as he entered.

It took his eyes several seconds to adjust to the gloom inside. As Jamie brushed the hail from his coat, he saw that he was in a narrow room filled with books. The walls were covered in shelves that reached from the floor to the ceiling, stuffed with fat leather volumes. Every available surface was taken up with piles of books, precarious towers rising into the air. Somewhere amongst the debris a heater whirred drowsily, and a pair of incense burners on the shelf behind the counter filled the air with cloying perfume.

A curtain twitched in the doorway at the back of the shop and a man appeared. He was completely bald, his head a smooth dome, and dressed in a tweed waistcoat over a patterned shirt with the sleeves rolled up. A pair of spectacles perched on the bridge of his nose.

"Good morning," he said politely. "What can I do for you?"

"Nothing," Jamie replied quickly. "I just . . . It's hailing and. . ." He trailed off apologetically.

"Ah." The man's face broke into a smile. He was younger than Jamie had first thought – around thirty, although his clothes made him look a lot older. "You're still welcome in Withershins anyway, even if you are only here to shelter from the storm. My name is Lawrence." He waited expectantly. "And you are. . . ?"

Jamie hesitated. Sarge didn't like him telling strangers a single thing more than he had to, but he reckoned he could trust a bookshop owner.

"Jamie," he said finally.

"Nice to meet you, Jamie," said Lawrence. "Feel free to have a look around until the weather eases."

With the hail still hammering its fists upon the window, Jamie didn't really have any choice. As he politely scanned the shelves, he realized that Withershins was different to the other bookshops he had been in. The books were older, for one thing, and stacked higgledy-piggledy under handwritten cardboard signs with strange titles like "Theosophy" and "Wicca". In a bookcase against the far wall Jamie found a stash of books about Alderston and other towns in the area. He could feel Lawrence's eyes following him as he wandered around the shop. Probably trying to check he wasn't stealing anything. Or maybe he was just bored.

"Is it always this quiet?" Jamie asked him.

"No, not always. . ." Lawrence paused, scratching the back of his neck. Then he smiled wryly and nodded. "Yes, most of the time it's just me in here. As you can see, we're not like other bookshops, and it turns out that the good people of Alderston aren't that interested in the world of the occult."

"Don't know why they would be," said Jamie. "Everything seems quiet and normal round here."

"That a fact?" Lawrence's eyes twinkled. "Hasn't anyone ever told you not to judge a book by its cover? It might not look like it, but if you dig beneath Alderston's surface you'll unearth a pretty dark past. It started with the Vikings, who terrorized the local coastlines for three hundred years, sailing their longships down the Irish Sea and coming ashore to murder and pillage. Ironically it was one of the most brutal raiders – a chieftain called Aldus – who eventually came to Alderston's rescue. He decided to settle in the town in 1150 and the raids came to an end. It was Aldus who built the church on the hill."

"Hang on a minute," said Jamie. "You're telling me that church was built by a *Viking*?"

"Soon after settling in the town Aldus converted to Christianity and never bloodied his famous spear again. He became so powerful that the town took its name from him: Aldus's town. We think he was buried in the churchyard but we don't know for sure. A year after Aldus's death, a terrible fire swept through the church graveyard, destroying all the graves that lay there. A monk who lived in the next town wrote that the fire was so fierce that burning corpses clawed their way out of the ground to escape it."

"Huh?"

"I *told* you this town has a dark past. And that's just the start of it. In the early 1600s, Alderston was at the centre of the Lancashire Witch Trials. Five local women, a coven led by a seventy-year-old known as Black Maggie, were found guilty of holding a Black Mass and were executed. The Witchfinder General himself came to Alderston to watch Black Maggie drown on the ducking stool." Lawrence's voice was rising with excitement. "Fast forward two hundred years – to the early Victorian period – and you find grave robbers known as Resurrection Men roaming the churchyards, looking for corpses to dig up."

"Why?"

"At the time medical schools were desperate for

a way to teach their students about anatomy and the human body. They were willing to pay good money for dead bodies, no questions asked. It made for a thriving black market."

Sounded like the kind of trade Sarge would be interested in, Jamie thought glumly.

"But then the body of a girl called Kitty Hawkins was taken from her grave by a gang led by a local criminal called George Rathbone. The town rose up in anger and chased Rathbone and his men from their homes. To make sure the Resurrection Men couldn't strike again, the church built a watch house in the cemetery, and protected the graves with giant iron cages called mortsafes."

"Iron cages? I think I saw some in the watch house," said Jamie, thinking back to the feverish night he had met Keeley.

"Impressive, aren't they? Imagine trying to break through one of them. You won't get very far."

"What about the girl's body?" asked Jamie. "Did they ever get it back?"

Lawrence shook his head. "I'm afraid not. Lost souls are something of a recurring motif in this town's history. During the First World War, a group of young men from the town signed up and formed their own battalion, the Alderston Pals. They were slaughtered almost to a man at the battle of Somme – hundreds of men mown down in the blink of an eye. Only a handful of soldiers saw the end of that day. There wasn't a family in Alderston who didn't lose a father, a son or a brother. For years afterwards it was said that the town was haunted by the spirits of the Pals, trudging home one by one from the battlefield. . ."

Lawrence's voice trailed off theatrically. In the silence that followed, Jamie realized that the rattling on the bookshop window had ceased. It had stopped hailing.

"Not bad," he said. "And all that really happened round here?"

Lawrence nodded. "Not that anyone cares," he sighed, pushing his glasses up on his nose. "The only history people want to hear about these days is Hitler and the Nazis."

There was a fizzing sound as one of the incense sticks burned out in the pot behind the counter. When he saw Jamie looking at them, Lawrence gave an embarrassed shrug.

"It's a bit hokey, I know," he confessed. "But some of my customers expect a certain atmosphere when they come in. And I need every customer I can get. You've just moved into the Lodge, haven't you?"

"How did you know that?"

"Small town grapevine. Nothing here stays a secret for long. Are you going to join the school?"

"I'm homeschooled," Jamie replied. The lie slipped out with practised ease. The truth was that he hadn't been to a lesson in over a year, but Sarge didn't want anyone letting the social services know. "My dad, Sarge, teaches me."

60

"Army man, I'm guessing?"

"His dad was."

"Well, tell him to come to me if he needs any textbooks ordering. I'll give him the local's discount."

Through the ceiling Jamie heard a phone begin to ring. Lawrence nodded back towards the curtain over the doorway.

"That's the flat phone," he said. "I'd better get that. Come back some time and I'll see if I can dig out a good book on Alderston for you."

"OK," said Jamie. "Thanks."

He walked out of the shop. The hailstorm had left the streets littered in sugary-white marbles, as though a sweetshop had exploded. Outside the gloomy bookshop and its shroud of incense, Lawrence's talk of Vikings, witches and ghosts seemed a bit unbelievable. Maybe he had exaggerated to impress Jamie. After all, he had said he needed every customer he could get.

Jamie trudged back to the Lodge to find the van pulling out of the driveway, its engine growling impatiently. Spotting Jamie, Sarge rolled down the window and gestured at him to hurry up.

"Where've you been, lad?" he yelled. "We're going! Get in!"

Jamie dashed up to the passenger side of the van and squeezed breathlessly in alongside Liam.

"What is it?" he asked. "Something happened?"

"Nothing," replied Sarge. "That's the problem. I'm not sitting around on my backside whilst some mystery man decides whether or not to get in touch. You're back on your feet, the clock's ticking and there's money to be made. I've packed our stuff – we're good to go."

Jamie glanced at his brother but Liam said nothing, his arms folded as he stared out of the window. The van pulled away down Church Lane and turned right at the bottom of the hill, heading up past the church and along the road towards the Moss. Looking up into the rear-view mirror as Alderston's roofs slipped out of sight, Jamie was struck by a mixture of sadness and inexplicable relief. Sarge turned on the radio and fiddled with the dial, filling the van with snatches of static and pop songs. Usually Liam would needle his dad about the choice of station but this time he stayed wrapped up in a cloud of surly silence.

As the removal van edged towards the small wood that marked the beginning of the Moss, the sound of a powerful engine roaring grew louder behind them.

"Hello, hello," Sarge murmured, looking into his rear-view mirror. "Who are these idiots?"

Twisting round to peer into Liam's rear-view mirror, Jamie saw a bright blob of red hurtling along the narrow lane behind them. It was Greg Metcalfe's sports car. The teenager zoomed up on the van's shoulder and slingshot past them, music blaring through the windows. Jamie caught a glimpse of long blonde hair in the passenger seat, and guessed it belonged to Donna, Roxanne's daughter.

"Thirty miles an hour!" bellowed Sarge, thumping

his palm on the van's horn. "That's the limit here, not sixty! Are you insane?"

The sports car sped away without reply.

"Honestly," Sarge said. "It's as if these idiots want to get themselves killed."

Liam muttered something under his breath.

"Mind repeating that, son?"

"All I'm saying is," said Liam, "if you cared as much about our health we'd be back in that house, not on the road again."

"We discussed this back in Alderston," Sarge said firmly. "I won't tell you again."

Liam's reply was interrupted by a screech of tyres from within the wood, and a loud bang. Sarge exchanged a glance with his eldest son and jammed his foot down on the accelerator. The van hurried into the trees, darkness folding in overhead. When they cornered the bend Jamie's mouth ran dry. Up ahead, where the road curved to the right, the red sports car had carried straight on, ploughing head first into a drystone wall. The force of the impact had concertinaed the front of the car, and the door by the driver's seat had exploded open. But all Jamie had eyes for was the arm hanging lifelessly down from the driver's side, the first drops of blood pooling on the ground beneath it.

CHAPTER SIX

SLEEPING DOGS

Afterwards, when he tried to unscramble the accident's aftermath in his head, Jamie was surprised how little he actually remembered. Only jagged scraps remained, as though they had been torn out of his memory like pages from a notebook: Liam on his mobile, urging the ambulance to hurry; Sarge crouching down by the sports car, murmuring reassuring words through the passenger seat window; hearing the sound of distant sirens, aware that they were heading straight for them; tree bark turning blue in the flashing emergency lights. Jamie recalled Liam's arm around his shoulder, and being led away to the other side of the van so he couldn't see the ambulance crew freeing the bodies from the mangled wreckage. Fragments of Sarge's conversation with the police returned to him: "I knew when they shot past me that they were going too quick, but you know what kids are like. . ."

Two ambulances left the scene of the accident, moving at very different speeds. One hurtled away to the nearest hospital within minutes of arriving, with Donna, the car's passenger, inside. The second ambulance crept away later with its lights off. There was no rush, no need to break the speed limit. Greg was dead.

It was then that Sarge finally relented, agreeing to turn the van around and head back for Alderston.

"But only for one night," he said. "You hear? We're off first thing in the morning."

No one argued with him. No one said anything. They returned to Alderston to find the house as they had left it – cold and cheerless, condensation streaming down the inside of the windows. There was no food left in the fridge, but then no one was hungry. Instead they slumped down in front of the TV, each lost in their own world. When Sarge went to the toilet during an advert break, Liam looked over at Jamie.

"You all right?" he asked.

"Yeah. Why?"

"Rough day, little bro. It's OK to be upset, you know."

They were interrupted by a shrill bleeping from the kitchen. The house phone was ringing. It had been so quiet during their stay that Jamie had almost forgotten it was there. He stared at Liam, who made no movement to get up. As the ringing echoed round the house Sarge's voice bellowed out through the downstairs toilet door.

"Someone bloody answer that, will you – and tell 'em whatever it is they're selling, we don't want it!"

Jamie hurried through to the kitchen and picked up the phone. The plastic receiver was cool against his cheek, the mouthpiece stale with the echoes of a thousand previous conversations.

"Hello?"

There was a loud, slow exhalation down the phone line, and then a gravelly voice said: "Hello, Jamie."

A prickle of unease ran down Jamie's spine. "Who's this?" he asked.

"All in good time, Jamie. Be a good lad and get Sarge for me, eh? And better put the speakerphone on. I want you all to hear this."

Jamie pressed the speakerphone button, fighting a sudden urge to put down the receiver. The toilet door slammed in the hallway, and Sarge appeared in the kitchen doorway.

"Why are you still on that phone?" he demanded. "You're supposed to tell them to hop it, not chat about the weather." He stopped at the look on Jamie's face. "What is it? Who is that?"

The speakerphone let off a loud crackle – a gust of wind through a mausoleum – and then the kitchen was filled with a mocking song.

"Any old iron, any old iron, any, any, any old iron. . ." The voice broke into rasping laughter. "Hello there, Sarge. How's business?"

"Can't complain," Sarge said cautiously. "Who am I speaking to?"

"I would say a friend, but it's a little more complicated than that."

"Why don't you explain it to me, then? It's been a long day and I'm a little old for guessing games."

Liam walked into the kitchen and pointed

questioningly at the phone. Sarge shook his head irritably and waved him away.

"Do you know what I heard today?" the voice asked mildly. "A little bird told me that you tried to make a run for it."

"Then you heard wrong," replied Sarge. "I don't run anywhere."

"You're lying, Sarge. If it hadn't been for those kids driving head first into a wall, you'd be halfway to Cornwall by now. Don't bother lying to me, it's a waste of time. Leaving town wasn't part of the deal. I said that you could stay in the Lodge but only if you did a job for me. Have you done a job for me?"

"We waited a week, but no one—"

"*Have you done a job for me?*"

"No," said Sarge.

"Then you owe me," the voice said forcefully, "and so you'd better do a job for me, or you'll force me to collect on your debt. Believe me, you don't want that."

"This might be easier if we knew who we were dealing with," said Sarge, playing for time. "Who you are?"

There was a long pause. "My name is Mr Redgrave."

Sarge sank down on to a chair and put his head in his hands. Liam went pale. For several seconds the kitchen was shrouded in disbelieving silence, and then the phone rattled into life again.

"I take it that you've heard of me," Mr Redgrave said. "Good. That should save us some time."

"Heard of you?" Sarge smiled grimly. "A man with your kind of reputation tends to acquire a certain amount of notoriety. You should have told us from the start. What can we do for you?"

"What do you think? Old iron, of course. Alderston's got a little treasure trove of iron that I want you to get your hands on."

"Where?"

"Where?" Mr Redgrave barked with laughter. "You're losing your touch, Sarge! Why do you think I put you in this house? It's right in front of you."

As Sarge and Liam exchanged baffled glances, in his mind's eye Jamie looked out through his bedroom window: over the fallen soldiers of gravestones strewn about the graveyard, the looming shadow of the church behind them, and then, tucked away by the far wall, the watch house, with its store of gleaming metal cages. . .

"The mortsafes!" he exclaimed.

Sarge glared at him.

"They're locked up in the watch house in the churchyard," Jamie said quickly. "Big metal cages. They must be worth a fortune."

"At least one of you is switched on, Sarge," Mr Redgrave said approvingly. "I'd heard your youngest was a bit slow but it sounds to me like he's the brains of the operation."

Sarge scratched his head. "Let me see if I've got this straight," he said slowly. "You want us to break into a *graveyard* to steal these things for you?"

"That a problem? Never had you down as a religious man, Sarge. Look, it's easy money – if you do it right, there'll be no witnesses except the dead, and they won't go round blabbing. A piece of cake, unless you're scared of the dark. You're not scared of the dark, are you now?"

Sarge walked over to the window and looked out through the blinds into the blackness outside. He scratched his cheek.

"We'll do it," he said finally.

"Of course you'll do it," laughed Mr Redgrave. "You didn't have any choice."

"Hang on a minute." Liam folded his arms. "How do we know this guy's for real?"

"That you, Liam?" the voice enquired. "I thought you might be there. You think I'm telling porkies, son?"

"I don't know," replied Liam. "I could go round phoning people and saying I'm Lady Gaga but it wouldn't make it true."

"It's proof you're after, then? That's a sensible lad you've got there, Sarge," said Mr Redgrave. "Lucky for me, I had a feeling you might need convincing, so I took the liberty of leaving you a little present while you were out driving. Reckon that should prove I'm serious. I'll be in touch."

"Present?" echoed Sarge. "What kind of present?"

There was a click on the other end of the line. Mr Redgrave had gone. Sarge slammed his fist down on the table, startling Jamie.

"I told you we should have got out of here when we

had the chance!" he yelled at Liam. "Now we're right in it, aren't we?"

"Calm down!" Liam urged. "The way I see it, we've got two options. We either do the job for this guy, or we get in the van and leave right now."

"Weren't you listening?" Sarge demanded. "Mr Redgrave knows that we tried to leave Alderston once already. He couldn't have known that unless he had people watching us. They're probably watching us right now. For all we know, it could have been him who caused that crash!"

"You think he arranged that accident? That's crazy!"

"You saw that crash site, just as I did. Greg might have been speeding but there was no reason for that lad to go off where he did! *Something* made him swerve into that wall. Who's to say it wasn't Redgrave?"

"What about his present?" asked Jamie. "Do you think that might have something to do with it?"

His dad and brother turned and stared at him.

"I'll check upstairs," Sarge rapped. "The pair of you check down here. Call me if you find anything, and for God's sake don't touch it."

They sprang into action, flicking on light switches until every room in the Lodge blazed with light. As he examined the front room, Jamie could hear the rattle of coat hangers and slam of cupboard doors from upstairs as Sarge searched the bedrooms. All Jamie managed to turn up was a remote control for the TV underneath the settee so he went back to the kitchen, where Liam had also drawn a blank. Sarge came downstairs to find them both peering through the window into the garden.

"Think there might be something out there?" he asked, joining them at the window.

"Only one way to find out," answered Liam.

Jamie dug out a torch in the kitchen drawer and took it into the garden with him. There was a frosty tang in the air, a whisper of wind playing on his bare skin. The garden seemed unfamiliar in the darkness, especially against the eerie stretch of fields beyond the back fence. Jamie torch's made a nervy examination of the shadows, its ghostly spotlight flitting from shrub to tree.

"Wait – what's that?"

Jamie shined the torch where Liam was pointing. In the loose soil beneath a rhododendron bush, someone had fashioned a makeshift cross from two twigs and stuck it into the ground.

"That wasn't here this morning," said Liam, uneasily.

"Get a spade," Sarge ordered. "Quickly."

"Shouldn't we call the police?" asked Jamie. "Whatever's there, it was nothing to do with us."

"Spade."

There was no arguing with the tone in Sarge's voice. Liam disappeared into the shed, and there were scrapes and screeches of rusty metal before he reappeared with a shovel in his hands. Sarge took the torch from Jamie and trained it on the cross as his son began to dig up the earth around it. As he watched his brother shovel

71

the earth to one side, Jamie realized he was holding his breath.

Liam grunted, and stopped digging. "Think I found something."

He dropped to his knees and carefully brushed away the soil.

"Jesus!"

Liam threw away the shovel and hastily backed away from the hole. As Sarge shined the torch upon the ground Jamie felt bile rise in his throat. A face was looking back at him, inhuman and twisted in rage. Although Jamie had only encountered it once before, he knew that its features were etched on his mind for ever, like the inscription on a gravestone, even though now its snapping jaws had been silenced, and its eyes locked in a glassy stare.

Mr Redgrave's present was the corpse of Mathers's beloved dog, Smiler.

CHAPTER SEVEN

IN MEMORIAM

Sarge dug Smiler a new grave in the field behind the Lodge, burying the dog in a deep unmarked hole. If he was shocked by Mr Redgrave's unpleasant gift he refused to show it, going about his work with a grim determination. It was Liam who paced nervously up and down the front room, peering out through the curtains. Jamie had never seen his brother rattled like this before. He didn't like it one bit.

"It was just a dog," Sarge said firmly upon his return, as he washed his hands in the kitchen sink. "A dumb mutt. Nothing to get all worked up about."

"That wasn't *just* anything," Liam retorted. "That was Mathers's pride and joy we just dug up in our back garden. How the hell did Redgrave get his hands on him? Jesus, Sarge, he killed a dog to prove a point. Who is this guy?"

"That's hard to say," Sarge said thoughtfully, drying his hands on a tea towel. "Redgrave's always been a bit of mystery. Occasionally you'll run into someone who claims to have worked for him, or worked for someone who was working for him, but I don't know anyone who's actually met him in the flesh. He's a bogeyman, a ghost."

"Yeah, well, whoever killed Smiler was very much alive," retorted Liam. "And where's Mathers in all this? He wouldn't let anyone harm that dog of his. Are we going to find him buried in the garden too?"

"That might not be such a bad thing."

"Sarge! This isn't the time for kidding around!"

"You're right. It's the time for calm heads and steady hands, so stop squawking and take a deep breath."

At that moment, looking into Sarge's hard, unblinking blue eyes, Jamie was glad that his dad was there. Whatever happened, Sarge wouldn't let them come to any harm.

"He sounded like an old guy on the phone," said Jamie, trying to sound brave. "He can't be that scary."

"That's more like it," said Sarge. "We've worked for people with big reputations before. So do everything the same as normal – prepare thoroughly, carry out the job professionally, get paid and get the hell out of this place. We'll be gone by the end of the week. Agreed?"

"Agreed," said Jamie. But even though Liam nodded along with them, Jamie could see the unease shadowing his brother's eyes.

The next evening word filtered through to the back bar of the Royal Oak that Greg Metcalfe's funeral was taking place the next morning. Sarge returned to the Lodge insistent that his family go to pay their respects.

"You sure?" Liam asked him. "It's not like we knew the lad or anything."

"Know him? We were the last people to see him alive," Sarge said adamantly. "That should mean something."

Although Jamie wanted to believe his dad, he couldn't help but think that the funeral also offered the perfect excuse to scope out the church and the graveyard behind it. Judging by the sceptical expression on Liam's face, he was thinking the same thing, but he knew better than to say anything. Instead they raided the small suitcases of clothes they carried around in the van with them. Liam changed into a black suit, and even Sarge looked smart in a blue shirt buttoned up to the neck. Jamie didn't have a suit of his own, so he put on a dark jumper over the white school shirt and black trousers he kept at the bottom of his suitcase.

They left the house just before eleven, joining the solemn trickle of mourners walking up the hill towards the church. The wind grew stronger as they climbed, sending the flag flying above the church tower into billowing distress. A crowd had already gathered outside the front porch, waiting quietly for the doors to open. Looking through the throng, Jamie saw Keeley Marshall standing to one side with a short, dark-haired woman he guessed was her mother. Even though everyone was dressed like her, all in black, there remained an aura around Keeley that seemed to set her apart from the rest. Nearby, a group of teenagers had formed a conspiratorial huddle next to one of the gravestones; they glanced over towards Keeley, nudging each other and stifling giggles. When one of the girls laughed out loud – a harsh, unnatural sound in the subdued air – Keeley shot them a scornful look and turned away. Before Jamie could go over and say hello, the church doors opened and the crowd began to file in.

The interior of the church was wrapped up in a respectful hush, backed by the soft, mournful strains of an organ playing. As he neared the massed ranks of wooden pews, Jamie had to crane his neck upwards in order to seek out the corners of the high vaulted ceiling. In the stained-glass window behind the altar, a giant, fierce-looking man with red hair stood by the church, a pouch around his neck and a spear and chest of gold coins lying at his feet. It had to be Aldus, the Viking chieftain Lawrence had told Jamie about in Withershins. Beneath the Viking's impassive gaze, a large framed photograph of Greg rested on an easel at the front of the nave, surrounded by bright explosions of flowers. A pair of football boots nestled amongst the bouquets. The coffin had been placed on a bier by the altar. There was something so simple and so horribly final about the white oblong box that Jamie couldn't bear to look at it.

Judging by the welcoming nods he received from some of the men in the crowd, Sarge's time down the Royal Oak had been well spent. As they shuffled into the church, the heavyset man from the reception of the Roxanne's Cabs came over and shook his hand.

"Sarge," he said.

"Don. Terrible business, this."

"You're not wrong there."

"Roxanne not with you?"

"She hasn't left Donna's bedside since the crash." Don's voice dropped to a whisper. "Between me and you, it's probably for the best. She blames the lad for what happened."

Sarge nodded. "A mother's grief," he said. "Still, this is no time for a scene. I wouldn't mind a word with Roxanne myself, as a matter of fact."

"You might be waiting some time," said Don. "She adores her girl. This accident has destroyed her."

"Understand completely, Don – I'm a father myself. Just let me know when she returns to the office, eh?"

The two men shook hands and moved away. Don joined the main group of mourners in the first few pews whilst Sarge, Liam and Jamie took a seat near the back of the church. When everyone had shuffled into the seats the vicar appeared: a solemn, grey-haired man with glasses. As he began to talk about Greg – how popular he was, how funny, always smiling and making people laugh – someone in the congregation began to cry, their sobs echoing around the church. Jamie wondered how many funerals had taken place in this building over the years. How many people had cried, how many tears had been shed. Enough to fill a lake – or a pond, maybe.

An icy draught blew against the back of Jamie's neck, sending a cold sweat of dread washing over him.

He turned round to find the girl from the Moss sitting in the pew behind him. She stared at him with dead eyes, her mouth set in a surly expression, a rotting weed plastered against her cheek. As their eyes locked Jamie felt his airways seize up, as though an invisible hand had reached out and grabbed him round by the throat. The girl gazed at him pitilessly as his eyes widened in silent alarm.

It took a sharp elbow in the ribs to free him. Jamie let out a loud explosion of breath and took in a large gulp of air. He looked up to see Sarge glaring daggers at him.

"Show some respect!" he hissed. "Sit still and stop messing about!"

Blinking back tears, Jamie saw that the pew behind him was empty. The girl had vanished. It was nothing, Jamie told himself, just another stupid daydream. But then why were his hands still trembling? All he wanted to do was run out of the church as fast as possible but he knew that Sarge would kill him if he tried to get up. Jamie forced himself to sit still, trying to blank out the sensation of ice against his neck. The vicar's speech seemed to take for ever, and there were several tearful readings and tributes from Greg's friends before the service finally came to an end.

The congregation were shuffling to their feet when the church door banged open and there was an unsteady tick-tock of heels upon the flagstones. Roxanne walked into the nave, her cheeks streaked with tears and her eyes vague. The whole building seemed to freeze at her entrance, the quiet taking on an awkward expectation.

"I told Greg about the woods," Roxanne called out, in a wavering voice. "I told him to keep away from them, and to keep my daughter away from them. Wouldn't listen, though, would he? Not our Greg. Always thought he knew best, that one. And now he's gone and my poor Donna's. . ."

The crowd gasped as one as Roxanne staggered. Jamie ran forward and caught her, just managing to keep her on her feet. She leaned on him like a dead weight, her eyes gleaming with sudden recognition.

"You feel the cold, don't you?" Roxanne asked him softly. "You know what it means. Winter's coming. They like it when it's cold."

"I don't understand," said Jamie. "Who likes it when it's cold?"

Roxanne smiled, tears glimmering in her eyes.

"Oh, love," she whispered. "You've no idea. Get out of here while you still can."

Suddenly they were surrounded by other people. Don took Roxanne's elbow, murmuring comforting words in her ears as he led her stumbling towards the church's exit. Jamie stood and watched them leave, his arm cold where she had clutched him.

CHAPTER EIGHT

TREASURE HUNTERS

The mourners followed Don and Roxanne outside the church, watching from a sympathetic distance as he helped her into the back seat of a car and hurriedly drove away.

"Look at her, poor thing," a woman whispered to her friend behind Jamie. "I don't think she knows what day it is."

"The hospital must have given her something," her friend replied. "By the looks of things she should have stayed there."

The crowd milled about in the glum daylight, humming with excitement over the funeral's dramatic interruption. As Sarge and Liam struck up a conversation with the landlord of the Royal Oak, a large man with a spiky black hair and a beer gut, Jamie caught sight of Keeley and her mum walking away down the church path. As their eyes met, Keeley's widened with surprise. She whispered something in her mum's ear and came over to speak to him.

"Well, well, well," she said slyly. "Jamie-Not-From-Around-Here. What are *you* doing here?"

"My dad made me come."

Keeley rolled her eyes. "My mum did the same," she said. "Apparently it doesn't matter that Greg never said a nice word to me, or that he and his cronies used to laugh at me in the street and call me Black Maggie. Because he drove like an idiot and crashed his car into a wall I'm supposed to pretend that we were best friends or something like that. It's stupid."

Jamie wasn't sure what to say back. He wished Keeley would keep her voice down – people were starting to look at them. A shaven-headed man in a dark suit was openly staring at her, a murderous glint in his eyes. Either Keeley hadn't noticed, or she didn't care.

"So have you been in hiding or something?" she asked Jamie. "I was starting to think you might have been a ghost."

"I was ill," said Jamie.

"That figures. You didn't look very well in the graveyard. Are you going to stick around in Alderston?"

"I don't know. For a little bit, I guess."

Keeley reached into her bag, scribbled something down on to a scrap of paper and pushed it into his hand.

"My mobile number," she explained. "If you decide to stay, give me a call and I'll show you around."

"Oh," said Jamie.

"You *do* have a phone, don't you?"

"Yeah," lied Jamie. Everyone had a phone, didn't they? Everyone normal, that is. "Of course."

"Well, there you go then." A car horn beeped impatiently from the other side of the street. Keeley rolled her eyes. "Mum's waiting. Gotta go."

She barged her way out through the crowd, ignoring the tuts and mutters that greeted her exit. Jamie waited until Keeley was out of sight before rejoining Sarge and Liam. Ordinarily Jamie would have expected his brother to be waiting with a smart remark about chatting up girls, but his face was serious. The funeral was over; it was time to go to work.

Sarge led his sons behind the church and down through the graveyard, his tie flapping in the breeze as he marched past the headstones. To the casual observer there would have appeared nothing untoward about their progress down the hill; just a family making their way home from a funeral. You had to know Sarge – or be a thief yourself – to know what was really happening. With little looks left and right he mentally mapped out the area, checking for potential traps and pitfalls, lines of sight from the road and surrounding houses. When they passed the watch house nestling against the cemetery wall Sarge slowed but didn't stop, a couple of casual glances all he needed to assess the strength of the padlock on the door and measure up the iron treasure visible through the grille over the window.

Jamie stayed silent as he trooped several paces behind his dad, preoccupied with gloomy thoughts. Roxanne's strange warning had been unsettling enough, but it was

82

the vision of the malevolent girl in the pew that was haunting him. That was the second time that Jamie had seen her. What did she want from him? Why could only he see her – was she a real threat, or just a figment of his imagination? As he looked out over the sloping roofs of Alderston, beyond the edge of the town and across the fields to the woods and the Moss beyond, Jamie felt suddenly very small: a trespasser on some bleak, unimaginably vast landscape.

At the bottom of the graveyard, they jumped down through the gap into the wall and crossed over the narrow road to their house. Sarge immediately strode up to Jamie's bedroom, where he stood staring out of the window at the church. There was a moody edge to his silence, as though his brain was chewing on a piece of gristle. Jamie and Liam lingered in the doorway behind him, waiting for their dad to speak.

"What do you think?" Liam asked finally.

Sarge didn't turn round. "About the funeral or the job?"

"The job."

"Not much *to* think," said Sarge. "It's child's play. There aren't any security cameras and the watch house isn't alarmed. The only house with a clear line of sight of the building is this one, so the chances of a law-abiding civilian spotting us are pretty slim. We can't get the van up close so it'll take a few trips to carry the mortsafes through the graveyard and down to the road, but that's about it."

"So it's an easy job," Liam said cautiously. "That's a good thing, right?"

"Maybe. But if the job's so simple any idiot with a hammer could do it, you have to ask yourself why everything else is so complicated. Why all the big mystery? Why this house? Why us?" Sarge tapped a finger against the window frame. "It doesn't make sense."

"Redgrave's a professional," said Liam. "He wants everything done properly, no shortcuts. I thought you'd appreciate that."

"I think there might be another problem," Jamie said slowly.

Now Sarge turned round. "What's that, son?"

"Keeley."

His dad looked at him blankly.

"That night when I was ill, I saw a light in the graveyard and went to see what it was," Jamie explained. "It was Keeley's."

"Was this the lass you were talking to outside the church?" asked Liam. "Funny-looking thing, with black lipstick?

"She's not *that* funny-looking," Jamie said defensively. "People don't like her because she's different, so she goes to the graveyard at night. No one bothers her there."

Liam shook his head. "Bloody goths," he muttered.

"What kind of girl spends her nights sauntering round a cemetery?" asked Sarge disbelievingly. "Doesn't she have a home to go to?"

"Her mum's a nurse," Jamie replied. "Maybe she works nights. Keeley didn't mention her dad, and he wasn't at the funeral. I'm not sure he's around."

"You were worried it was too easy," Liam told Sarge, with gloomy irony. "Happy now?"

Sarge shot his son an irritable look and turned to Jamie. "It's down to you, son," he said. "Didn't I see her give you her number?"

"Um, yeah."

"That's easy, then," Liam said casually. "Ask her out on a date."

"No!"

"Why not?"

"I don't want to!"

"Scared she'll turn you down?"

"No! I just. . ."

Sarge strode over and wagged a finger in Jamie's face. "I don't care how you do it, lad," he said threateningly, "but I want Marilyn Manson out of that churchyard tomorrow night. If you can't make it happen then I will. Understand?"

Jamie nodded. He understood, all right.

That afternoon Sarge carried his toolkit in from the van, laying out his apparatus on the kitchen table for inspection and selection. There were thin lockpicks and a bunch of skeleton keys, pliers and hammers, a crowbar and a set of heavy-duty bolt cutters. The display of metal tools made the kitchen look like some kind of medieval torture chamber, with Sarge poring over his implements with the terrible carefulness of an executioner.

Jamie left his dad to it, changing out of his funeral clothes before heading back into Alderston. As he walked down the arcade of shops towards the main square he saw a van parked outside Withershins. Two old men appeared in the bookshop doorway, examining a fold-out map. One of them was carrying a metal detector under his arm. He glared suspiciously as Jamie walked past, and folded up the map.

Withershins felt as though it had somehow shrunk since Jamie had last been there – or perhaps the unruly stacks of books had just grown. In the middle of the cramped cubbyhole, Lawrence was sitting cross-legged on the floor, a long red scarf draped around his neck. He was going through a stack of books in a large cardboard box. When the bell above the door tinkled, he looked up and smiled.

"Hi, Jamie," he said. "How's it going?"

"OK, I guess. I went to Greg's funeral this morning. I didn't see you."

"I'm not sure anyone wanted me there."

"I'm not sure anyone wanted me there either," said Jamie. "But we went anyway."

"That's Alderston for you," said Lawrence, with a rueful smile. "Unless your great-great-grandfather used to drink in the Royal Oak they don't want to know you. I could live here until I was a hundred, I'd still be an outsider."

"Who were the guys with the metal detectors?" asked Jamie, pointing out through the door. "What did they want?"

"The usual," Lawrence said dismissively. "Maps. X marks the spot. Wealth beyond their wildest dreams."

Jamie frowned. "Sorry?"

"The countryside round here is crawling with treasure hunters," explained Lawrence. "They spend their time pacing up and down fields with their metal detectors, desperately waiting for that precious bleep. They're not interested in the past. All they're interested in is money."

"Money? What money?"

"I take it you haven't heard about Aldus's hoard, then," said Lawrence, brushing his hands as he climbed to his feet. "The Viking sagas claimed that, when he was a young man back in Scandinavia, Aldus broke into a chieftain's burial mound. It was a terribly reckless act – the Vikings believed that graves were protected by powerful, vengeful spirits. Aldus was gone for the whole night, and when he returned to his feasting hall he was carrying a spear and a hoard of priceless silver jewellery and coins."

"So Aldus was a grave robber too?"

Lawrence smiled thinly. "Our very own Viking Resurrection Man, yes. There's something about this town that seems to draw thieves and vagabonds to it like a magnet."

Jamie looked quickly at Lawrence to see what he

meant by that, but the bookshop owner was walking back behind the counter.

"Anyway," Lawrence continued, "when Aldus settled in Alderston he brought his spear and his hoard with him."

"I saw them in the stained-glass window in the church," said Jamie.

"Right. It was thought that he was buried with them, but the fire that engulfed the graveyard the year after Aldus died meant that we don't know for sure if that was actually his final resting place."

"I get it," Jamie said slowly. "So these treasure hunters go around searching for Aldus's grave."

"They have been for nearly a thousand years now, and I'm guessing they still will be a thousand years from now. Some things never change: greed is one of them." A phone started ringing in the flat upstairs. Lawrence sighed, running a hand over his bald scalp. "Here endeth the lesson," he said, disappearing through the beaded curtain. "Come back soon, though. You're my best customer!"

"But I haven't bought anything!" Jamie called after him.

"Don't remind me!" Lawrence called back.

Jamie left the bookshop and headed back to the Lodge. He crept in through the front door and immediately made for the stairs, hoping to make it up to his bedroom before anyone realized he was back. The TV was on in the living room, masking the creak of the stairs beneath his feet. As he tiptoed towards the landing, Jamie glanced over his shoulder, smiling with satisfaction at the empty hallway. He turned back, and started.

Sarge was standing at the top of the stairs, his arms folded. "You asked that girl out yet?"

Jamie shook his head.

"Why the hell not? I ask you to do one thing, Jamie. One simple thing!"

Sarge grabbed Jamie and marched him downstairs into the living room, where Liam was sprawled across the settee, staring at the television.

"Phone," ordered Sarge, holding out his hand.

Liam rummaged around his tracksuit pockets and tossed his dad his mobile, which Sarge pressed into Jamie's hand. Jamie wasn't used to texting, his fingers stumbling across the tiny keys, and it took him several attempts to type out his message.

"There," he said. "Done."

Liam examined his message.

Hi. Want to do something tomorrow night?
Jamie

"Steady there, Casanova," said Liam, grinning. "You don't want her fainting from the romance of it all."

"You're not funny, Liam."

"Not as funny as you, little bro."

Taking the scrap of paper Keeley had given Jamie, Liam typed her number into his phone and pressed send. They didn't have to wait long for a reply. Within a minute the phone buzzed into life, and a terse message flashed up on the screen.

The War Memorial. Midnight. K

A leathery smile snaked across Sarge's face.
    "Perfect," he said.

CHAPTER NINE

THE WITCHING HOUR

The minute and the hour hands were creeping ever closer to the top of the dial as Jamie hurried beneath Alderston's clock tower. He kept to the shadows of the main square, aware of his loud footfalls in the empty hush. The only sign of life in the whole town was outside the Royal Oak, where light and laughter spilled out from the pub on to the pavement. For once Sarge wouldn't be at his usual station in the back bar, though. Tonight there was business to take care of.

Back in the Lodge, the family had eaten their dinner in silence, Sarge's knife scraping against the plate as he scooped gravy into his mouth. The night's business had hung in the air like a chill fog. When Sarge and Liam disappeared upstairs to change into dark clothes, Jamie's nerves began to jangle and his stomach lurched queasily. Secretly, guiltily, he found himself praying that something would happen at the last second to stop them from going ahead – a call from Mr Redgrave cancelling the job, or a police car driving past the church. Even if it was just for one night; anything to stop his dad and brother going to the graveyard.

But the phone didn't ring and no police cars appeared, so Jamie said goodbye to Sarge and Liam in the hallway and walked on his own through the town. Following the directions his dad had given him, he turned left at the road at the bottom of the main square, crossing a bridge over a trickling brook. The rows of shops came to an end, and on the other side of the road the buildings were replaced by a long hedgerow, with two sets of rugby posts jutting into the sky behind it.

Slipping through a gap in the hedge, Jamie found himself in the middle of a large playing field, the majority of which was taken up by a rugby pitch. To the right of the pitch, a squat clubhouse with a sloping roof sat in a patch of scruffy wasteland. The building's windows were boarded, crumpled cans and discarded newspaper littering the tangled grass around it. In front of the clubhouse, surrounded by a foot-high railing, stood a stone obelisk covered in carved names. This was Alderston's war memorial, a single, solemn finger pointing towards the heavens.

There was no one waiting for him by the clubhouse. Jamie checked his watch. It was well past midnight. Either Keeley was playing a trick on him or something had stopped her from coming. If she had tried to text him at the last minute it would be Liam who received the message – and Liam would be in the graveyard by now, hard at work. Jamie was alone. He shivered.

"Mwwaaaaaaaaahhhh!"

Jamie jumped as Keeley darted out from behind the monument. She was shining a torch into her face, casting an eerie glow over herself as she cackled loudly.

"Ha ha," Jamie said. "Very funny."

"I know." She flicked off the torch, her face melting into the darkness. "I *am* a witch, after all."

"I thought witches spent their time stirring cauldrons and casting spells," Jamie retorted. "Not jumping out at people shouting 'Boo'."

Keeley laughed as she jumped down from the memorial, stepping lightly over the railing. "What are you looking so nervous for? Don't worry – it's not like we're on a date or anything."

"I'm not nervous," Jamie said quickly. "Just cold. It's freezing out here."

The wind was whipping mercilessly across the rugby pitch, sending pages of newspaper cartwheeling across the wasteland. Now that Jamie was here with Keeley, he realized he didn't know what to say to her. It didn't really matter, he thought – as long as he kept her as far away from the church as possible.

"You promised to show me the sights," he said, nodding at the obelisk. "Is that it?"

"It might not look like much," Keeley admitted. "But almost everyone in this town knows a name carved on it. A family member who died in the war."

"The Alderston Pals, you mean?"

Keeley looked impressed. "How do you know about them?"

"Lawrence told me."

"Mr Withershins? You sure can pick your friends, can't you? He's almost as unpopular as I am."

"He's a nice guy."

"He's an idiot," Keeley said dismissively. "What did he think was going to happen, coming from nowhere and opening a shop with books on witches and old murders and stuff like that? People round here don't want attention drawn to that sort of thing. They don't like other people meddling in their business."

Jamie walked over to the memorial and peered at the rows of names covering the obelisk.

"Can't see any Marshalls here," he told her. "Did any of your relatives die in the war?"

Keeley shook her head. "My mum's granddad Frank was one of the Pals who went to France during the First World War, but he was one of the lucky ones. Apparently he was a different guy when he came back from the trenches – wouldn't say a word about what had happened out there. Mum tried to ask him about it once but he went all weird and she didn't try again. There's a tape of it somewhere: if you're interested I can dig it out for you."

Jamie shrugged. "Sure."

He had no idea why she was so keen to give him a tape of her granddad, or why she had brought him to the deserted war memorial. Maybe it was because Jamie was an outsider, but every time he talked to Keeley she gave him the impression she knew more than she was willing to let on.

"When we first met at the graveyard," he said, "you told me to be careful in the Lodge. Why was that?"

"There was a man called George Rathbone who used to live in Alderston years and years ago," Keeley told him. "He was a real villain, a thief who'd steal anything he could get his hands on. Everyone else in the town hated him, which kind of makes me feel like we had something in common, but *anyway*, Rathbone had this long-running feud with another guy called John Hawkins. One day Hawkins's daughter, Kitty, went for a walk in the woods and drowned in the pond. This girl was all perfect and pretty so everyone was cut up about it. Everyone except Rathbone. The night after her funeral him and two cronies crept into the graveyard, killed a watchman and dug up Kitty's body."

"Yeah, the Resurrection Men. I've heard about them before," Jamie told her. "What's it got to do with our house?"

"George Rathbone's house," corrected Keeley. "He lived in the Lodge for years before Kitty died and he had to leave town in a hurry."

Jamie had been sleeping in a grave robber's room. No wonder there was such an unearthly cold in the house. Maybe Smiler wasn't the only body buried in the back garden. Jamie shuddered. He hoped Sarge and Liam had got to work. The sooner they could leave this place, the better.

Jamie turned away from the obelisk. Something about Keeley's story was nagging at him. He'd said he'd heard about it before, but he hadn't heard *all* of it. There was something new here, something important.

"How did Kitty die again?" he asked.

"I told you, she drowned. There's a pond in the woods, you know, where Greg crashed his car. She slipped and fell in, got her dress caught up in the weeds."

Jamie went numb, nightmarish images flashing through his head. A dripping shadow in the sunshine on the Moss. A demon in a church pew. A finger pointing at him like a dagger.

"Jamie? What is it?"

"I've been seeing things," he said quietly.

"What kind of things?"

"A girl." Jamie hesitated. "A dead girl. Soaking wet and covered in weeds."

Keeley looked at him sharply. "Are you messing about?"

"No! Why would I?"

"I don't know."

"I haven't told anyone else," said Jamie. "I didn't want them thinking I was crazy. Do you think it was Kitty?"

"I don't know," Keeley said slowly. "The dead have a funny way of coming back to haunt Alderston. Why d'you think I brought you here to see the memorial? Best off keeping your mouth shut, though. If word gets out an outsider's been seeing the ghost of Kitty Hawkins, people might get nervous."

"I can talk to you though, right?"

"Of course," said Keely, offhand. "Isn't that what friends are for?"

"I don't know," said Jamie. "I've never had one."

Keeley grinned. "Me neither."

Jamie hadn't seen her smile before – it changed her face, softened it. Before he could say anything Keeley had turned away, picking up her bag from behind the memorial.

"Come on," she said, slinging her bag over her shoulder. "Let's go to the graveyard. I'll show you Kitty Hawkins's grave. They left her headstone there in case anyone ever recovered her remains."

"No!" Jamie said quickly.

Keeley stopped, surprised by the urgency in his voice. "Why not?"

"I want to stay here. I don't like that graveyard."

"You big baby!" scoffed Keeley. "It's all right, I'll be there to protect you from the ghosts and ghouls."

"I'm not scared! I just don't want to go!"

"Suit yourself. You can do what you like, but *I'm* going to the churchyard."

"Wait!"

He grabbed her hand. The amusement faded from Keeley's face, and her eyes became serious. "What is it, Jamie? Why don't you want me to go there?"

"I can't tell you."

"Yes, you can. I told you, I'm your friend."

Jamie slumped down on the steps, his shoulders

sagging. "My dad and my brother will be there. In the watch house."

"Why? There's nothing there but—" Realization dawned on Keeley's face. "It's the mortsafes, isn't it? You were looking at them when I first met you."

"You don't understand! I didn't know then!"

"Didn't know what?"

"That we were going to have to steal them," Jamie said miserably.

Keeley's eyes widened. "You *are* criminals!" she breathed. "I should have known!"

"We didn't have any choice!" Jamie protested. "This crazy guy let us stay in the Lodge, but now if we don't do what he wants he says he's going to kill us."

Keeley was pacing up and down in front of the memorial, her face creased in thought.

"That's why you texted me, wasn't it?" she said softly. "That's why you met up with me – to keep me away from the graveyard. So your family could get on with stealing without being interrupted."

"No! I mean, it wasn't *just* that. . ."

As he trailed off, Keeley nodded, biting her lip. Then she stalked away without another word, crossing the wasteland and slipping through the gap in the hedgerow. Jamie picked himself up from the memorial steps and hurried after her. Already he knew that there was no way he could talk her out of going back to the church – Keeley was too stubborn, too angry with him to listen. His only hope was that the mortsafes were already safely stored away in the removal van and Sarge and Liam were back in front of the TV. If they saw Jamie and Keeley while they were still working – it was too awful to even think about. Jamie would have failed Sarge, again.

The two of them walked moodily through the empty town, a solitary car roaring past them on the main road, its headlights piercing through the darkness. They reached the church to find the front gate unlocked, and skirted round the side of the building towards the graveyard. When the watch house came into view Jamie could barely dare to look, but then his heart gave a little skip of relief. The door remained closed, the padlock still clasped tightly around the chain. Pressing his face against the grille over the window, Jamie saw the silent ranks of the mortsafes still standing to attention against the wall.

"O–Kayyy," said Keeley. "Nothing to see here."

But as Jamie looked around the graveyard, his initial relief was replaced by a growing sense of unease. In all the years he had spent following Sarge around the country, he had never seen his dad walk away from a job. Once he had given them the green light that was it – there was no turning back. If Sarge and Liam had been caught in the act then there would be people here, the police even. Noise and flashing lights. But instead the graveyard was empty.

"Tell me something, Jamie," said Keeley. "Was all this some weird attempt to impress me, or are you *actually* delusional?"

Jamie turned and stared at the surrounding headstones. The wind rustled conspiratorially through the branches of the oak tree behind the watch house.

"Something's wrong," he said quietly.

"You got that right," retorted Keeley, tapping her temple. "Something's wrong up there, if you ask me."

Jamie ignored her. He turned his back on the watch house and walked away through the graves, his mind occupied by a sudden terrible possibility. As he continued uphill, to where the most recent graves had been dug, Keeley followed behind him complaining.

"Hellooooo? Earth to Jamie? Where are you going now? Look, if you think this is going to scare me it's not going to—"

Keeley paled.

They were standing in front of Greg's grave, the boy's name etched on a dark marble headstone. The ground in front of the headstone had been the subject of a violent disturbance, a coffin rising into the air as though it had been coughed up from the earth in a shower of loose earth. The lid of the coffin had been wrenched open, revealing its pale white innards. Greg's body was nowhere to be seen.

CHAPTER TEN

POST MORTEM

Jamie and Keeley fled the graveyard together, their footsteps stumbling and stuttering away through the darkness. At the church gate Keeley slipped away without a word, and when she glanced back over her shoulder at Jamie he saw fear and uncertainty etched across her face. He couldn't blame her. What had Sarge and Liam done?

He ran all the way home, the soles of his trainers pounding on the pavement and his head churning with unanswered questions. The Lodge was shrouded in darkness, its front windows dormant. Jamie didn't even bother trying the front door; instead he slipped around the side of the house, trying to catch his breath as he pressed himself against the icy stonework. Lights shone through the kitchen window; raised voices were floating out into the night.

"What the hell is going on here?" Liam shouted.

"How should I know?" Sarge yelled back. "You think that I had anything to do with this? Eh?"

Jamie flinched at the sound of a sharp bang, a fist

slamming into a fridge or a cupboard door. When Liam spoke again, his voice was calmer.

"Course not, Sarge," he said. "But since we've set foot in this place everything seems to have gone wrong."

"Tell me about it. I've seen some things in my time I wish I hadn't, but nothing like this. Grave-robbing? What kind of freak goes around digging up coffins?"

"I don't know . . . kids?"

"Kids?" Sarge's voice with thick with incredulous sarcasm. "The same kids who threw that bloody great rock at our windscreen? Or the kids who made that boy's car crash? Or the kids who killed Mathers's dog and buried it in our back garden?"

"You got a better explanation?"

"The way I see it, there are only two," said Sarge. "Either Mr Redgrave didn't care about the mortsafes and was deliberately trying to set us up. . ."

". . .or this is just a coincidence, he *does* care about the mortsafes and we haven't got them."

"That's about the long and short of it. Either way we're in trouble."

"What do we do, then?"

"Nothing." Sarge's voice was hard. "We do absolutely *nothing* until I'm sure what it is we're actually dealing with. We keep this between ourselves, understand?"

There was a long pause.

"I wish we'd never stepped foot in this bloody town," said Liam.

"That makes two of us, son."

102

The light in the window flicked off, and Jamie heard his father and brother leave the kitchen. He waited until he was breathing normally before walking back round to the front door and entering the Lodge. Liam and Sarge were in the front room, still dressed for work in their all-black uniforms, Sarge's bolt-cutters propped up against the side of one of the armchairs.

"All right, Jamie?" asked Liam. He was trying to sound upbeat, like everything was fine. "How did it go with Keeley?"

"OK."

"Get a kiss out of her?"

"No." Jamie refused to rise to his brother. "How did the job go?"

Liam and Sarge exchanged glances.

"We had to call it off," Sarge said finally. "There was a problem when we got to the watch house – a civilian out walking his dog. I don't think he saw us but the dog was raising all kinds of hell so we thought it best to come back to the Lodge."

"What about the mortsafes?" asked Jamie. "It sounded like Mr Redgrave wanted them pretty badly."

"And Mr Redgrave's going to get them," Sarge said smoothly. "But he's a professional too. The last thing he wants is a botched job and the police crawling over the place. We'll give it a couple of days and then we'll try again."

"Things went all right with Keeley?" checked Liam. "She didn't suspect anything?"

Jamie shook his head. "We just hung out at the war memorial for a bit and then went home. It was a bit boring, really."

Liam nodded, apparently satisfied. Jamie didn't like deceiving his brother but if Sarge and Liam were going to lie to him, then he was going to lie right back. The family went to their separate rooms soon after, each wrapped up in their own thoughts. Even as he shivered beneath his blankets, Jamie felt hot with indignation, too angry to sleep. He was sick of being treated like a little kid. It might be dark now but did Sarge think he somehow wouldn't notice there had been a grave robbery? Jamie's bedroom looked out on the cemetery! By morning there would be blue-and-white police cordons fluttering in the breeze around the remnants of Greg's grave, men in white overalls combing the area for clues. The whole town would be alive with the news.

Jamie wasn't the only one having trouble sleeping that night. A burst of movie gunfire erupted from the TV downstairs, where Sarge was supposed to be sleeping. In the next room, Liam's bedsprings creaked as he shifted restlessly in bed.

When morning did finally arrive, it had a surprise for all of them. Jamie opened his bedroom curtains to find there were no policemen examining the graveyard. There was no one there at all. What was more, where only hours earlier a coffin had jutted out from the earth like the hull of a shipwrecked liner, now the soil was smooth and serene. Even from this distance, Jamie could make out the yellow glow of a fresh bunch of flowers laid at Greg's headstone.

"You've got to be kidding me!" Liam's muffled voice, rising up through the grating into Jamie's bedroom. "Is this some kind of joke?"

"If it is, I'm not laughing," Sarge replied grimly.

It felt like a long time since anyone had laughed or even smiled in the Lodge. The temperature had dropped even further, turning each room in the house into a frozen cell. Sarge took his frustration out on the broken boiler, disappearing into the cupboard under the stairs with a toolbox he had found in the shed. Judging by the loud bangs and oaths emanating out through the door, he wasn't having any luck fixing it. Liam took the removal van over to Caxton to use the gym, leaving Jamie on his own. He had thought about borrowing Liam's phone to text Keeley, but he had no idea what he could say to her. What with nightmarish visions and coffins rising up and sinking back into the ground, it was getting harder and harder for him to believe his own eyes. *What kind of freak goes around digging up coffins?* Sarge had asked disbelievingly. If only he had learned about Alderston's history like Jamie had, he could have answered his own question. But George Rathbone and his men had been run out of town nearly two hundred years ago. And if some modern Resurrection Man had decided to pick up his shovel, why was there no sign of their crime? None of it made any sense to Jamie.

He left Sarge hammering angrily in the cupboard and

drifted into town. The sky was a barren white landscape above his head. It was market day in Alderston's main square, rows of stalls creating a narrow warren filled with clothing and second-hand CDs and DVDs around the clock tower. A white van was parked in front of a charity shop, a chalkboard propped up on the serving hatch advertising fish caught fresh from the sea that morning.

As Jamie threaded his way through the stalls, hands plunged in his pockets, he detected an uneasy edge to the bustling atmosphere. A young woman was arguing with a trader in a woolly hat over the price of a dressing gown, jabbing her finger into his chest. An old man glanced up warily at the swollen white clouds piling in overhead and spat on the ground, muttering darkly to himself. One trader had already started to pack his goods away, even through it was barely midday. When the man at the neighbouring stall pointed this out, he merely shook his head and continued ferrying boxes back to his van. Roxanne's warning came whistling back to Jamie on the breeze: *Winter's coming. They like it when it's cold.*

"Oi, lad!"

Jamie turned round to see a trader in a wax jacket eyeing him thoughtfully. He was in his twenties, broad-shouldered and shaven-headed. There was something vaguely familiar about him.

"Know you from somewhere, don't I?" the trader asked.

"I don't think so," Jamie said hesitantly. "I'm not from around here."

"Maybe so, but I've definitely seen you somewhere before." The man grinned. "Don't look so frightened, lad, I'm not taking you in for questioning. You're Keeley Marshall's new friend, aren't you? I saw you talking to her at the funeral."

Suddenly Jamie realized where he had seen the man before – he had been the one giving Keeley a black look outside the church. Jamie nodded, feeling suddenly uneasy.

"I thought so," the trader said. "Well, listen, lad, since you're new in town, let me give you some advice: stay the hell away from her."

"What?"

"You heard me. There's hatred running in that one's veins. I heard her bad-mouthing our Greg at the funeral, the little cow."

Jamie backed away, stumbling over an upturned crate. The trader leaned over his counter, his voice dropping to a threatening murmur. "So you tell Black Maggie to watch her step, right? Tell her Richie Metcalfe knows where she lives."

Jamie nodded and quickly walked off, trying not to look scared even though he was desperate to get away. He cut between two stalls and hurried down a narrow alleyway that ran down the side of the bank, not caring where he was going. It was only when he reached the end of the alley that he realized he had come out on to the small car park behind Roxanne's taxi firm. A couple of cars sat idly in the spaces by the back door to the office.

A dark green 4×4 was parked next to them.

Jamie pulled sharply back from the alleyway's entrance, his heart thumping against his ribcage. His head rang with the echoes of a dog snapping and biting as it fought against its chain, and a giant man's mocking laughter. The last time Jamie had seen that vehicle it had been parked in front of the Portakabin in Mathers's rain-swept scrapyard. What on earth was it doing here?

Peering around the corner, Jamie's heart sank when he saw the scrap dealer leaning against the side of his 4×4. Mathers had ditched his high-vis vest but apart from that he was dressed as usual, in a pair of blotchy grey overalls and wellington boots. His face, too, was as before; set in an idly mocking sneer. Mathers's companion was obscured behind the 4×4 – when they stepped forward to shake the scrap dealer's hand, Jamie realized how much trouble they were in. It was Don, Roxanne's right-hand man. If Mathers was looking for Sarge, then Don could tell him exactly where to find him.

Laughing obligingly at a parting crack from Mathers, Don stood back as the scrap dealer got into his 4×4 and the engine rumbled into life. Jamie was halfway up the alleyway before the vehicle had swept powerfully out of the car park. He raced through the market, the stalls blurring into one as the traders barked out their offers –

three for a fiver, cheapest in town, get your bargains here. By the time Jamie had left the market behind and reached the bottom of the hill, where the road forked beneath the shadow of Alderston church, he had given himself a stitch. He stopped to catch his breath, clutching at his sore side, his eyes alert for a glimpse of a green vehicle amongst the traffic. Up on top of the hill, the church stood resolute in the face of the cold wind: Aldus's fortress, unbowed by fire and ice, and the crushing weight of passing centuries.

Sarge and Liam wouldn't be happy when they heard the news that Jamie was rushing home to bring them. It didn't matter – he had to tell them. There was no telling what kind of danger they were in, but it felt as though the walls of the town were closing in around them, cutting off their escape routes. As he stumbled down the lane towards the Lodge, Jamie felt a soft, cold kiss upon his cheek. Looking up into the sky, he saw large white flakes spiralling lazily down towards the ground.

It had started to snow.

PART TWO
HEL-BLÁR

CHAPTER ELEVEN

THE SNOW

All of a sudden the air was alive with white flakes, a thick flurry descending upon the roofs and roads of Alderston. There was none of the noisy drama, the crash and crackle that accompanied thunder and lightning, or the rain's slippery patter. The snow fell in stealthy whirls, landing on the ground as silent as a feather. By the time Jamie reached the house at the end of the road, the pavement was already covered in a fine white dusting. The bumper of the removal van was poking out through the driveway gates, and through the front-room window Jamie could see the flicker of the TV screen.

He hurried inside the house, kicking off his trainers and leaving them in a pile in the hallway. Liam was lying beneath a blanket on the sofa in the front room, his hair damp from the shower. He didn't acknowledge Jamie as he burst in.

"Liam?"

His brother grunted.

"Liam!"

"Not now, eh? I'm watching the snooker."

"But it's important!"

His brother reluctantly looked up from the screen. "This had better be good," he warned.

"It's Mathers. He's here."

"Here?" Liam sat up. "In Alderston?"

Jamie nodded.

"Are you sure? I mean, absolutely *positive*?"

"Yes!"

"'Cause I know sometimes you space out and go into your own little world. That's all right, but this is too important to—"

"I wasn't spacing out!" interrupted Jamie, exasperated. "I saw the green 4×4, and I saw Mathers! He was in the car park talking to Don from the taxi firm. I couldn't hear what they were saying, but they looked pretty friendly."

Liam's face darkened, and he switched off the TV.

"What's he doing here, Liam?"

"I don't know," Liam admitted. "But I doubt it's to bring us chocolates and flowers. I'll talk to Sarge when he gets back. Don't worry about it, OK? I'll take care of it. I'm not scared of bloody Mathers."

Jamie was relieved to hear his brother sound so confident. But although Liam turned the TV on again, his eyes kept flicking away from the snooker to the front window, and later that afternoon Jamie heard the handle of the kitchen door rattle as his brother checked it was locked. Maybe Liam wasn't scared of Mathers, but he wasn't taking any chances.

114

They waited all evening for Sarge to come home, but the curtains had long been drawn by the time Jamie went to bed and still his dad hadn't returned. A part of Jamie was secretly pleased – it had been a long day, and the last thing he wanted was another angry interrogation from Sarge, as though spotting Mathers was somehow *his* fault. Huddled beneath an extra duvet, Jamie tumbled into an exhausted, dreamless sleep.

The snow kept falling.

When he woke up the next morning and climbed out of bed, his bare feet wincing at the cold floor, Jamie pulled back the curtains to find the world buried beneath a thick layer of crisp snow. The headstones in the churchyard had acquired white fringes, while a deep drift had formed around the base of the watch house. Shivering, Jamie gathered up some clothes and went into the bathroom, where he showered, dressed and brushed his teeth. Downstairs, he found a note in his brother's handwriting waiting for him on the kitchen table. It read simply: *Outside. Now.*

Jamie's shoulders sank. He knew it. Either Sarge hadn't believed his story, or he was blaming him for it. Glumly he retrieved his shoes from the hallway and struggled into his coat, trudging back to the kitchen like a condemned prisoner on his way to the firing squad. When he opened the back door, the dazzling white sheen covering the outside world made him blink. The snow lay in a perfect carpet around him. Jamie stepped out into the garden, his feet sinking in the snow with a satisfying crunch.

There was no one there.

"Liam?"

A snowball whizzed through the air, smacking Jamie in the temple. He stumbled backwards, brushing the icy powder from his face. From somewhere in the bushes came the sound of mocking laughter.

"Hey!" cried Jamie. "No fair! I wasn't ready!"

He ducked, too late to prevent a second snowball clipping the top of his head. Liam's voice rang out around the garden.

"Take cover, little brother!" he called out. "I'm coming for you!"

There was a flash of movement behind one of the bushes, and this time Jamie was able to dodge the snowball that flew past his ear and smacked into the wall behind him. This meant war. Dropping to his knees, Jamie began scooping up snow and fashioning his own ammunition. He came under fire at once, white missiles raining down around him. Liam could hurl his snowballs faster and more accurately, so Jamie had to pick his moments to go on the attack, taking shelter behind bushes and trees before leaping out to take aim himself. When one glorious shot caught his brother squarely in the face, Jamie punched the air in triumph as Liam spluttered and wiped the snow from his eyes. Without any gloves to protect them Jamie's fingers were soon stinging with the cold, but he forced himself to carry on scraping up snow, refusing to be the one who stopped first.

Finally, when they had both run out of breath and their fingers were red and burning, Liam charged towards Jamie, roaring at the top of his voice, and rugby tackled him to the soft ground. Jamie was pinned to the floor, although not before he had the satisfaction of shoving a handful of cold snow down the back of his brother's coat.

"Give in?" Liam demanded, breathing heavily.

Jamie nodded.

"I'm the best and you're a little squirt?"

Jamie nodded again.

Liam grinned and hauled him to his feet. "Not a bad shot earlier," he said admiringly. "You still throw like a girl, mind, but that's not your fault – seeing as you are a girl."

Jamie tried to shove him away but Liam wrapped an arm around him, drawing him into a half-headlock, half-hug.

"It'll just be me and you for today," he told Jamie. "Sarge is in town checking the grapevine to see if there's any word about our friend being in town."

"Oh."

For a few fleeting moments, it had just been Jamie and his brother messing about and everything had been all right. But now the real world had returned, with its mortsafes, thieves and dead dogs, and the snow didn't seem quite as dazzling as it had before. Jamie glanced up to find Liam looking at him thoughtfully.

"There should have been a bit more of this, eh lad?"

"A bit more of what?"

"Snowball fights. Kickabouts. You know . . . fun."

"Oh." Jamie shrugged. "I guess. Not much you can do when you're in a van all day."

"It was easier for me, see – being a bit older and that. I can remember when Mam was still around, before she got sick. Things were different then, normal. We lived in a house, for starters; it wasn't big or anything, but it was better than the van."

"I'd like a house like this one," Jamie said eagerly. "We could all live there and not have to move all the time. And I could go to school and—"

"You *want* to go to school?" Liam's eyes crinkled with amusement. "You really are a weirdo, Jamie, you know that?"

In the kitchen they peeled off their wet coats and left their shoes to dry out on the doormat. Jamie's fingers stung as the circulation returned to his veins. As the afternoon went on the snow returned – harder this time, until the flakes fell in a continuous white curtain. Around four Jamie heard a key turning in the front door. He and Liam hurried out into the hallway to find Sarge stamping the snow from his feet, his hands full of shopping bags from the local supermarket.

"I brought supplies," he explained. "Not sure how long this weather's going to last."

"Any news?" Liam asked quickly.

Sarge shook his head. "Nothing – so far as I can tell.

If he is about, I don't want him knowing that I've been asking for him."

No one seemed to want to mention Mathers's name out loud, but Jamie knew what they were talking about. He wasn't stupid.

"What about the boiler?" asked Liam. "Any luck finding someone who can fix it?"

"I found someone," Sarge replied. "Only problem is, they're in Caxton."

"Why's that a problem?" asked Jamie. "It's only a few miles away. Liam was there yesterday."

Liam let out a groan. "The road across the Moss is snowed under, isn't it?"

"Completely impassable," Sarge told him. "No one can get in. And no one can get out."

"Great," said Liam. "We'd be bloody warmer in the van. Why didn't we get it fixed *before* it started snowing?"

"Don't start, son," Sarge replied ominously. "Not today."

Biting back a retort, Liam took the shopping bags through to the kitchen and began to unpack them. They heated up ready meals in the microwave for dinner and ate them camped around a heater in the living room, toasting their hands and feet in the warm draught. That night, when Jamie went upstairs he piled another couple of blankets on to the bed, but no matter tightly he curled up into a ball he couldn't escape the chill. It sank into his bones and seeped into his mind, plaguing him with bad dreams. As he slept, Jamie watched through someone else's eyes as he prowled a landscape black as midnight, the slim shadow of trees all around him. It felt as though a great furnace had been lit in his chest, fuelled by rage and a deep, unspeakable envy. He could hear the ragged, animal breaths coming from his mouth, could feel the rippling strength in his muscles. Hunger so strong it felt like an ancient need. His thoughts were consumed by the urge to rip, and to crush . . . and to kill.

Jamie woke with a start. His skin was clammy with sweat and his muscles ached from the constant huddle for warmth. Cold air gnawed at the tips of his ears. Dawn was painting the bedroom in a watery grey colour. All Jamie wanted to do was roll over and go back to sleep but he needed the toilet. Reluctantly he climbed out of bed and padded across the landing to the bathroom. The Lodge was encased in frozen silence. As he washed his hands, Jamie found himself staring at the curtain across the bathroom window. Wondering if it was still snowing, he opened the bathroom curtains, wiping away streams of condensation from the glass with his pyjama sleeve, and peered outside. The blizzard had finally stopped, but not before submerging Alderston in a thick white blanket. In the garden below, all traces of Jamie's battle with Liam the previous day had been wiped clean. The snow was pristine once more.

Almost.

A single set of tracks made a dark line across the garden, snaking from the back fence to beneath the bathroom window, where they came to a sudden halt.

Not animal tracks – human footprints. Goosebumps broke out across Jamie's skin. Someone had walked all the way across the fields and climbed over the fence just to stand beneath the window. As Jamie looked down the sky seemed to darken and return to night, and he could see a shadowy figure in the garden below, its breath forming frosty clouds as it stared up at the bathroom.

Yanking the curtains closed, Jamie ran back to his room and dived under the bedcovers, shivering uncontrollably.

CHAPTER TWELVE

BLACK MAGGIE

It was the grating in the bedroom sideboard that woke Jamie up again, voices carrying up from the kitchen through its small, wrought-iron mouth.

"Jesus!" he heard Liam say. "Have you seen outside, Sarge?"

"Aye," Sarge replied. "Looks like Mathers paid us a visit in the night. I guess he's searching for his beloved pooch."

"He'll have a job finding him. Smiler's six feet under all that snow."

"Maybe so, but he's closer than he's any right to be," Sarge said darkly. "He shouldn't even know what postcode his dog's buried in. You think it's a coincidence that Mathers is creeping round our garden? Someone must have pointed a finger in our direction."

"Don," spat Liam. "That little—"

"My thoughts exactly," interrupted Sarge. "Don't worry, we'll take care of our good friend from the taxi firm. But first of all we deal with Mathers."

"How?"

"How do you think? It shouldn't be that hard to find him. As long as the snow holds he can't go anywhere. Even that 4×4 couldn't manage the roads as they are at the moment."

"So why hasn't anyone seen him?"

"Maybe he's not staying in town. Did you see where the footprints were coming from?"

"Straight from the wood on the Moss. You think he's hiding out there?"

"It's a possibility. Mathers is as tough as old boots – a bit of winter camping isn't going to bother him. And if he is trying to stay out of sight it's the perfect hiding place. All you have to do is mention those woods and people round here get the jitters. They aren't going to poke their nose in."

"What are you going to tell Jamie?"

"Nothing yet. The less he knows the better. Lord knows I want to be able to trust the lad – he's my son, just like you are – but we all know what he can be like. Did you see the way he was acting at Greg's funeral? Speaking of which, better go out now and brush those tracks away before—"

Sarge was interrupted by an unexpected jangle of the doorbell. The grating fell pointedly silent.

"You expecting visitors, son?" Sarge asked carefully.

"Nope," Liam replied.

"Me neither. Come on."

Jamie rolled out of bed and quickly pulled a jumper and a pair of jeans over his pyjamas before leaving his bedroom. From the landing he heard the murmur of voices from the front door. He peered down the stairs and saw Liam looking back at him, a broad grin upon his face.

"You've got a visitor, Jamie lad," he said.

Liam stepped to one side to reveal Keeley standing on the doorstep. She was immersed in a thick duffel coat, with a black woollen hat and matching gloves. Her arms were folded, her bag slung over her shoulder.

"Hi," she said.

"Um, hi," replied Jamie.

"Come on in, love," Liam said easily. "You'll catch your death out there."

She stepped uncertainly into the hallway as Jamie walked down the stairs, aware of Sarge standing in the kitchen doorway, his face schooled into a polite smile.

"Hope I'm not disturbing you," said Keeley.

"Not at all," Sarge replied. "My boy's told me a lot about you. Always nice to put a name to the face. We'll leave you two youngsters to it."

He pushed Liam towards the living room; Jamie flinched as his brother ruffled his hair on the way past. He took Keeley through into the kitchen and closed the door behind them.

"Sorry about them," he said.

"Don't worry about it," Keeley replied. "You should see what my mum's like. One foot through the door and she'd be stuffing food down your throat and asking you a million questions. It's awful."

"Doesn't sound so bad to me," said Jamie. "You not at school?"

"It's closed. Half the teachers can't get in. Don't know if you've heard, but there's been a bit of snow round here lately."

"Of course, yeah."

"Shouldn't stop you, though," Keeley said slyly. "You being 'homeschooled' and all."

There was an awkward silence.

"Look, about the other night..." said Jamie. "I'm sorry things got so weird."

"Yeah." Keeley looked back towards the kitchen door, drumming her fingers on her bag strap. When she started speaking again, the words came tumbling quickly out of her mouth, hot with embarrassment. "When I got home from the churchyard I didn't want to see you again, ever, but then I thought about it and you seemed as freaked out as I did, and even if it was your family who ... you know ... it didn't mean it was *your* fault..." She took a deep breath. "I just wanted to check that you were all right."

"I'm fine," said Jamie. "Thanks. And it wasn't anything to do with Sarge and Liam, I swear. Did you see the graveyard the next day? It was like nothing had ever happened."

Keeley nodded. "That's Alderston for you. I tried telling my mum about it but she was too busy stressing about not being able to get to the hospital for work. As if it doesn't matter that someone's going around digging up dead bodies." She sighed. "So what are you doing today? Do you want to hang out?"

Did you see where those footprints were coming from? Sarge had asked Liam. *The less he knows the better. . .*

"I'm going for a walk," said Jamie. "To the wood on the Moss."

Keeley arched a single eyebrow. "And why would you want to go there?"

"Why not?"

"There's nothing there!"

"Fine! Don't come with me!"

Keeley glared at him for what felt like an age. Then she strode over to the back door and opened it.

"Are you coming then, or what?" she demanded.

Jamie smiled. "Give me five minutes to get ready," he told her.

They left the Lodge together, following the road as it wound up the hill and around the church before leading out of Alderston towards the Moss. Behind them, on a hill on the other side of the town, there were dark spots of movement as children built snowmen and bombed down the slope on sledges. Jamie and Keeley kept going in the other direction, past hedgerows crowned with white powder. They didn't talk much, concentrating on keeping their footing in the treacherous drifts. The wood lay up ahead, a dark shadow on a brilliant white canvas. Something about the slender congregation of trees made Jamie feel uneasy. When all was said and done, Mathers was a criminal, and if he *was* hiding out in the woods there was no telling what he might do if he caught them.

Jamie wondered whether he should have told Keeley about Mathers before setting out. Then again, it wasn't as though she had been that keen on coming to the wood in the first place, and Jamie was glad of her company. It wasn't just that, though. Keeley might know about the failed robbery of the mortsafes, but Jamie didn't want to have to explain about the scrapyard dealer and his dead dog buried deep beneath the cold earth. That was his family's secret, no one else's. All Jamie needed was a glimpse of Mathers and they'd leave the wood immediately. Then he could go back to the Lodge and tell Sarge and Liam that he had found their man – maybe then they'd stop treating him like a little kid and trying to hide everything from him.

The drifts deepened as they neared the wood, until Jamie saw that even Mathers's 4×4 wouldn't be able to force its way through. Alderston was going to be cut off for a while. When they reached the edge of the trees, Keeley stopped.

"You all right?" asked Jamie.

"Fine."

"Then what is it?"

"Nothing," said Keeley, briskly adjusting her hat. "Just . . . watch your step, OK?"

It was too late for Jamie to ask her what she meant –

Keeley had already plunged into the gloom. He hurried after her, the shadows enveloping him. Although Jamie had been driven through the wood twice before, he soon realized that entering it on foot was a different matter entirely. Wedged in the front seat of the van, with his father and brother on either side, he had been safe, protected. But inside these trees, the outside world didn't seem to matter any more. They could have been walking through the wood a thousand years ago, or another thousand years in the future. In here, the trees seemed to whisper, nothing would ever change.

With Keeley hurriedly tramping through the snow ahead of him, Jamie had to concentrate on keeping up. The crisp tread of their footprints were the only sounds – no birds sang in the bare, skeletal branches; no animals scurried through the frosted undergrowth. There was a hollow absence of life in the wood that seemed due to more than just the changing of the seasons. Instinctively, Jamie was certain that Mathers wasn't here. He found himself wishing that they had kept the road in sight – then he remembered the twisted wreckage of Greg's car, and thought better of it. Maybe this hadn't been such a clever idea after all.

Almost as if she could hear his thoughts, Keeley stopped.

"Woods," she said bluntly, gesturing at the trees. "Happy now?"

Jamie shrugged. "I guess."

"Great. Let's get out of here."

As they ploughed on through the snow, the ground to their left began to rise, forming a steep bank. Keeley, Jamie noticed, kept her eyes fixed straight in front of her. If anything, she seemed to have picked up her pace.

"What's the big hurry?" he asked her.

Keeley nodded ahead. "If we keep going this way we'll soon come out the other side," she told him. "We can walk back to town around the edge of the fields – hey, where are you going?"

Jamie was already scrambling up the bank.

"I'll be back in a second!" he called out.

"Jamie! Don't!"

He crested the bank, and looked out breathlessly over the scene on the other side. The ground fell away in front of him, sloping down towards a large pond – a dark gem set into the snowy ground. The surface of the water was a still, inky mirror. On the far edge of the pond the outline of a large rock was visible beneath the snow. The silence was total, deafening; the cold somchow more bitter and intense.

As Jamie stood and stared, he heard the reluctant crunch of Keeley's boots as she followed him up the bank and stood beside him.

"Well, now you've seen it," she sighed. "Welcome to Black Maggie's pond."

"Lawrence told me about her," said Jamie. "She was a witch, wasn't she?"

Keeley gave him a cold stare. "Of *course* she wasn't a witch, dummy."

"But ... I mean, that's what everyone thought, wasn't it?"

"Just because everyone thinks something, it doesn't mean it's true, Jamie," Keeley said, exasperated. "OK, Maggie had a sharp tongue and wouldn't keep her mouth shut, and she argued with everyone in Alderston at one point or another. So people didn't like her, and for years people had been accusing her of silly stuff, like making the cows dry up so they couldn't produce any milk. But then one day her oldest enemy was found dead in her bed, her bones all broken. Maggie was arrested and accused of making a pact with the Devil. At her trial it was said she brought the dead back to life and sent them out to kill people in the town who had crossed her."

"What happened?"

"They found her guilty, of course. Maggie was sentenced to the ducking stool as punishment. The next morning a crowd of people dragged her from her cell and brought her here. It was winter, just like now. An old woman, in her bare feet. She would have been so cold."

As Keeley spoke, Jamie could hear the echoes of the crowd – the jeers and the taunts, the mocking laughter as Black Maggie stumbled, her bony frame shivering, through the snow.

"When they reached this pond they strapped her into a chair on the end of a long beam and plunged her into the water."

130

Jamie stared at the blank surface of the pond.

"I can't imagine what that must have felt like," Keeley said softly. "The shock of it. Freezing cold water streaming into your nose and mouth. Fighting to breathe but being unable to break free. Five times they lifted her out, five times they stuck her back in again. Maggie stopped screaming after the third time. By the time they were done with her she was dead."

Jamie shuddered. "That's horrible."

"That's Alderston for you. They have their own way of taking care of things here. Black Maggie had the last laugh, though. The day after she died the town mayor was found dead in his bedroom, his neck broken and his ribcage shattered. People have stayed away from the pond ever since."

"Apart from Kitty Hawkins," said Jamie.

"She did." Keeley gave him a meaningful look. "And look what happened to her."

"You think Black Maggie had something to do with Kitty's accident?"

"Course not! I think 'Black' Maggie was just a harmless old woman who was picked on and murdered by a cruel mob. But that doesn't mean I don't think that there aren't monsters in this town, and I don't come here more than I have to."

"You seem to know an awful lot about her."

Keeley blew out her cheeks. "It's a family thing. I'm Maggie's great-great-great-whatever-granddaughter."

"Hang on," Jamie said incredulously. "*That's* why

people think you're a witch? But that's crazy! Who cares what happened hundreds of years ago?"

"In this town?" Keeley laughed. "Everyone. Don't you see, Jamie? The past doesn't go away here. It's like the snow, trapping us all — only this snow won't ever thaw, and it won't ever go away. I won't ever be free from it."

"You could always leave. Go somewhere else."

"It's not as simple as that. We don't live like you, Jamie. We can't just hop in a van and leave every time we feel like it. They're making cutbacks at the hospital and Mum's fighting for her job. I can't ask her to run away because some idiots are being mean to me."

"I guess not," said Jamie. "Well, I'm not from around here and I don't care what anyone else says. *I* don't think you're a witch."

"Great," Keeley said gloomily. "You're weirder than I am."

Jamie smiled, and after a second, so did she. Suddenly he was aware that it was just the two of them by the side of the pond and that they were standing close together, their breath clouds brushing against each other. As Jamie gazed at Keeley the blush of colour in her cheeks seemed to deepen, and there was a look in her eyes that he couldn't quite decipher.

"Don't even think about it," Keeley said quickly.

"What?"

"You know."

"I don't!" But Jamie could feel his own face reddening, and his voice squeaked with indignation.

"Was that why you wanted to come here?" Keeley demanded. "So we'd be 'alone'?"

"No, I wanted to see the wood!"

But it was too late — Keeley had already marched away down the bank and was stomping off through the snow. As he stumbled after her Jamie wasn't sure whether she was actually angry with him or just embarrassed, or whether in fact she was just desperate for a reason to get out of the wood — to leave the glassy pond behind them and return to the bright white world beyond the trees' edge.

CHAPTER THIRTEEN

THE PALS

On the way back to Alderston Jamie trailed after Keeley like an embarrassed shadow. He knew she was waiting for him to apologize but he wasn't entirely sure what for – whatever Keeley might have thought, he hadn't been planning on trying to kiss her. Jamie had never kissed a girl before; he had never even had the chance, although he would never have admitted it. So they walked home in silence, before sharing an awkward goodbye in front of the church. The wind ruffled Keeley's fringe as she reached into her bag and handed Jamie an old cassette tape.

"What's this?" he asked.

"I said I'd give you this back at the war memorial, remember? I found it in a box up in the attic. Take care of it – it's my mum's, and she'll go spare if she finds I've taken it."

Jamie shrugged. "OK," he said. Keeley had already started walking around down the hill. He called out after her: "Will I see you again?"

"Maybe!" Keeley called back, without turning around. "Listen to the tape, Jamie-Not-From-Around-Here!"

He watched her disappear down the road towards the town centre before walking home to the Lodge. There was no sign of Sarge, but Liam was lounging on the sofa in front of the TV, buried beneath several layers of blankets. He grinned at the sight of Jamie.

"Welcome home, lover boy! How did your date go?"

"It wasn't a date!"

"Oh aye?" Liam's eyes twinkled. "Give you the knock-back, did she?"

"No, I didn't. . . !" Jamie shook his head. There was no use talking to his brother when he was like this. Liam enjoyed tormenting him too much. "Can I have the keys to the van?"

"Course you can," Liam said breezily. "Drive her carefully, though, and fill up the tank before you bring her back."

"Ha ha," said Jamie. "I'm not driving anywhere. I just need to listen to this."

He passed his brother the cassette tape. Liam turned it over in his hands. "This is old school," he murmured. "What's on it?"

"Don't know yet, do I?" Jamie said impatiently. "But the van's the only thing old enough to have a cassette player I can use. Go on, give us the keys!"

"I tell you what," said Liam, tapping the cassette against his cheek. "How about I keep the keys, and we'll listen to it together?"

Jamie shrugged, defeated. "Whatever."

Liam climbed out from beneath his blankets and

pulled on a jacket, playfully rebuffing his brother's attempts to snatch the cassette tape back. They went out into the driveway, where the van was sitting idly in the snow, and climbed up into the front seat, brushing crumbs from the worn leather on to the floor. The view through the windscreen was dominated by the crumbling graveyard wall on the other side of the lane. Blowing into his hands, Liam turned the key in the ignition and inserted the tape into the cassette player. For a few seconds there was silence, and then a loud click signalled the beginning of a recording. Murmuring voices; a television blaring in the background. Someone wheezing close to the microphone, exhausted breaths like a tyre slowly deflating.

"Are you sure you're all right to do this, Granddad Frank?" a girl's voice asked. Keeley's mum, Jamie guessed. "I can always come back tomorrow, you know."

"I'm fine, Jennifer," an old man insisted, in a voice like crackling parchment. "Fire away, my girl."

"OK, if you're sure. Like I said on the phone, our history teacher Mr Roberts wants us to do a project on the First World War. Seeing as you were actually in the trenches, I thought if I could come to the nursing home and ask you a few questions that would be much more interesting than just reading a load of books."

"Well, this is going to be fascinating," Liam said sourly. "You made me come out here to listen to some girl's homework project?"

136

"Shhh!" said Jamie. "I'm trying to listen!"

"Sooooo. . ." There was a rustle of paper as Jennifer looked through her notes. "Dad told me you went to France as a member of the . . . Fourteenth Lancashire Battalion."

"The Pals," the old man said proudly. "Everyone called us the Alderston Pals. We came from all around the area — from Caxton and Wellesby too, and the surrounding villages — but it was Alderston lads at the heart of it. Everyone knew not to mess with the people from our town. Now it was time to show the Germans a thing or two. We were looking forward to it. What silly boys we were."

"So you went with your friends?"

"Aye, there were the Illingworth brothers, Charlie and Christopher; Dick Stevens; Harold, the fishmonger's lad. And my best friend Jack came too, on the toss of a coin would you believe. As a lad he had found the coin in the woods near his house at Lark Farm, and swore blind it was lucky. Well, it couldn't have been that lucky: he called heads for the Front, and tails to stay home, and heads it came up."

"What was it like when you got there?" asked Jennifer. "In the trenches, I mean?"

The old man wheezed painfully. "Boiling in summer, freezing cold in winter," he said. "Knee-deep with churned-up mud; rats scurrying everywhere. Exploding shells, dead bodies. They weren't trenches, Jennifer, they were the tunnels of Hell. We were there six months

137

before the order came to go over the top into No Man's Land – it felt like a lifetime."

"Were you scared?"

"Scared? I was petrified – we all were! The order was a death sentence. We were sitting ducks out in No Man's Land; target practice for the Germans. Shells were exploding all around me, earth flying up into the air and bodies tumbling to the ground, but I kept walking. We all kept walking. What else could we do? In the blink of an eye over three hundred Pals died, including most of the boys from Alderston. Somehow I survived. I don't know why I didn't get hit – whether it was just plain old good luck, or something else. You'd have to ask Him Upstairs, and I'll be seeing him long before you will."

"What about your friend Jack?"

"He took a piece of shrapnel in the head," Frank told her. "A lesser man would have died right there, in a churned-up field in France, but my pal Jack was a fighter. The medics found him bleeding in a ditch and managed to patch him up enough to bring him away from the Front. Jack survived the journey back to England, but his injuries were too severe for even him to overcome. He died in Caxton Hospital three months after coming back from France, still clutching his lucky coin."

"That's so sad!" Jennifer said sympathetically. "You must have been devastated."

"We all were. But that was the Great War for you. There wasn't a family in Alderston who hadn't lost a loved one: a son or a husband or a brother. When I eventually came home two years later the town was still in mourning."

"In 1918? After the war had ended, you mean?"

There was a long pause on the tape. "The war didn't end in 1918."

"I'm pretty sure it did, Granddad," Jennifer told him gently. "Look, it's here in my notes: 'The First World War ended when the Germans signed an Armistice on 11 November, 1918.'"

"Not for us, it didn't," the old man said obstinately.

"I don't understand—"

"You're an Alderston girl!" he snapped, suddenly angry. "I shouldn't have to tell you! People can't just leave out the bits of history they don't like!"

"You're not making any sense, Granddad! What are you talking about?"

The old man erupted into a hacking cough that crackled over the speakers. When he spoke again it was more slowly, each breath an audible struggle.

"I'm talking about what happened when the Pals came back to Alderston," he said quietly. "The living *and* the dead."

"My auntie used to tell me stories about ghosts of some of the dead soldiers haunting the town. Is that what you mean?"

"Ghosts!" The old man's voice was thick with contempt. "Ghosts are nothing to be frightened of. They can't lay on a finger on you. I thought I had seen the worst the world was capable of in the trenches, but

I came home to Alderston to find a killer on the loose who was meaner and stronger than ten German soldiers. A creature of pure evil."

"A killer? Granddad, I've never heard anything about this!"

"Of course you haven't! That's the problem with this town – it's obsessed with keeping secrets. It was the same in those months after 1918. No one wanted to face up to the fact that people were disappearing and not coming back. It was left to the handful of boys who had survived the Front to band together and hunt down the killer. We finally cornered it in a barn on the edge of the town. It was so strong; it took all eight of us to bring it down. We had to chop its head off to keep from getting up again."

"Granddad!" Shock echoed in Jennifer's voice. "You didn't!"

"We didn't have a choice. If we hadn't, it would have carried on killing."

"I don't understand this," Jennifer said desperately. "What are you talking about? Who was this killer?"

"It was Jack," Frank replied miserably. "My poor pal Jack. . ."

The old man became choked up, and he started to cry. There was an awkward pause, and then a nurse's voice interrupted the tape.

"I'm going to have to ask you to stop whatever it is you're doing," she said sternly. "Frank's clearly not well enough for this."

Jennifer stammered an apology and the recording hurriedly clicked off, leaving a soft hiss echoing around the van as the tape continued to play. Jamie pressed eject and turned to Liam.

"What do you think?" he asked.

"I think Frank forgot to take his medication that day."

"Be serious!"

"I am! Haven't you heard Sarge talking about soldiers coming back from wars? Half of them are a complete mess. They end up with Gulf War Syndrome or something like that. Your man Frank there sounds like he was suffering from shell shock. He came back to Alderston and found his dead friend was going around killing people, so he chopped his head off?" Liam tapped his the side of his head. "Yeah, right."

"If none of it happened, why did Keeley give me the tape?"

"How should I know? The inner workings of the teenage goth mind . . ." Seeing Jamie's serious expression, Liam punched his brother lightly on the arm. "Don't let all this local mumbo jumbo get to you, little bro. Alderston's a funny old place but it's not—"

Liam paused, looking up through the van's windscreen. Following his brother's gaze, Jamie saw a procession of figures walking in single file through the graveyard towards the watch house.

"Hello, hello," Liam muttered. "What's going on here, then?"

Jamie recognized the grey-haired vicar at the head of the procession. Don was also there, along with Richie Metcalfe and the paunchy landlord of the Royal Oak – and a couple of other men Jamie didn't know. At the watch-house door the vicar produced a set of keys and unlocked the building. Don and Richie went inside, and reappeared carrying a mortsafe between them. Even at this distance Jamie could see that they were struggling with the weight of the iron cage.

"They're taking the mortsafes," said Liam. "Sarge isn't going to like this."

But as Jamie watched, he realized that they weren't going far. Slipping and sliding in the snow, their faces reddening with the effort, Don and Richie manoeuvred the mortsafes over one of the graves and lowered it into place. The other men followed suit, carrying the cages out of the watch house and securing them over the tops of the graves.

"What are they doing?" murmured Liam.

"Protecting the graves," Jamie told him. "I guess they're expecting the grave robber to strike again. They did the same to stop George Rathbone and the Resurrection Men."

"And when was that, then?"

Jamie nodded. "About two hundred years ago. Why?"

Liam pointed at the gleaming iron cages. "Because those mortsafes aren't two hundred years old. They look pretty new to me – five, ten years old at the most. So it's a bit convenient that they just happened to have some on site. Unless they were expecting this."

Jamie glanced across at his brother, and back at the cassette tape.

Liam shook his head. "I'm getting as bad as you," he muttered. "Come on, lad, let's go inside."

CHAPTER FOURTEEN

EARTH AND MOSS

Jamie lay back in the bath and let out a long sigh of satisfaction. Steam was rising up from the water in great clouds, wreathing the bathroom in humid fog. Droplets of condensation were running down the white tiles, and the mirror had misted up. Peering over the edge of the tub, Jamie could barely see his pile of clothes in the corner through the steam. The wind buffeting the house only made the bathroom feel more like a sanctuary.

The Lodge's shower might still be working but the bath was connected to the broken boiler, and it had taken Jamie the best part of half an hour and several trips upstairs to fill the tub with water he had boiled in the kettle. It had been worth every second. Ever since his family's arrival in Alderston he had felt besieged by the cold, and it was glorious to lie stewing in the bath's warm embrace, to feel the heat passing all the way down from his head to his toes. Jamie felt like he could have stayed there for ever, until his skin was wrinkled like an old man's and he was too weak to clamber out of the tub.

His dad and his brother had headed out to the Royal

Oak an hour earlier, continuing their careful search for information on Mathers's whereabouts. Liam had looked uneasy at the prospect of leaving Jamie on his own, but there was no way Jamie was going to ask him to stay. Sarge waited impatiently in the doorway as Liam wrote his mobile number down on a piece of paper in the kitchen, telling Jamie to call him if there was any trouble. Secretly Jamie was grateful for the prospect of an evening to himself. And if Mathers was stalking the streets of Alderston, Jamie didn't want Sarge walking alone through the town at night.

Wherever the scrap dealer was hiding, it wasn't in the woods – Jamie's trip with Keeley had convinced him of that. Perhaps he should have felt reassured, but if anything the opposite was true. Hours after he returned home, Jamie had had the uneasy feeling that he had brought something back with him, like a stone wedged in the soles of his trainers. Added to the unsettling tape of Keeley's grandfather and the sight of the townspeople breaking out the mortsafes, and Jamie was left with more questions than ever.

The wind had picked up outside, rattling the windowpanes in their settings. Jamie was resting his head against the tub when a loud thud on the roof made him sit up. It sounded as though something had fallen out of the sky and crashed into the Lodge. He sat very still, until the ripples in his bathwater had died away and the water was a glassy sheen. *Must have been the wind*, Jamie told himself.

There was another thud on the roof, and a painful crunch of tiles. The bathwater winced and quivered. Jamie held his breath.

Crunch. Crunch. Another jarring thud, louder than before.

It wasn't the wind. There was someone on the roof.

Jamie stood up in the bath, water dripping from his body, and pulled a towel off the handrail. He dried himself quickly, his skin still damp as he slipped into his clothes. The thuds and crunches above his head had stopped, plunging the house into an ominous silence, a snatched breath between screams. Jamie slowly opened the bathroom door, tendrils of steam curling around his legs and snaking out into the cold corridor as he peered into the darkness.

"Hello?" he called out softly, hoping to hear Sarge's gruff bark from downstairs, or Liam's laughter. But there was no reply. Jamie was half tempted to lock himself in the bathroom and wait until the noise died away, but if there was a problem and he needed to call for help, the phone was downstairs. He couldn't spend the whole night trembling in the bathroom.

Jamie crept along the landing, leaving the drowsy warmth behind him. Floorboards creaked uneasily beneath his feet. Shadows clutched long-held secrets. The house seemed larger in the darkness, older and steeped in a sullen air – no longer Jamie's home but the solitary lair of George Rathbone. In his mind's eye Jamie could hear the echo of the Resurrection Man's footsteps as he paced through the lonely halls, readying himself for another midnight trip to the graveyard. A swig of spirits to warm the chest and steady the nerves; a muttered oath for courage; the spit and crackle of wood as the fire burned low in the grate. . .

There was a loud bang on the front door. Jamie froze.

Tiptoeing to the top of the stairs, he peered down the hallway. The noise had been pregnant with threat – less of a knock than a slammed fist. Could someone really have scrambled down from the roof to the door so quickly? Or was there more than one person outside? Jamie didn't want to think about that possibility. He racked his brains, trying to remember whether Sarge had locked the front door before he had left.

There was nothing for it – he had to check. Jamie tiptoed down the staircase and along the hallway, each footstep as soft as a breath. Reaching out a trembling hand, he tried the door handle. It was locked. He let out a sigh of relief. The window by the front door was made of frosted glass, preventing Jamie from seeing outside clearly, but he couldn't make out any silhouettes on the doorstep.

He walked into the kitchen, resisting the urge to turn the lights on as he went. If it looked like there was nobody home, perhaps whoever was outside would get bored and go away. Moonlight was pouring in through the kitchen blinds, collecting in a pool in the sink. The fridge let out a dull hum as it ticked over. The back door was also locked. For the time being, at least, he was safe.

It was then that the house phone started ringing. Jamie stood and stared at it. Something about the timing of the call gave it a sinister, insistent edge. Each ring was a separate taunt, daring him to pick it up. Jamie watched the phone for a whole minute, and then another, silently praying in vain for it to stop. Whoever was calling seemed happy to wait for him to pick up. Maybe they knew he was there. Maybe Liam was calling on his mobile with an urgent message. Finally Jamie's nerve broke. He ran over and snatched up the receiver.

"Hello?"

"Jamie, Jamie, Jamie," a voice rasped. Jamie's heart sank. It was Mr Redgrave. "Bad time, is it?"

"What do you mean?"

"It took you a long time to answer the phone. You kept me waiting."

"I was in the bath."

"What about Sarge and Liam – they in there with you?"

"They're not in," said Jamie, instantly regretting it.

"You're home alone?" Mr Redgrave tutted slowly. "Parents these day."

"They're coming back any minute now," lied Jamie.

"No they're not, you little whelp," Mr Redgrave said viciously. "Sarge is propping up the bar in the Royal Oak and he *and* your brother will be there until last orders. There's no one there to help you, son. Not a living soul."

Goosebumps broke out across Jamie's skin. "What do you want?" he asked.

"You know what I want. We had a deal. If you stayed in the house, you did a job for me."

"I know, but—"

"*We had a deal!*" A voice like a snakebite. Venom dripped from the receiver. "I don't care about excuses. I want my mortsafes!"

"We tried to get them, honest!" pleaded Jamie. "But someone got there before us. They dug up Greg's body and took it. We couldn't stick around after that!"

There was a strange, strangled noise down the phone line. It took Jamie a few seconds to realize that Mr Redgrave was chuckling.

"So it was grave robbers who stopped you, was it?"

"Yes!"

"You've spent too much time listening to local ghost stories, Jamie. It's been two hundred years since the Resurrection Men were last abroad in Alderston. You don't have to worry about grave robbers, or the police, or anybody else. You only have to worry about *me*. Tell Sarge that I want my mortsafes by the end of the week. Or there'll be penalties."

Jamie nervously ran his tongue over dry lips. "Penalties?"

"It's nothing personal, son," Mr Redgrave told him. "It was nothing personal with Mathers, either. But in our business, you have to have penalties. Else people think they can get away with murder."

"It's not fair!" said Jamie. "Why us? What did we ever do to you?"

"You stole from me," Mr Redgrave told him sharply. "You and your dad and Liam took a whole load of copper wire from the railway – from *my* railway. You and Mathers had been making a pretty penny dipping into my pocket, so I thought it was time you did something for me in return."

Jamie thought back to the rainy morning in the scrapyard, and Mathers' warning that the railways were off limits: *There are some serious characters in the scrap metal business these days. . .*

"We didn't know, I swear!" Jamie told Mr Redgrave. "Not until afterwards!"

"What difference does that make? The word was out – that's all that matters. So tell Sarge that he either brings me what I want, or next time it'll be one of his sons he's digging up in the garden."

"He doesn't like it when people threaten him."

"It's not a threat. It's a promise. Tell me this, son: are you *sure* you're home alone?"

The line went dead before Jamie could reply. He put down the receiver and looked around the empty kitchen, his blood turning to ice. The moon withdrew its pale fingers behind a cloud, returning the kitchen to darkness. Where was Liam's phone number? Jamie began rifling through the scraps of paper by the phone, tossing aside old shopping lists and takeaway menus until he located the piece of paper with Liam's number on it. He picked up the phone.

The kitchen door creaked, and a large shadow detached itself from the gloom. A hand flew out of the darkness, knocking the receiver from Jamie's grasp.

Stumbling backwards, Jamie took a shuddering blow to the temple and collapsed to the floor. The world reeled and buckled around him. His nostrils were flooded with the smell of outdoors; of earth and moss and frozen rain. A hand grabbed him around the throat, cutting off his cry for help before it could escape his mouth. His attacker knelt down, driving a knee into his chest. The pressure was unbearable; it felt as though Jamie's ribcage would snap like a handful of dead twigs. He clutched feebly at the man's arm as he throttled him, but it was no use. The grip was total, absolute.

Darkness was falling across Jamie's vision when he heard the sound of the front door opening, and then the house was filled with voices – Liam and Sarge, calling out his name. Jamie's attacker paused and then lurched up into a standing position, releasing the terrible pressure from Jamie's throat and chest. Air flooded back into his lungs, overwhelming him. There was a loud crash as the back door flew open and then Jamie was alone in the kitchen, coughing and sprawled across the kitchen floor like a drowning man washed up on a linoleum shore.

CHAPTER FIFTEEN

LARK FARM

"Jamie? You all right?"

Slowly, grudgingly, the world began to swim back into focus. Jamie was lying on the sofa in the front room, his head propped up on something soft. His chest and his throat were aching and there was a deep thudding inside his skull where he had been hit, but he was alive. Two familiar faces were hovering over him like concerned clouds.

"You're back," Jamie murmured.

"And not a moment too soon, by the looks of things," Sarge said grimly. "Liam rang to check you were all right, and when he couldn't get through we figured something was up. Came back to find you on the kitchen floor."

"There was a man," Jamie said haltingly. "In the dark ... I didn't see him. He ran away ... the back door. .."

Liam nodded. "We saw, little bro."

"The footprints were headed across the fields," Sarge told him. "There's no point trying to follow them

152

in the dark. Mathers won't be coming back tonight, at any rate."

"I'd love it if he did," Liam said darkly. "I'd wipe that smirk off his face once and for all. Was it him you were talking to on the phone?"

Jamie shook his head. "Mr Redgrave."

"This gets better and better," said Sarge. "What did he want?"

"The mortsafes. He says if he doesn't get them by the end of the week he'll kill me or Liam. The copper we took from the railway was his – that's why he dragged us all into this."

Sarge rubbed his face wearily. The lines around his eyes seemed to have deepened over the previous week – for the first time that Jamie could remember, his dad looked old.

"I'm sorry," said Jamie. He blinked back the tears threatening his eyes. "I wanted to fight him off, but he was so strong!"

"Hey, hey, hey, it's all right, son!" Sarge's grizzled face crinkled into a smile as he patted Jamie's arm. "This was my fault – I should never have left you on your own with Mathers around. There's a line I thought he'd never cross, but I was wrong. But I'll take care of everything, don't you worry about it. You rest now. I'll take care of everything."

The last thing Jamie heard before he slipped gratefully into unconsciousness was Sarge's voice, whispering a hoarse lullaby:

"No one lays a hand on one of my boys and gets away with it. No one."

The next morning Jamie woke to find himself smothered in blankets, warm waves from the portable heater on the floor lapping over him. Gingerly he pushed himself up into a sitting position, wincing at his sore ribcage. Sarge was sitting in the armchair opposite, watching him calmly.

"How are you feeling?"

"OK."

"Well enough to come out with me and Liam? We've got to take care of some things but I'm not leaving you on your own until this . . . situation is resolved."

Jamie nodded.

"Good lad," said Sarge. "We'll wait for you while you get ready."

In the bathroom Jamie gingerly inspected his battered body in the mirror as the shower thundered down behind him. There were purple bruises on his chest where his attacker had driven his knee into his ribs, and his throat was covered in fingermarks. Closing his eyes, Jamie could see Mathers lurching out of the gloom towards him. He might not have been able to make out his face in the darkness, but it had to have been the scrap dealer, dancing to Mr Redgrave's macabre tune like a vicious puppet. One thing was certain – if they didn't find a way to stop Mathers, he would return sooner rather than later.

Jamie felt better for a hot shower and some breakfast. As he spooned cereal into his mouth, Liam sat across from him at the kitchen table, idly surfing the net on his phone. Sarge stood with his back to them, leaning against the sink and staring out of the window. He was frozen in an icy, deliberate rage. Usually Jamie would have been frightened by the palpable threat of violence in the air, but this time it gave him a small, guilty thrill. The truth was, this was the closest Sarge had come to showing Jamie that he cared about him for a long time.

They left the house soon afterwards, slipping past the stranded removal van in the gateway and tramping through the snow towards the town centre. The hillside, which yesterday had been dotted with children playing, was quiet. It seemed to Jamie that every time he stepped out of doors he saw fewer and fewer people. But when he walked past Withershins he was surprised to see a couple of people browsing the shelves. The rest of the town may have closed down, but for once Lawrence had customers.

As they left the town centre behind them the white snow lost its lustre until it became mottled and grey, flecked with stones. Outside Roxanne's Cabs Liam peeled off without a word, heading around the side of the building. His heart quickening in his chest, Jamie followed Sarge inside. The chairs in the reception were empty as usual, the stack of local newspapers left unread on the table. Behind the glass partition Don was tucking into a hot bacon and egg sandwich. At the sight of Sarge he hastily wiped the runny yolk from his mouth with the back of his hand and put the rest of the sandwich down on the counter.

"Wasn't expecting visitors," he said. "Roxanne's still not back to work, I'm afraid."

"Not here to see Roxanne," Sarge replied. "It was you I wanted a word with. Buzz us through, will you?"

Jamie spotted a flicker of unease in Don's eyes.

"No can do," he said, apologetically spreading his hands. "Employees only when the boss isn't around. Roxanne worries about people in her office, see."

"Roxanne isn't here. Let us in."

"I can't!"

Sarge leaned against the counter, his mouth set in a dangerous smile. "Let's put it this way, Don," he said casually. "You've got precisely five seconds to open that door before I pick up one of those chairs and make my own, chair-shaped door in the glass. Are we clear?"

Don stared at him, apparently trying to work out whether Sarge was bluffing. Then the burly man sprang up from his seat and bolted away down the corridor. Sarge watched him flee with a contemptuous shake of the head.

"Quick smart, lad," he told Jamie, and marched out through the front door. Jamie scurried after Sarge as he headed round the side of the building and into the car park behind. It was as far as Don had got − Liam was pressing him up against the side of one of his taxis, a handful of his shirt in each fist.

"Nowhere to run, Don," Sarge called out.

"Get off me!" Don shouted. "What do you want?"

Sarge strode over and pushed his face into the cab driver's. "Where is he?" he demanded.

"Where's who?" croaked Don.

"Mathers."

"Who?"

Sarge scratched his stubbled cheek. "Don't be stupid, Don. We saw you talking to him right here. And maybe talking to people isn't a crime, but last night Mathers came round to the house when Liam and me were out and attacked my youngest. See the marks on the lad's neck?"

Don's eyes flicked over towards Jamie. "You've got it wrong!" he protested. "I've known Mathers for years. He wouldn't do that!"

"He did," Sarge said firmly. "Believe me: I've known him for longer than you have. So I what I need from you, Don, is an address."

The man stared miserably up at Liam, and then across at Sarge.

"Lark Farm," Don said finally, with a slump of the shoulders. "If you keep on past the cab firm and follow the road out of town, you'll see it on your left. Mathers has been staying there since he came to town."

"And why did he come to town?" Liam demanded. "Why did he jump our Jamie?"

"I don't know!" said Don. "Honest! He said he had a score to settle and needed to in a place somewhere out of the way. Something about a dog . . . but I didn't know it was anything to do with you, I swear!"

"It wasn't," Sarge said ominously. "But it is now."

At a glance from his dad, Liam let go of Don's shirt, letting the cab man slide down into a sorrowful heap in the snow.

"Be seeing you, Don," Sarge said crisply. "'Specially if your little tip leads us up the garden path."

"You don't know what you're getting mixed up in," Don said sorrowfully. "No one does – until it's too late."

"Thanks for the warning," said Sarge. "We'll take our chances."

He marched out of the car park, shaking his head. "This bloody town," he muttered. "Not an honest man to be found anywhere."

They followed Don's directions, turning right at the car park exit and walking on until they left the boarded-up buildings behind and the countryside reclaimed the land. The street became a narrow lane, bordered by hedgerows; the snow deepened until it was almost knee-high. Jamie struggled to keep pace with Sarge and Liam as they ploughed onwards. Snow was seeping into his trainers and his socks were wet through. Home suddenly seemed a very long way away.

Ahead the lane began to curve to the right, and a wooden gate interrupted the hedgerow. It guarded a rutted path that forked off to the left, hobbling past a couple of trees and up the hillside. Liam nudged Sarge, pointing at the set of tyre tracks leading up the path.

"Reckon that could be a 4×4?" he asked.

"Reckon so," Sarge agreed. He looked back at Jamie. "Stay alert now, lads," he said. "No wandering off."

As they clambered over the gate and started along the path a bird started singing among the trees, as though they had set off a strangely melodic burglar alarm. Their silence took on a wary edge now, Liam glancing over his shoulder as they tackled the hillside. Jamie was panting and out of breath by the time they reached the brow, where they found Lark Farm waiting for them.

The farmhouse was a low, sullen-looking stone building with the curtains drawn firmly across the windows. Behind it two large sheds loomed over its shoulder like bodyguards, and then there was nothing but a snowy wasteland of fields leading all the way to the coast. The tyre tracks led up to a dirty patch of land in front of the farm, where they became lost in an indecipherable churn of mud and snow. There was no sign of life anywhere.

"Nice place," Liam remarked. "Very homely."

"Mathers would fit right in," said Sarge.

"I'm just glad the bloody dog's dead."

Here, on the exposed hillside, the wind was free to roam, stalking across the ground like a wild animal, its call a high-pitched shriek in Jamie's ears. They fanned out around the farmhouse, trying to peer in vain around the curtains in the windows. Both the front and the back doors were locked.

"This place is deserted," Liam said. "You think Don was lying to us?"

Sarge shook his head. "Mathers was here, all right. I can smell him." He turned and scanned the horizon beyond the barns, a seemingly endless line broken only by the solitary silhouette of a scarecrow in the field, its clothes rippling in the breeze. "Keep looking."

Jamie walked past the farmhouse and entered the cavernous barn on the left. A savage draught was blowing in through the door, the corrugated iron roof rattling in the wind. The floor was covered with brown, lumpy sacks of produce, loose potatoes spilling out across a worktop against the far wall. In the corner of the barn a thick tarpaulin had been draped over a large object. Carefully lifting up the tarpaulin, Jamie was rewarded with a dark green gleam.

"Over here!" Jamie cried out. "I've found it!"

Sarge and Liam came running in seconds; together they pulled away the tarpaulin to reveal Mathers's 4×4. The vehicle was splattered with mud and snow; the door was unlocked and the keys were still in the ignition. The driver, however, was nowhere to be seen.

"Well, wherever Mathers is," said Liam, "he went on foot."

"This isn't right," Sarge said warily. "Something's happened here."

He marched out of the barn and looked out over the fields, searching the sweeping expanse of countryside for answers. The wind had picked up, making the scarecrow sway as it continued its lonely vigil. Sarge's eyes narrowed.

"What's that scarecrow doing there?"

"I'm no expert, Sarge," replied Liam, "but I think it's something to do with scaring away birds."

"In the middle of winter? Look at the ground, lad! You think there's any crops growing underneath a foot of snow?"

"Maybe the farmer forgot to move it," suggested Jamie.

"Maybe," Sarge said grimly. "Maybe not."

He strode off across the field.

"Where's he going?" Jamie asked Liam.

"God knows," his brother replied. "I think he's starting to lose it."

The wind let out a banshee screech as Sarge covered the short distance to the scarecrow. He reached into his pocket and brought out a knife, a bright flash of silver in the murky afternoon light. Sarge cut away at something above the scarecrow's right arm and the limb slumped free. Another flash of silver, a flick of the blade above the left arm, and the scarecrow tumbled to the ground. Jamie realized with a sudden chill that it wasn't a scarecrow after all, but a lifeless human body.

CHAPTER SIXTEEN

CORTEGE

Even death hadn't been able to wipe the smirk from Mathers's face. He grinned lifelessly up at them, mocking their horrified expressions. Liam paled and turned away; Sarge swore and kicked the snow. Jamie just stood and stared. He had seen Greg's limp arm trailing out of his sports car but this was the first time he had been confronted with the face of death. Mathers's throat was bruised so badly it was almost black. *How strong must his attacker have been*, Jamie thought, *to squeeze the life from a giant?* Suddenly he was back in the darkened kitchen in the Lodge, with a hand on his throat and a knee driving into his chest. Unexpectedly, he felt a surge of pity for the giant scrap dealer.

Something soft and cold brushed the end of Jamie's nose. He looked up into the sky. It was snowing again. Sarge reached down and hooked his arms underneath Mathers's armpits, hoisting him into a sitting position.

"Look sharp," he said to Liam. "Grab his legs. We're not leaving him here."

Liam stared at his dad. "Why not?"

"Look at him!" Sarge pointed at Mathers's crushed windpipe. "Don't you think the police might have a question or two about what happened here? Who do you think they're going to want to talk to first? I'll wager it'll take our good pal Don all of two seconds to drop us right in it."

"Drop us in what?" Liam protested. "We didn't do anything!"

"Really?" Sarge barked with laughter. "And what about that shiny pile of copper wiring that's probably still sitting in Mathers's scrapyard? Or had you forgotten you helped me nick it? No, we're taking care of this now. Come on, Jamie, stop gawping and shake a leg."

The snow was swirling down around them, dappling Mathers's frozen face with white flakes. Jamie's hands were turning bright pink in the cold. He blew on them in a futile effort to warm them up.

"He was strangled too," he said softly.

"What's that, son?" rapped Sarge.

Jamie looked across at his dad. "We all thought it was Mathers who attacked me in the Lodge because it kind of made sense but I never actually saw his face. And now he's strangled, just like someone tried to strangle me. All I'm saying is, maybe it wasn't Mathers who attacked me. Maybe it was someone else."

"Like who?" Liam demanded. "It wasn't Mr Redgrave – you were talking to him on the phone."

Sarge turned and scanned the horizon, scratching his shaven head. "Save the guessing games for later," he said. "Whoever killed Mathers might still be in the area, and we're sitting ducks out here."

Liam relented, picking up Mathers's legs whilst Sarge grabbed the scrap dealer's arms. They carried the body across the field through the billowing snow with Jamie following close behind, trying not to look at Mathers's grey rictus grin. It was a relief when they reached the shelter of the barn and could escape the wind and the snow. They wrapped up the body in a blanket before laying it to rest in the back of the 4×4, Sarge closing the boot down over it like a coffin lid. Then they hurried inside the vehicle. Jamie climbed into the back seat while his dad and brother sat up front. Unlike their battered van, the 4×4 was scrupulously clean, with scrubbed leather seats and an air freshener dangling from the rear-view mirror.

As Jamie buckled his seat belt Liam peered out through the open barn doors at the thickening white deluge enveloping Lark Farm. "You reckon this thing can make it through the snow?"

"If we hurry," said Sarge, turning the key in the ignition and rousing the engine into snarling life.

"Where are we going?" asked Jamie.

Sarge tapped his fingers on the steering wheel. "Home," he said, reversing the 4×4 out of its bay and swinging it around to face the barn's exit. The windscreen wipers scraped into life as the vehicle ventured out into the snow, leaving the grim protection of Lark Farm to face the elements on their own.

"You sure that's a good idea, Sarge?" asked Liam. "This respecting the dead stuff is all very noble, but if anyone finds out we've got Mathers's body in cold storage it's going to look like we're the ones who did him in. We've already got his dead dog buried in the field behind the Lodge, remember?"

"Unlikely to forget," Sarge replied quietly. "It was me that buried it."

The 4×4 rattled down along the path towards the main road, bouncing Jamie around in the back seat. In other circumstances the journey might have felt like some kind of exciting fairground ride, but with every bump he could hear the corpse in the boot thudding against his seat. Jamie leaned forward, trying to keep close to his dad and brother. An aura of intense concentration enveloped Sarge as he steered the van up the main road towards Alderston, the vehicle's windows milky blind eyes in the growing blizzard.

The weather might have made for treacherous driving, but Jamie realized it was also a useful accomplice, throwing a cloak of invisibility around them. The roads were deserted but even the nosiest of neighbours would have struggled to identify Mathers's 4×4 as it jolted past their house – let alone who was in the driving seat. For the first time Jamie felt a glimmer of gratitude for the harsh, unrelenting winter. Still, as the van bumped and skidded its way through the town, he wished that they had left Mathers where they'd found him. The atmosphere in the Lodge was foreboding enough without throwing a dead body into the mix. But Sarge had been insistent. It was strange – only an hour ago his dad had been hell-bent on destruction; now, upon finding his old friend and adversary already dead, Sarge looked pensive and shadowy.

They were all relieved when the silhouette of Alderston Church loomed into view on the horizon, and the 4×4 skidded down the road past the cemetery. Sarge pulled up outside the front gate of the Lodge but left the engine running.

"So we're home," said Liam. "What now?"

"Take the van and go and dump it somewhere," Sarge told him.

"Where?"

"I don't care, as long as it's far away from here. Take it back to the farm if you have to. The boy and I will take care of Mathers."

Sarge opened his door, allowing a gust of snow to come howling into the vehicle, and jumped down on to the pavement. Liam rubbed his hands together and shifted over into the front seat.

"Now we're talking," he murmured, adjusting the rear-view mirror.

Jamie got out, shielding his eyes from the blizzard, and trudged round to the boot of the 4×4. Sarge had already opened it, and was wrestling with Mathers's blanketed body. Jamie hurried over to take the corpse's feet, grunting with the effort as he helped share the burden.

"You going to be able to carry that?" Sarge had to shout to make himself heard above the wind.

Jamie nodded. He'd let his arms fall off before he dropped it. Sarge walked backwards through the front gate, checking over his shoulder every few steps. Even though he knew his dad was shouldering most of Mathers's weight, Jamie struggled to keep up with him. He bent low, trying to avoid the full force of the bludgeoning wind, keeping his eyes firmly fixed on the front door.

"Not in the house!" Sarge shouted, with a shake of the head. "Round the back!"

Jamie followed his dad around the side of the house, the snowy bushes leaving brilliant white smears on his coat like icy bloodstains as he brushed past them. The snow was falling so rapidly he could barely make anything out except for vague shapes. His arms were really tired now, and he had to stop to change his grip. Sarge didn't say a word, waiting patiently until Jamie was ready. They made for the shed in the corner of the garden, where Sarge propped Mathers against the side of the small building and opened the door. The interior was a rusty jumble of tools and garden furniture.

"We'll leave him here for now!" shouted Sarge. "Until the weather breaks!"

As his dad began to manoeuvre the corpse inside, Jamie felt a prickle on the back of his neck. He turned and looked up towards the bathroom window.

And saw a face looking back at him.

Jamie blinked, and the face vanished. The shed door slammed behind him and Sarge's hand was on his shoulder, firmly steering him towards the Lodge. Jamie looked up again towards the bathroom window, but it remained a blank shadow.

The longer he spent in Alderston, the more grateful Jamie became for his dad's presence. Reassured by the sound of Sarge making tea in the kitchen, Jamie went upstairs to check the bathroom and the rest of the house. There was no sign of any intruder – whoever or whatever he'd seen had vanished. As he looked out at the church through his bedroom window, Jamie could see the blizzard begin to ease. It had stopped snowing altogether by the time Liam returned, grinning from ear to ear having navigated the 4×4 through the snow.

"I put it back where we found it," he told Sarge proudly. "Figured we didn't want anyone trying to follow its tracks here."

Sarge barely seemed to be listening. He ate dinner in silence, and sent his sons up to bed early so he could lie out on the living room settee. Jamie didn't bother changing into his pyjamas, getting into bed fully dressed and burrowing beneath the duvet until he was completely covered. It had been another long, strange day in Alderston, and as cold as the bedroom was, Jamie could feel his exhausted limbs melting into sleep. But just as he felt himself drifting off, a noise made his eyes ping wide open.

Someone was in his room.

Peeping out from beneath his duvet, Jamie saw a figure hunched down on its hands and knees by the skirting board. A pool of water gave off a slick glint on the floorboards beneath it. A squeak of fear escaped Jamie's mouth, and the figure's head slowly turned until Jamie was face to face with Kitty Hawkins.

It could only be her; he was sure of it now. The Victorian clothing, the long blonde hair bedraggled with pondweeds. He had been told that in life Kitty had been beautiful; there was no trace left of that now, with her puffy discoloured skin and hateful gaze. She let out a long, drawn-out hiss of contempt as she stood up, her bloated body edging towards Jamie's bedside. Too terrified to move, a cry for help frozen in his throat, all Jamie could do was watch as Kitty climbed on to his bed and lay down on top of him. She was heavy in a way that was impossible, inhuman – so heavy that he would crumble to dust beneath her. . .

Jamie woke up with a strangled yell, his arms flailing around his head. His skin was clammy with sweat and he was gasping for breath. But he was alone.

Just a bad dream, Jamie told himself. *Bad dreams can't hurt you.*

He reached over and flicked on the bedside lamp for reassurance. As he scanned the bedroom for movement, his eyes fell on the iron grating in the skirting board where Kitty's ghost had been crouching. His eavesdropper's ally, the gateway to Sarge and Liam's kitchen conversation. What had Kitty been doing down there?

Slowly Jamie pulled back his sheets and got out of bed. Lying flat on the floor, he peered through the grating, but couldn't make anything out in the gloom beyond the ironwork design. At first glance the grating seemed to be set firmly into the wall, but when Jamie examined it he could see deep scores in the floorboards by its bottom edge. One person, at least, had been able to move it. He wrapped his fingers around the ironwork and tried to pull it free, but the grating wouldn't budge. Jamie frowned. He could have used Liam's help but there was no way he was going to wake his brother up in the middle of the night just because he'd had a bad dream.

Jamie braced his feet against the wall and took another grip on the grating, pushing with his legs as he tried to pull it free. Nothing happened for several seconds, and Jamie was about to give up when gradually he felt the heavy grating give, reluctantly scraping free from its resting place. Jamie placed it carefully to one side and peered inside the opening, feeling its chill breath blowing in his face. Something was definitely there, an object wedged halfway along the duct.

Jamie reached inside the opening and tentatively felt around, trying to fight off the inexplicable fear that something was going to grab his hand and drag him inside the duct. Then, at the very edge of his reach, Jamie's fingers closed around a rectangular object. A small smile of triumph crept across his face. He slid his hand out from the duct to find himself holding a book wrapped in a dusty white cloth. With trembling fingers he unwrapped the volume and leafed through its pages. They were covered in tight lines of spidery handwriting. On the first page was written: *The Diary of George Rathbone.*

Jamie opened the book and began to read.

CHAPTER SEVENTEEN

THE DEVIL'S DESCENT

5th December, 1821

The night sky is as black as a grave. The search party has returned from the woods carrying Kitty's body. She fell into the pond and drowned amongst the weeds. My chest feels as though it has been pierced with a shard of ice.

8th December, 1821

I come to my diary having only now emerged from the mindless fog that enveloped me. For two days I staggered around the Lodge, clawing at the walls and howling like a cur in the madhouse, swigging gin from the bottle in the hope of achieving some kind of numbing stupor. No one in this accursed town can know the grievous pain Kitty's death has caused me. Alone in the world, she was able to look beyond my crimes. I loved her as an angel, beyond life itself — and she loved me right back. But for her father's certain disapproval, our affair would have been common knowledge. Instead our pounding hearts were compelled to silence, and we were forced to meet in secret refuges far from prying eyes. Barns, abandoned farm outbuildings, secluded country lanes.

The woods.

Only a month previous, I had knelt down upon the banks of Black Maggie's pond and asked for Kitty's hand in marriage. Unable to speak, she simply nodded, watching through tears of joy as I slipped the engagement ring upon her finger. We talked of eloping, of starting a new life afresh. But all that is gone now, burned to bitter ashes. All the future holds now is my beloved's funeral on the morrow. The fact that my bedroom looks out over the church graveyard is a source of both untold anguish and the coldest of comforts. If nothing else, I will see Kitty's resting place from mine: the last thing before I go to bed; the first after I rise.

9th December, 1821

My Kitty has been taken from me for a second time.

I was forced to watch her funeral from my own front gate; my reputation allowed me no further. John Hawkins has been telling anyone who'll listen that he'll not let me near her grave — myself, Silas and Lucas are suspected of robbing a tailor's grave in Caxton. As the mourners departed I saw John Hawkins deep in conversation with the farm boy Tom McNally, who is equally ill-disposed towards me. Little did they know I was already aware of the topic of conversation – in secret my man Lucas has been romancing the Hawkins's housekeeper, and she had told him that the master of the house was leaving for Manchester that evening on pressing business, and that he had decided upon leaving McNally in his stead as a guard dog. As if that would stop me from saying farewell.

That night I waited with Silas and Lucas in the back bar of the Royal Oak, warming my frozen veins with ale until it was late, and then we stepped out into the night. I led my companions to the churchyard, intent on removing McNally by whatever means proved necessary. Yet when Kitty's headstone drew into sight I stumbled to a halt, gorge rising in my throat. Kitty's coffin had erupted from her grave, its lid flung open. The body of my beloved was nowhere to be seen.

As we turned and fled from the hellish scene, Silas stumbled over Tom McNally's body. The farm boy was lying beside the grave, his throat crushed like a stalk of corn. He can rot, as far as I care. If I had been the one standing guard over Kitty's grave, the Devil himself would not have got by me.

10th December, 1821

The damned butcher has been flapping his trap, telling everyone about the sharp words I had exchanged with McNally in the Royal Oak the night

174

of his death. I had a mind to pay the gossiping fool a visit but Silas begged me not to. He says that we are suspected of being the authors of both McNally's death <u>and</u> Kitty's missing body. The Resurrection Men, they call us. Silas may fret and wring his hands but I care not a jot for the chatter of fishwives and tattletales. I care for almost nothing, now.

11th December, 1821

Kitty visited me in a dream last night. I was sitting in the Lodge parlour staring into the fire when she came laughing and dancing into the room. I enquired as to the cause of her happiness but she would not reply, pressing a finger to her lips to indicate that it was a secret. I rose from my chair but Kitty pushed me back down. Clutching me to her chest, she whispered in my ear that I was not to worry and that everything would be all right. Her words pulled the shard of ice clean from my heart, and I felt my spirits soar. I was so elated it took me time to become aware of the light tap of water droplets upon my head. Looking up at my love, I was horrified to see that Kitty's smile had twisted into a hateful sneer, whilst her soft hair had become bedraggled and her skin had turned black and blue. I tried to break free but she had gained the strength of a monster, leaving me helpless in her nightmarish embrace. Prising open my jaws, Kitty forced a small metal object into my mouth. As it lodged in my throat I realized, choking and gagging, that it was the engagement ring I had given her.

I awoke screaming in my bed, the taste of sour pond water in my mouth. I did not sleep again that night.

12th December, 1821

This evening Lucas and I were turned away from the Royal Oak by the landlord, who refused to serve us our usual drinks. I was prepared to tell the lumbering idiot exactly what I thought of him and his watered-down ale, but the mood in the back bar was turning ugly and Lucas dragged me away before I could say my piece. As we left I caught sight of John Hawkins amongst the gathered men, a look of grim satisfaction in his eye. He blames me for the disappearance of his daughter's body and will not rest until I pay with my blood. What does he want from me – to sink to my knees and plead my innocence? I would not give him the satisfaction. I will own to all manner of crimes and dark deeds; in search of fortune I have descended to the lowest depths, committed the most base and brutal acts of criminality and sin. I was the author of the Caxton grave-robbing, travelling to the cemetery under the cover of night with Silas and Lucas and digging up the tailor's body, before hurriedly exchanging it for a purse of coins with a shifty-eyed medical man. For Kitty's sake I had sworn it would be my final criminal deed, and I have stayed true to that pledge despite her death.

More important than my own innocence, however, is the nagging question haunting my wakeful nights – if we were not responsible for Kitty's desecration, then who was?

13th December, 1821

I did not sleep this night. Some time in the small hours I was disturbed by a tremendous clamour upon the roof, and there followed a sharp rap upon my front door that echoed around the Lodge. I went down to the hallway and threw open the door but there was no one waiting for me upon the doorstep. If John Hawkins wishes to play hide-and-seek with me, let him try. There is nothing left I care about in this world, and it will give me great pleasure to tear him apart with my bare hands.

14th December, 1821

Snow fell in the night, covering Alderston in a thick white blanket. A chill has settled into the Lodge's bones, and no matter how high I build the fire in the grate I cannot get warm. This morning I watched from my bedroom window as a shivering crowd gathered in the church graveyard, edging round the spoiled remains of the grave where Tom McNally was recently laid to rest. It seems that the farm boy's body has now also been stolen. I was wearily unsurprised to see John Hawkins at the head of the aggrieved crowd, jabbing an angry finger towards the Lodge as he addressed the others.

Several hours later, an ironmonger's cart braved the Moss to deliver a consignment of iron cages to the church. These "mortsafes" were fastened into place over recent graves to protect their occupants from being disturbed. Some animal instinct within me tells me this is too little, too late.

15th December, 1821

Silas appeared at my door at first light, pale as a ghost and shivering in the dawn cold. He is leaving Alderston at once, meaning to cross the Pennines for Yorkshire, where his uncle has a farm. Silas tried to convince me to leave with him, snivelling that there was violence brewing in the town, and that our lives were in danger. I chased him away like a dog, hurling stones at him as he fled. Let Silas go off and become a milkmaid for his uncle: George Rathbone flees for no man.

I spent the afternoon shovelling the deep snow from my garden path, taking solace in hard physical activity. As dusk fell, I looked out across the fields and spied a small figure in the distance, a smudge on the horizon. Even from so far away, I was struck by the unnerving sensation that the figure was watching me. There was no way of knowing whether it meant good or ill – or indeed, whether it was a figure at all, or just some trick of the winter

twilight. All the same, I was relieved when I had
finished clearing the path and could retire inside the
Lodge, and I locked the door behind me as I went.

I walked into Alderston to find the streets deserted
and the shops closed. The town is waiting for
something. Curtains trembled in windows. Doors
looked the other way. Chimneys held their breath.

My enforced solitude has given me pause to puzzle
over the terrible events of the past month. I remain
haunted by the nightmare in which Kitty attacked
me, the rattle of the silver ring against my teeth
still ringing in my ears. Was there a message in this
terrible vision? Did Kitty appear to me one final time
to reject me? Why did she want to give me back the
ring she had accepted with such blissful happiness?
Alone among my possessions, the silver ring was
untarnished, innocent of any criminal associations.
It belonged to my mother, who stumbled across it in the
woods near Lark Farm as a young girl. She gave it
to me on her deathbed, pressing it into my palm with
her stiff, cold fingers. Smiling, she told me that my
life would find a righteous course in time. My mother
died – as Kitty did – before I could justify that faith.
Bitterness threatens to eat me away from the inside.

18th December, 1821

A still, moonless night. As I write by candlelight at my desk I can see torches dancing in the graveyard as the menfolk of Alderston march down towards the Lodge. Like a pack of hounds, they have the scent of blood in their nostrils, and soon they will come barking and clawing at my door. Lucas was murdered this afternoon, set upon by a mob in the town square and punched and kicked to death. This town has long wielded a gavel like an axe, dispensing justice after its own fashion. Yet in this matter – if not in any other – I can proclaim complete innocence. If the mob believes that with our deaths the dead can rest peacefully in their graves, they are much mistaken.

Oh my darling Kitty, what have I done to us? If I had been a better man I could look forward to our being reunited in the afterlife, but my many crimes have put paid to that. Rest assured that wherever you tread in Heaven, I shall be forever gazing up at you through the flames.

The mob nears my door. I shall leave this diary in a safe place and prepare to receive my guests. If they are set on sending me to Hell, I'll not go alone.

CHAPTER EIGHTEEN

RAIN OF STONES

Jamie read through the night, blowing on his hands to keep them warm as he turned the pages. Hampered by George Rathbone's crabby handwriting and the old-fashioned spelling, it took him a long time to reach the diary's solemn end. The window was brightening behind the curtain by the time he had closed the book and carefully replaced it behind the grate for safekeeping.

Although Jamie was tired, there was no question of going back to sleep – his brain was ticking over too quickly for that. It felt as though he was slowly beginning to prise Alderston's secrets from its cold, grudging grasp. According to his diary, George Rathbone had had nothing to do with Kitty's grave-robbery. He could have been lying, Jamie supposed, but why bother lying in his own secret diary? Looking around the bedroom, Jamie imagined George Rathbone hurriedly scratching his final entry at his desk as the torches grew ominously larger in his window. What had happened, he wondered, when the mob had reached the Lodge? Everyone had told Jamie that the Resurrection Men had been chased out of Alderston, but it seemed this was a convenient version of events, cleaned up and polished for later, more squeamish generations. *Lucas was murdered this afternoon, set upon by a mob in the town square and punched and kicked to death. . .*

A thoughtful air had descended upon the Lodge. Sarge was preoccupied and monosyllabic, spending the afternoon cleaning and oiling his toolkit. He barely touched his dinner, rising from the table and putting on his coat with barely a grunt before leaving the Lodge. Usually Jamie would have expected Liam to make some kind of smart comment, but this time, he noticed, his brother kept his mouth shut.

"What's up with him?" Jamie asked.

"What do you think's up with him?" said Liam. "He's got Mathers's dead body in the shed, for Chrissakes!"

"But I thought Sarge didn't like him?"

"He didn't. Doesn't mean he wanted him dead, though. Doesn't mean he won't miss him."

Jamie scratched his head. "I don't get it."

"I know you don't, little bro," said Liam, with a grim smile. "I'm not sure Sarge does either."

A tinny dance tune interrupted him. Liam pulled his mobile out from his pocket and checked the display, frowning.

"Who's this, then?" he wondered.

A prickle of unease swept across Jamie's flesh. "You think it's Mr Redgrave?"

"Only one way to find out," Liam replied, pressing *answer*. "Hello?" He rolled his eyes. "All right Keeley. No, it's not Jamie, it's his brother Liam. He's . . . erm, in the shower."

Jamie had forgotten that he'd pretended to Keeley that he had a mobile. He reached out to take the phone, but Liam knocked his hand away.

"Slow down, love," he said. "What is it? You sound a bit—" He paused. "OK, we'll be right over."

Slipping the phone back into his pocket, he went into the hall and began putting his trainers on. Jamie watched him curiously.

"What's going on?" he asked.

"Some idiots are hanging round outside Keeley's house," Liam told him. "Kids, mainly, but they're freaking her mum out."

"Why don't they call the police?"

"No police to call until the Moss clears, and it doesn't sound like Keeley and her mum have got many friends in town. We'd better go over there and make sure they're all right. Get your shoes on – you're coming with me."

As Jamie hurried into his coat and shoes he was filled with a combination of nervousness and another, more unexpected emotion – pride. Even though Liam barely knew Keeley, he hadn't blinked when she had asked for help. *So what if he helps Sarge steal stuff?* Jamie thought. *Nobody's perfect. It doesn't mean Liam can't be a good person too. Does it?*

They set out immediately, Jamie struggling to keep pace with Liam's long strides as he loped down Church Lane. Keeley lived on an estate on the edge of Alderston, but with Liam hurrying along it didn't take them long to reach the right street. A small knot of people had gathered outside the terraced house at the end of the row, a dark storm cloud on the horizon. There were ten, maybe fifteen people: mostly teenagers with their hoods up, hungrily circling the front gate like wolves. At the back of the pack a handful of older men and women looked on, including Greg's brother Richie Metcalfe, who stood with his arms folded and a look of sour satisfaction on his face. The street rang with crowing, high-pitched laughter, insults ricocheting off pebble-dashed walls. As Liam and Jamie approached the throng a teenager in a red tracksuit cupped his hands together and called out:

"Come out, Black Maggie!"

"Witch!" came the cry from the hooded figure beside him – a girl's voice this time. "Grave robber!"

The curtains stayed firmly drawn inside Keeley's house, the taunts falling on deaf ears. The lack of response only seemed to make the crowd angrier. Egged on by his friends, the boy in the tracksuit dug a stone from the snow and hurled it at the front window of the house. A cheer went up around him as the stone smacked into the glass.

Jamie glanced nervously at his brother. "Are you sure we shouldn't wait for Sarge?" he asked.

"I left a message for him in the Oak," Liam told

him. "He won't be long. I can handle this lot anyway. Just stand behind me and try not to look like you're crapping yourself like usual, eh?"

Jamie swallowed nervously. Easier said than done. A slow, murderous chant had gone up among the crowd: part nursery rhyme, part murderous threat.

"Kill the witch ... Kill the witch ... Kill the witch..."

A curtain twitched in the upstairs window and was greeted with hooting catcalls and a shower of stones. Breaking into a jog, Liam forced himself through the crowd. As the teenager in the red tracksuit picked up another stone, Liam caught his arm and knocked it from his hand.

"Careful with that, lad," he said pleasantly. "You might hurt someone."

Abruptly, the chanting died. The teenagers broke away from the gate, forming a jostling ring around Liam. Jamie stayed close to his brother and tried to look confident, praying that no one could see that his legs were trembling.

He shouldn't have worried. It was Liam everyone was looking at, and he couldn't have looked calmer.

"Evening, all," he said, with a nod.

Richie Metcalfe stepped angrily forward. It made sense that he was the ringleader, thought Jamie.

"Who the hell are you?" Richie demanded.

"You know who we are," said Liam. "We're Sarge's lads."

"Outsiders," spat Richie. "You've no business being round here."

"Free country, isn't it?" Liam retorted nonchalantly. "I was just out stretching my legs and wondered what all the fuss was about."

"Nothing that concerns you. Just taking care of some Alderston business."

"What, getting all your mates to pick on a teenage girl and her mum?" Liam laughed. "Nice one, tough guy."

Unfriendly eyes narrowed. The circle tightened around them.

"I warned your brother," said Richie, pointing at Jamie. "I told him to stay away from that girl if he knew what was good for him."

"News to me," Liam replied coolly. "And if you know what's good for *you*, you'll stay away from Jamie."

"You know what happened to my brother!" Richie said angrily. "You know what she did to his body!"

"Are you really telling me it was *Keeley* who broke out the shovels and dug Greg up?" asked Liam incredulously. "Or is she just the easiest target you can find?"

"She's a freak who spends all her time in that churchyard," hissed Richie, through gritted teeth. "No one else round here would be weird enough to do something like that. Everyone else loved Greg."

"Oh, well that settles it," said Liam. "The prosecution rests."

"It's not funny."

"It's hilarious, mate. You're hilarious."

Jamie wished Liam would go easy. Trying to protect Keeley was one thing – insulting an angry mob another. His brother's mocking contempt had only succeeded in drawing all the crowd's venom in their direction. A hand pushed Jamie in the back, shoving him into his brother. Was this how it had started for Lucas Forshaw, Jamie wondered – the exchange of insults, the ratcheting up of tension before the first blow landed?

"Maybe you're right," Richie told Liam slowly. "Maybe it wasn't her. All this started happening when your family came to town. Maybe it was you who dug up my little brother."

Jamie didn't doubt for a second that Liam could take Richie in a fight, but if the whole mob jumped on them they were in serious trouble. Looking up, he saw Liam's jaw tighten: his brother knew it too. Then Richie hesitated, and took a sudden pace back. He was looking over Liam's shoulder.

When Jamie turned round his heart gave a little stutter of relief. Sarge was marching briskly up the road towards them. Jamie's dad wasn't a large man, but there was something about the way he moved – straight-backed, purposeful, blue eyes unblinking – that gave him an air of instant authority. The ring around Jamie and Liam reluctantly parted to let him through.

"Richie, right?" said Sarge, addressing the ringleader.

"What's it to you?"

"I've been with your old man in the Oak. He wants a word with you."

Richie's face fell.

"I wouldn't keep him waiting if I were you," Sarge told him. "He's had enough to deal with losing one son without the other pulling a stunt like this. Your old man told you he didn't want any trouble, didn't he?"

Richie muttered something under his breath.

"It's a hard thing, losing someone you care about," Sarge continued. "You don't have to tell me that, son – my wife died ten years ago and I still have to live with it every day. But this doesn't help anyone. That girl you've got trapped in her house had nothing to do with what happened to your brother. She was with my youngest the night Greg's body was dug up. Isn't that right, Jamie?"

Jamie nodded.

"So stand down, Richie, take a breath, and go see your old man."

It was as though a sudden gale had whipped down the street, blowing away the storm clouds. The jostling ring around Jamie slackened and began to move off. As Richie's shoulders sagged, defeated, Sarge grabbed him by the neck and pulled him close, whispering into his ear just loud enough for Jamie to hear: "You *ever* threaten my sons again and I will snap every single bone in your body. Do you understand me?"

Richie nodded. The other adults were retreating to their houses on the other side of the road, whilst the teenagers had already melted away into the evening shadows. Within the space of a couple of minutes the street was empty except for Jamie, his brother and his dad.

"Cowards are like dogs," Sarge remarked. "Slap the biggest one on the nose and the rest will back down."

"I know," said Liam. "I was handling it."

Sarge stared at his son, his eyes cold sapphires. Liam hastily held up his hands. "Doesn't mean I don't appreciate the back-up," he said.

"Good," said Sarge. "'Cause from where I was standing, you were about to get your backside handed to you on a plate."

He opened the gate and marched up the path to Keeley's house, rapping smartly on the front door. The curtain twitched again, and after a few seconds the front door swung cautiously open and Keeley's mum appeared. She was a small woman with dark hair; pretty, but with dark circles under her eyes and a pensive expression on her face.

"You must be Keeley's mum," said Sarge, offering his hand. "I'm Sarge, Jamie's dad."

"Nice to meet you," she replied warily. "Jennifer Marshall."

"Don't worry about the mob. They've put down their pitchforks and won't be coming back."

Keeley's mum looked up and down the street for herself before opening the door. "Would you like to come in?" she said.

The Marshalls' house was small and neat, the walls dotted with smiling photographs of Keeley and her mum. After years of constant travelling in the removal van, and then the cold, musty atmosphere of the Lodge, Jamie had almost forgotten what a real house – a *home* – felt like. The busy smell of housework: freshly hoovered carpet and damp clothing on the dryer, delicious wafts of food from the oven. Jamie took a deep breath, trying to take it all in. As they walked through the hall he saw Keeley sitting at the top of stairs, warily watching them through the banisters like a cat.

"Hi," said Jamie.

"Hi."

"You OK?"

Keeley nodded.

"Drama's over," Jennifer Marshall told her daughter. "I want that bedroom of yours cleaned before tea, understand? It's like a pigsty up there."

"Mum!" Keeley protested.

"A pigsty," Jennifer repeated firmly. "Go on."

Keeley flounced away to her bedroom, slamming the door shut behind her. Jennifer shook her head and led them into the front room. She went immediately to the window, biting her lip as she peered around the net curtains at the empty street.

"Nasty business, that," said Sarge, sympathetically. "How are you holding up?"

"I'm doing all a mother can do," Jennifer said bitterly. "Pretending everything's all right when it's going to hell in a handcart. For years the people in this wretched town have picked on my Keeley, and for what? Because of her clothes? Because of the *music* she listens to? I wasn't like her – I kept my head down and my mouth shut and did everything I could to try and make people forget who I was. And all because some poor old woman scowled at the wrong person five hundred years ago and was drowned for her troubles. Tell me, please – what terrible crime have my daughter and I committed to deserve a mob at our door, and stones hurled at our windows?"

Keeley's mum sat down on a chair, wiping angry tears from her eyes.

"Sorry," she said quietly. "You come over here to help us and all you get is me shouting at you."

"No need to apologize," Sarge told her. "Need to let it out somehow."

"We don't mind a bit of shouting," Liam added. "We're always shouting at each other."

Keeley's mum smiled gratefully. "Thank you," she said. "For everything. Ordinarily we'd take care of ourselves but this terrible business with Greg has got the whole town acting crazy. Did you see they've brought out the mortsafes in the churchyard? The sooner this snow melts the better. I was telling Roxanne the other day, at this rate someone's going to get hurt."

Sarge looked up sharply. "Roxanne's in Alderston?"

Jennifer nodded. "She only came back to town to change her clothes and now she's trapped here, and with

Donna still in the hospital. The poor thing's going out of her mind. She's been saying a lot of things . . . strange things." Jennifer gave Jamie a curious look. "Have you said anything to her recently?"

Inquisitive eyes turned in Jamie's direction. He flushed.

"Roxanne? No! I mean . . . at the church during Greg's funeral, but I didn't really say much. She seemed pretty out of it. Why?"

"She's mentioned your name several times. She wants to talk to you. Says there's something important she's got to tell you."

CHAPTER NINETEEN

THE SPIDER

"You sure this is a good idea?"

Liam glanced around the car park behind Roxanne's Cabs. Someone had built a grimy snowman next to one of the snowbound cabs, a brainless grin spelled out in stones across its face. The blinds were drawn over the window of Roxanne's office, but the lights were on. Someone, at least, was home.

"What if it's Don in there?" Liam asked Jamie. "We know he was mixed up with Mathers. God knows who else could be in there with him. Maybe Sarge was right – maybe we should come back another time."

Back in the Marshalls' front room, Sarge had greeted the news that Jamie wanted to talk to Roxanne with a grimace and a scratch of his stubbled cheek.

"It's not the time to go gallivanting across town, son," he said briskly. "Another time, perhaps."

"She's not across town," said Jennifer Marshall, faltering slightly. "I mean, just so you know. She was at home but Donna's empty room upset her too much, so she went to stay at the cab company."

"Roxanne's been through a lot," Sarge said pointedly to Jamie. "Not sure she wants bothering, son."

"I won't stay long, Sarge," pressed Jamie. "If she doesn't want to talk to me I'll go right away."

He found it hard to explain why he was so keen to talk to a woman he had barely spoken to. It was their exchange in the church during Greg's funeral – something about Roxanne's dreamy speech and the way she had looked at Jamie, like she understood him completely. If there was something important she wanted to tell him, he wanted to hear it.

"How about if I go with Jamie?" suggested Liam. "I'll make sure he doesn't do anything daft."

Sarge scratched his cheek even more fiercely. He looked like he could have happily throttled both of his sons, but the presence of Keeley's mum was forcing him to keep his temper on a tight rein.

"I want you back at the Lodge by eight *sharp*, you hear me?" he told Jamie, pointing a finger straight at him.

"No problem," Jamie had said quickly. "Thanks, Sarge."

They had said goodbye to Jennifer and Keeley and left the house, parting at the end of the street and crunching off through the snow in different directions. Jamie knew that Sarge was angry with him but for once he didn't care. As long as his brother was by his side, grinning and teasing him, everything would be OK.

Not that Liam was grinning now.

"I have to see if Roxanne's in," Jamie told his brother. "Trust me, I think it's important."

Liam shook his head. "Sometimes I think you and this town are a perfect match," he muttered. "You're both as crazy as each other."

Jamie smiled.

"Well, go on, then!" Liam said, jerking his head towards the office door. "Yell if you need me." He drew back into the shadows. "Don't hang about though, eh?" he added, rubbing his hands together. "It's bloody freezing out here."

Nodding, Jamie stepped up to tap on the back door of the cab company. There was no reply. He tapped again, and this time he heard a chair creak and slow footsteps shuffle towards the door. The door opened, and Roxanne's silhouette filled the doorway.

"Hi," said Jamie, suddenly nervous. "My name's Jamie. I don't know if you remember me but—"

"I remember you," said Roxanne, in a flat voice. "Come in."

She trudged back to her desk, settling down in a seat and wrapping herself up in a thick blanket. Jamie had no idea how she could have been cold because the radiators were on full blast, flooding the room with heat. The first time Jamie had met Roxanne he had been surprised how she had switched from mild-mannered parent to no-nonsense criminal – a candyfloss bubble wrapped around a steel core. But now her face was drawn and her make-up smudged. She looked exhausted, hollowed out inside. The television near the wall was on mute, a chat-show audience laughing silently. Roxanne's mobile phones lay dormant on the desk in front of her.

There was a long silence as Roxanne gazed into space. Jamie unzipped his coat and took it off.

"Um, how's Donna?" he asked finally.

"The doctors tell me she's 'out of the woods'." Roxanne laughed, a harsh noise utterly devoid of humour. "Can you believe that's the phrase they used?"

"But that's a good thing, right?" Jamie said uncertainly. "It means she's going to be OK."

"It means she'll recover from the crash, yes. But my girl isn't out of the woods yet. The woods are still all around her."

"I know you must be really upset," Jamie said cautiously. "It must be horrible, having your daughter suffer a horrible accident—"

"It wasn't an accident! Don't call it that!" Anger flashed in Roxanne's eyes. "I need to go to the hospital," she said, drumming her fingers on the desk. "I need to get out of this bloody office and out of this *bloody* town and be with my daughter."

"At least she's not on her own," said Jamie, trying to sound positive. "There are doctors and nurses if she needs anything."

"They don't know about *him*, though. I can't tell them about *him*." Roxanne's voice became softer and more fragile. She sounded frightened. "Every night I'd be standing in Donna's room and I knew that all I had

196

to do was look out of the window and I'd see him, standing in the darkness. Watching. Waiting."

"Waiting? Who?"

"Who d'you think?" snapped Roxanne. "Greg, of course!"

The office was plunged into silence. Jamie swallowed, his mouth suddenly dry. He waited for Roxanne to burst out laughing but there was no smile hiding in the corners of her mouth. Instead she opened her desk drawer, pulled out a bottle of vodka and poured a large measure into a glass.

"Greg died," Jamie told her hesitantly. "I saw him . . . you know, afterwards. In the car."

"I know he died!" Roxanne took an unsteady gulp of vodka. "His heart stopped and they put him in a coffin and buried him in the ground. *And then he came back up again.*"

"That's crazy!" said Jamie. "It was grave robbers!"

Roxanne gave him a withering look. "Don't give me all that Resurrection Man nonsense. I've been hearing those tales since I were younger than you. It's just a cover story, something to tell outsiders. There aren't any grave robbers in Alderston. The dead disturb themselves."

It couldn't be true. *Of course* it couldn't be true. Roxanne was grief-stricken and drunk, and she didn't know what she was saying. Yet as Jamie stared at her, he realized that part of him believed her. If this one incredible, impossible thing could somehow be true, could it not explain the strange atmosphere that hung over Alderston like a fog?

"That's why there were mortsafes in the watch house," said Jamie. "It's not to protect the dead from the living. It's the other way around."

"Alderston's little secret," said Roxanne, her voice thick with contempt. "No one talks about it, but everyone knows, all right."

"But I'm not from Alderston. Why are you telling me all this?"

"You're less of an outsider than you think you are. I remember when I came into the church during Greg's funeral. The look on your face – like you had seen the dead, too."

Jamie shivered, remembering the icy, hateful presence of Kitty Hawkins in the pew behind him.

"I don't know what Sarge has got you mixed up in," Roxanne told him, "but you're all alone in the Lodge on the edge of that graveyard, and winter's closing in around you. They like it when it's cold, Jamie. Get out while you still can."

A phone buzzed loudly on the desk, making both of them jump. Roxanne's jaw tightened when she checked the incoming caller. She wiped her eyes.

"Hello?" she said. A voice crackled angrily down the line back at her.

"I know," said Roxanne. "I'm sorry, I just . . . OK." She rubbed her face and handed Jamie the phone. "It's for you, love," she said.

There was a note of apology in her voice that made Jamie feel uneasy, and he only took the phone reluctantly. "Hello?"

A voice like a gust of wind answered, flinging gravel into his eyes. "Jamie, my boy!" said Mr Redgrave. "What brings you to the spider's lair?"

"Nothing," said Jamie. "I just wanted to say hi to Roxanne."

"Comforting a distressed mother in her hour of need. Very commendable of you."

"If this is about the . . ." Jamie looked across at Roxanne, but she was looking in the distance, ". . . stuff you wanted Sarge to get for you, there's a problem. They've taken them out of the watch house and are using them. There's no way we could get them for you now."

"I know that, Jamie. The sooner you realize I know everything you know the easier this will be. I know exactly who you've been talking to, where you've been: the bookshop, the war memorial, the woods. . ." Mr Redgrave chuckled. "Your old man thinks he's so clever, setting himself up at the Oak, making contacts, putting out feelers . . . if only he knew, it's his youngest who's been asking the right questions all along."

"What questions?"

"Don't play dumb, Jamie. Everyone else might think you're stupid but I'm not buying it. It's you – not Sarge, not your brother – that's beginning to understand what's truly going on here in Alderston. It's the only reason

I'm giving you and Liam a second chance. Forget about the mortsafes; they were only going to be a trial anyway. I wanted to see if your family was up to the task. What I really want from you is much more important than that."

Jamie's throat had gone dry. "What is it?" he managed.

"Something lost for centuries. Something very old, and very precious, and very hard to find. Buried treasure, if you like."

Even as the answer came to Jamie, his heart sank. "Aldus's hoard."

"Bingo."

"You can't be serious!" Jamie protested. "People have been looking for it for years. Treasure hunters, with metal detectors and everything! How am I supposed to find it?"

"The same way you've found out everything else: keep asking the right questions. I've got every confidence in you, Jamie. Has anyone ever said that to you before? I bet they haven't. I bet Sarge hasn't."

"Hang on," said Jamie. "Earlier, you said you were giving me and Liam a second chance. Why just us? What about Sarge?"

"What about him?"

"Where's his second chance?"

"Sarge used up his chances a long, long time ago. There's nothing more I can do for him."

"What do you mean?" Jamie asked urgently. "You're

not going to hurt him, are you? I'll get the hoard for you, I promise!"

"I know you will. As for Sarge, that's beyond my control. He's dug his own grave."

"Please don't hurt my dad!" pleaded Jamie.

"I told you, I'm not going to," Mr Redgrave chided. "You still haven't put it all together, have you? If you had, you'd have known to leave Mathers exactly where you found him. . ."

The line clicked as Mr Redgrave rang off. Jamie stood numbly, his heart thumping against his ribcage. Roxanne refused to look at him, her gaze fixed on the muted television screen. She drained her glass with a large swig and poured herself another measure of vodka.

Dropping the mobile on to her desk with a clatter, Jamie sprinted out of the office. Liam was shivering in the shadows of the car park, stamping his feet in an attempt to keep warm. He wasn't alone – Keeley was standing with him, her arms folded across her chest, and an obstinate expression on her face.

"Don't ask me what she's doing here," Liam started, nodding at Keeley. "I tried to tell her—"

"Forget about that!" cried Jamie, cutting him off. "We've got to save Sarge!"

CHAPTER TWENTY

BEYOND THE FENCE

"What d'you mean, we've got to save Sarge?" said Liam.

Both he and Keeley were staring at Jamie. What was he supposed to tell them? That he was worried someone was coming back from the dead to attack Sarge? They'd think he'd lost it. And maybe they'd be right.

"There isn't time to explain," said Jamie, grabbing Liam's arm. "We have to go now!"

"Where?"

"To the Lodge! Haven't you been listening?"

"I'll come with you," Keeley said quickly.

"You can't," Jamie told her. "It's too dangerous – you'll have to go back to yours."

"Split up?" she scoffed. "Yeah, right! You two will go running off and it'll be me who gets jumped. Haven't you seen any horror films?"

"No one asked you to come," snapped Jamie. "Find your own way home!"

"Enough!" Liam rubbed his face wearily. "You're doing my head in, both of you." He turned to Jamie. "Keeley's right – we can't leave anyone on their own right now. Whatever's out there, we'll face it together. Come on."

They hurried out of the car park and up the alleyway into the main square, Jamie and Keeley struggling to keep up with Liam's loping stride. They returned to the Lodge to find it swathed in darkness. Liam tried the front door, rattling the handle.

"It's locked," he reported. "I told you there was nothing to worry about. Sarge probably stopped in at the Oak on his way home."

"He said he wanted us back sharp at eight," insisted Jamie. "He wasn't stopping anywhere. Let's try round the back."

They crept through swaying trees round the side of the Lodge into the garden. The rear of the house was as dark as the front, the back door locked and all the windows intact.

"I told you he wasn't home yet," said Liam, but there was a tinge of uncertainty in his voice. The problem was clear in the moonlight: there were cross-currents of footprints in the snow, suggesting that *someone* had been here. As they fanned out around the garden, examining the shadows for the unexpected, the wind picked up and there was a loud bang behind them. Jamie whirled round to see the shed door swinging on its hinges.

"Thank God for that," Keeley said with relief. "That made me jump right out of my skin."

But as Jamie looked over towards the shed door his creeping unease grew. Sarge had been extra careful to lock it after they had stored Mathers's body in there – the last thing he wanted was someone accidentally stumbling over a dead body. So why was it open now? Jamie crept over to the shed, the hairs on his neck beginning to rise, and peered into the darkness. The shed was a jumble of objects – folded-up garden chairs, a DIY workbench, the saggy carcass of a deflated football – but there was no sign of the blanket shrouding Mathers's dead body.

"Why the worried face?" asked Keeley, looking over Jamie's shoulder. "It's just a shed."

"That's exactly the problem," Liam replied grimly. "There's something missing that shou—"

"Shh!"

Jamie held up his hand, and Liam fell into a surprised silence. As the three of them stood frozen in the garden's icy shadows, Jamie could make out a faint noise coming from the fields beyond the Lodge. Stepping softly through the snow, he pushed through the trees and looked out over the fence.

A single silhouette was standing tall against the horizon, half-illuminated by a lantern placed on the ground next to him. The man was frantically digging a hole, flinging handfuls of cold earth to one side with his shovel. Beyond the outer fringes of the lamplight, Jamie could just make out a second figure lying prone in the snow.

"Sarge?" Liam called out warily. "What are you doing?"

The man didn't look up. He was totally engrossed in his shovelling.

"The ground must be frozen solid!" Keeley whispered in amazement. "How strong *is* your dad?"

"He's burying Mathers next to Smiler," groaned Liam. "He's lost the plot."

The figure straightened up and stopped digging, hurling the shovel to one side. As the man reached down and grabbed the prone body by the feet, Jamie's breath caught in his throat.

"What is it?" asked Liam.

"That's not Sarge," Jamie said hoarsely.

He didn't even need the lamplight to see it – the digger was too tall, his shoulders far too broad for Sarge's wiry frame. But the figure lying on the ground had a shaven head, and was wearing fingerless gloves on his hands...

"Jesus, that's Sarge on the ground!" gasped Liam. "He looks in a bad way."

"He's not dead, is he?" asked Jamie, in a horrified whisper.

"If he is, he's not going to be the only one," Liam replied grimly. "Stay here."

He vaulted the fence, landing easily on the other side, and began striding towards the figure.

"Oi!" he yelled. "Back off!"

The figure straightened up, letting go of Sarge's feet. As the man slowly shuffled around to face Liam, his features passed through the faint aura of the lamp, and suddenly Jamie was aware of the full horror of the situation.

It was Mathers.

Mathers was dead. Jamie had seen the scrap dealer's crushed throat. He had helped carry his lifeless body. It couldn't be him, and yet it was: the same hulking frame, the same sneer imprinted on his face. His flesh had decayed from pallid grey to a dark, bruised blue. Already a giant of a man, in death Mathers seemed to have only filled outwards, rolls of flesh and flab pushing against the straining seams of his overalls. Jamie saw now that he had dug his hole next to where Sarge had buried Smiler. *An eye for an eye. . .*

If Liam was unnerved by this nightmarish vision he managed to hide it, striding on without breaking step. As he watched his brother, Jamie felt a sharp elbow in his ribs.

"What are you waiting for?" Keeley hissed. "Go and help him! You're not going to let him face that thing on his own, are you?"

"What can I do?" Jamie retorted. "Liam told us to stay here. I'll only get in the way." He couldn't tell her the truth – that he was so scared his legs had turned to jelly, and he was desperate to go to the toilet.

Rolling her eyes, Keeley scrambled over the fence and dropped down into the snow on the other side.

"Leave him alone, you big baboon!" she called out, through cupped hands. "Pick on someone your own size!"

"Get back, Keeley!" Liam shouted. "I've got this!"

She ignored him, jogging across the field until she caught up with Liam. Jamie swore under his breath. There was no way he could stay here now. He swung his legs over the fence, landing with a crunch on the other side, and ran after Keeley and his brother. As he neared Mathers, his heart in his mouth, Jamie could see the crimson swathe where Sarge had been dragged through the snow. Blood was seeping from a wound in his head. Jamie's dad was out cold.

Confronted by three enemies, Mathers turned and let out a low growl. He lunged at Liam, but Jamie's brother skipped easily out of reach. They had the advantage of speed and numbers, but how could they hurt such a giant? As he looked across at his brother, Jamie saw Liam thinking the same thing, his eyes flicking over towards the shovel that Mathers had hurled to one side. At the moment it was still too close to the scrap dealer to reach, but if he moved. . .

Jamie bent down and scooped a handful of snow into a ball.

"Hey, you!" he cried at Mathers. "Leave my dad alone!"

He drew back his arm and hurled the snowball, landing a direct hit on the giant's chest. Mathers looked at him curiously, as though distracted by a buzzing fly. Quickly Jamie dropped to his knees and made another snowball, aware that Keeley was staring at him like he had lost his mind.

"Help me!" he hissed at her.

His second shot flew even truer than the first, smacking into Mathers's cheek with a satisfying thud. As Mathers took a lumbering step towards them, Keeley caught on, flinging her own snowy missiles in his direction. Together they peppered him with snowballs, slowly drawing him nearer. Soon Liam was able to dart forward and pick up the shovel. Running up behind Mathers, he swung the heavy tool into his back with murderous intent.

"Agh!"

It was Liam who cried out in pain, dropping the shovel and clutching his wrist. Mathers grunted and stopped, turning round as though someone had politely tapped him on the shoulder.

"What happened?" Jamie called out to Liam.

"I think I broke my bloody wrist!" he shouted back. "It's like he's made out of iron or something!"

"What do we do now?"

"What do you think? Run for it, the pair of you!"

The brothers stared at each other a second too long, allowing Mathers to pounce. He swung a monstrous fist at Liam, who raised his hands to defend himself only to take a glancing blow to his left arm. He cried out, staggering away. Mathers had hurt him without even connecting properly. Liam came back with a vengeance, ducking another bludgeoning glow and connecting with a solid right across the monster's jaw. Mathers didn't even flinch, thumping Liam in the gut and hurling him to the ground. Tears of helpless frustration welled in Jamie's eyes. Unless he did something fast, Mathers was going to kill his brother. But how could you hurt someone who was already dead?

"Jamie!"

Blinking with surprise, Jamie looked back towards the Lodge to see Lawrence scrambling over the fence. The bookshop owner cut an unlikely figure as he ran through the snow, pressing his glasses down on his nose, his red scarf streaming out behind him.

"Help!" cried Jamie. "We can't stop it!"

"The lamp!" Lawrence shouted back. "Use the lamp!"

Jamie looked down at the lantern perched on the edge of the grave near Sarge. He picked it up and hurled it at Mathers, and was rewarded with a loud shattering of glass as the lantern broke against the creature's back. Mathers let out an angry growl, breaking away from Liam to brush off the glittering shards. A dark patch of liquid spread out across his shoulders, spicing the air with the sweet smell of kerosene.

As Mathers wheeled around and glared at Jamie, Lawrence stepped in-between them. Fumbling through his pockets, the bookshop owner produced a silver lighter and struck the flint. When the lighter blossomed into fiery life, he threw it straight at Mathers.

The flames went up immediately, a beacon against the night sky. Mathers let out a bellow of pain, his arms flailing around wildly. Jamie watched with a mixture of horror and dark satisfaction as the creature staggered and writhed, fire wreathing his back and shoulders. With a final, primeval roar, Mathers lurched away across the fields and into the darkness.

No one said anything for a long time after that. Lawrence was bent double, catching his breath; Keeley was still staring after Mathers's retreating form, her eyes wide and her face ashen. Jamie ran past them and skidded to a halt where Liam crouched in the snow, his left arm hanging uselessly by his side. Gingerly Jamie helped his winded brother to his feet, taking some of his weight as they hobbled over to where Sarge was lying prone. Their dad hadn't moved a muscle throughout the whole ordeal. His eyes were open and he was staring blankly up at the night sky, a reddening halo forming in the snow around his head.

"Jesus, Jamie," Liam whispered, a sob of fear in his voice. "What the hell is going on?"

CHAPTER TWENTY-ONE

DRAUGR

Jamie and Liam carried Sarge inside the Lodge, Lawrence and Keeley following closely behind them. Sarge's limbs were stiff, his skin freezing to the touch. It was as though he had been encased in ice. They had done the same with Mathers's body, Jamie remembered with a shudder, hauling him through the blizzard at Sarge's insistence. At the time Sarge hadn't realized – how could he have? – that each step was another pen stroke on his own death warrant.

He can't die, Jamie told himself furiously. *Not like this.*

They brought Sarge inside the house and laid him down on the sofa, wrapping him in blankets in an attempt to melt the chill from his bones. As the rest of the room looked on, Liam turned on the heater and placed it near his dad's motionless body. Sarge barely blinked, his blue eyes cold and lifeless.

"What's wrong with him?" Jamie asked Liam. "Is he in a coma or something?"

"How should I know?" Liam snapped. "Do I look like a doctor to you?"

He anxiously gnawed on a fingernail, staring at his dad. Keeley took her phone from out of her bag and began scrolling through her address book.

"There's no point phoning for an ambulance, love," Liam told her. "It can't get here from Caxton, can it?"

"No," said Keeley. "But my mum doesn't live in Caxton, does she?"

"Your mum? Keeley, you can't ask her to come down here!" said Liam. "Did you not see that thing out there?"

"I saw it running away across the fields with its head on fire, if that's what you mean," Keeley said archly. "I think Mum's safe for the time being."

"Mathers isn't the only one out there," Jamie told her. "I think . . . I think Greg's the same. Alive and dead at the same time."

Perhaps he should have expected them to be more surprised, but nobody in the room blinked. After fighting Mathers's animated corpse, nothing seemed impossible any more.

Liam gave Keeley a dubious look. "You heard Jamie. This isn't a good idea, love."

"You helped us, didn't you?" Keeley retorted. "You could have got hurt but you came anyway. So let us return the favour, *love*."

Defeated, Liam threw up his hands and let Keeley go upstairs to phone her mum. Jamie watched his brother pace across the front room, muttering to himself. Lawrence was a pensive shadow in the corner of the room, fidgeting as he stared down at his feet. He looked up to find Liam eyeballing him from across the room. The bookshop owner smiled weakly.

Too late, Jamie realized what was going to happen. Liam marched over to Lawrence and grabbed his jacket with his good arm.

"Hey!" cried Jamie. "What are you doing?"

Liam had already bundled the protesting Lawrence out of the living room and was striding away down the corridor. Jamie ran after them into the kitchen in time to see his brother slam Lawrence up against the fridge.

"Leave him alone!" Jamie cried. "It's not his fault!"

Liam ignored him, pressing his snarling face up against Lawrence's. Jamie had never seen his brother so angry.

"I want some answers, yeah?" said Liam, through clenched teeth. "You were the only who knew that fire would work on that thing in the field. How? What else do you know? It feels like everyone round here's been keeping secrets but you're going to tell me everything. 'Cause I just saw a corpse come back from the dead to attack my dad, and I'm *this* close to losing it!"

"You're not losing it," Lawrence said solemnly. "Though it might be easier for you if you were."

The calmness of his reply seemed to puncture something inside Liam. He relaxed his grip on Lawrence's jacket, and allowed Jamie to pull him away. Lawrence adjusted his glasses and smoothed his rumpled shirt before continuing.

"I can't give you all the answers you want, I'm

afraid," he said. "I don't know what's wrong with your father and I can't make him better. I can only tell you what I've managed to piece together since I moved to this town. Since I realized that there was something very wrong here, lying just beneath the surface."

As Lawrence took a seat at the kitchen table, Keeley appeared in the doorway. Seeing Liam's angry glare, she glanced at Jamie, but he shook his head as if to say, *Not now*. Unusually for Keeley, she didn't press the matter. Instead she quietly joined them at the table and sat down.

"Go on," said Liam.

"It began a thousand years ago," Lawrence told them, "with Aldus, the Viking who founded this town. Back in Scandinavia, he committed the deed that made his name – trekking to a distant barrow where a notorious and wealthy chieftain lay buried, and descending into its depths to plunder the hoard of treasure within."

"Right," said Liam. "With you so far."

"Aldus never said a word about what happened in that barrow. But his actions in the following months tell us that *something* had taken place that had changed him to his very core. During the next Viking raid on Britain, Aldus turned his back on the raiding party and settled in what became Alderston with his hoard. He lay down his weapons and embraced Christianity. He never returned to his home country. The Norse sagas claimed that Aldus had been cursed as punishment for his act of desecration. By the *draugr*."

Liam frowned. "Drow-ger? Enlighten me."

214

"In English the name translates roughly to 'afterwalkers'," Lawrence explained.

"Afterwalkers? Walking after what?"

Lawrence looked down at his hands. "After death."

There was a long silence, and then Liam laughed aloud. "*Please* tell me you're not talking about zombies," he said.

"Of a kind," said Lawrence. "The Haitian *zombi* has become famous around the world, but many cultures have their own names for the undead. In Tibet they are called *ro-lang*, lurching corpses with seized-up limbs. In order to protect themselves the local villagers build their houses with very low doorways, because the *ro-lang* aren't flexible enough to bend down and enter. There's the Hindu *vetala*, malicious spirits who take possession of corpses, and the *ghül* of Arabic myth — a terrifying monstrosity that hunts graveyards feeding on the undead. And then there are the *draugr*."

Jamie leaned forward as Lawrence's voice dropped. The bookshop owner had the whole room under his spell now.

"The *draugr* are Viking undead," Lawrence continued, "condemned to forever haunt the location of their death like guard dogs of Hell. The sagas describe them as *hel-blár*, 'blue as death', and cloaked in a terrible odour of rotting death. As you've seen, they are blessed with incredible strength. Their bodies become bloated and heavy — one of their favourite methods of attack is to crush their victims beneath their own body weight."

"I had a nightmare where that happened to me!" Jamie blurted out. "I could feel my ribs cracking in my chest."

Lawrence nodded. "*Draugr* can control the dreams and visions of the living. They can also control the weather."

"That's the one thing that makes any sense," Liam said gloomily. "The weather in this town is bloody awful. OK, so we're talking about some pretty mean Viking zombies. But what are they doing *here*?"

"It's difficult to be certain," mused Lawrence, "but I believe that when Aldus broke into the chieftain's barrow he encountered a *draugr*. Although he managed to escape, he was cursed afterwards. Aldus brought the stain of the *draugr* with him to England, and they've been terrorizing Alderston ever since." Lawrence turned to Jamie. "Remember the first day we met, when I told you about the history of this place? The fire that swept through the church after Aldus's death, so fierce that the dead rose. The trial of Black Maggie for 'bringing the dead back to life'. The Resurrection Men supposedly digging up Kitty Hawkins's grave. The ghosts of wounded soldiers after the First World War. Do you see? Over and over again, the same pattern – the dead returning. The *draugr*."

Jamie nodded thoughtfully. It all made a certain kind of terrible, incredible sense. "What do the *draugr* want, Lawrence?"

"They are driven by an insatiable hunger."

"Which is?"

"Hate," Lawrence said starkly. "The *draugr* hate humans to the very core of their soul, because they have the one thing they want the most – life. So the *draugr* hunt, and the *draugr* kill, and since anyone who dies at their hands becomes a *draugr*, the cycle continues."

"OK," said Liam, blowing the air out of his cheeks. "Let's pretend for a moment that this isn't all insane. What's Mr Redgrave got to do with it?"

It was Lawrence's turn to look confused. "Who?"

"He's a local criminal," Liam explained. "A real bigwig. He's been threatening us, making us do jobs for him."

"He's the one who set Mathers after us," Jamie added. "The thing you just saw in the fields."

He quickly told them about his conversation with Mr Redgrave in Roxanne's office. Lawrence looked thoughtful.

"I don't know who this man is," he said, "but if what he claims is true, and he does have some kind of control over the *draugr*, you'd do well to do what he says."

"But he wants Aldus's hoard!" Jamie protested. "People have been hunting for it for centuries. You think we can find it overnight?"

"I'm not saying it's easy," Lawrence told him. "But isn't there *something* you've got to work on?"

Jamie felt the eyes in the kitchen turn on him. Everyone was waiting for him. Counting on him. He took a deep breath. His mind was racing so quickly the thoughts were elbowing and jostling one another for attention. If Lawrence was right, then Alderston's inhabitants had been turning into *draugr* for centuries. And his description of the *draugr* matched exactly the visions Jamie had been having of Kitty Hawkins. But everyone agreed that Kitty's death had been an accident – so what could have triggered her transformation?

And then he had it.

"The ring!" Jamie cried out. "Kitty's ring!"

Lawrence leaned forward, light shining in his eyes. "Go on," he said.

"You said you think Aldus was infected or cursed somehow when he broke into the chieftain's barrow," Jamie said quickly. "What if it was the treasure he found there? His hoard? George Rathbone gave Kitty an engagement ring but he swore he didn't steal it, that his mum had found it. If the ring was part of Aldus's hoard, and Kitty died wearing it. . ."

"Are you saying you think *Kitty Hawkins* became one of these *draugr* things?" Keeley said sceptically.

"I'm sure of it," said Jamie. "So if we can find out where George Rathbone got hold of the ring, wouldn't that give us a clue to where Aldus's grave is?"

"It's a possibility," Lawrence admitted. "But how do you propose to do that?"

"Easy," said Jamie, with a grin. "Check his diary."

"Wait a moment." Lawrence stared at him. "Are you telling me you have George Rathbone's diary?"

Jamie nodded excitedly. "Upstairs – I'll go and get it!"

He ran to his bedroom and retrieved the diary from its hiding place behind the grating, bringing it down to the kitchen and laying it in front of Lawrence on the table. The bookshop owner carefully unwrapped the diary from the white cloth and began to pore over the pages.

"Incredible!" he murmured.

"So where did he find the ring, then?" asked Liam, almost unwillingly. Hurriedly Jamie began flicking through the pages. "Here it is," he said. Lawrence cleared his throat and began to read out loud, in a deep, clear voice:

"*Alone among my possessions, the silver ring was untarnished, innocent of any criminal associations. It belonged to my mother, who stumbled across it in the woods near Lark Farm as a young girl. . .*" He looked up from the diary. "You think this is a clue?"

"It's not exactly X marks the spot, is it?" Liam said dubiously. "One ring doesn't necessarily mean—"

"It's not just one ring though!" interrupted Jamie. "Jack's lucky coin!"

Liam scratched his head. "Now I'm totally lost."

"Don't you remember the cassette tape we listened to in the van – the one Keeley gave me, with her great-grandfather Frank on it? He said his best friend Jack came back from the dead after he had been injured in the war. Frank kept talking about Jack's lucky coin, which he had found ... yes, you guessed it, at Lark Farm!"

"I thought we'd agreed that Great-Grandfather Frank had been suffering from a bad case of shell shock."

"After what you've just seen, you can't believe that!" cried Jamie. "Frank was telling the truth – it all fits together! Jack's lucky coin was from Aldus's hoard, just like the ring George Rathbone gave Kitty. And they were both found in the same place – Lark Farm." He tapped the diary excitedly. "*That's* where Aldus's hoard is!"

CHAPTER TWENTY-TWO

THE BARROW

The night sky above Lark Farm was a velvet sheet sprinkled with distant stars. As Jamie followed his brother up the hill towards the farmhouse he gazed up at the heavens, lost in thought. Had the stars looked the same for Aldus all those years ago, when he had left his warm feasting hall to go in search of a chieftain's barrow? Had the night been as cold when George Rathbone stumbled out of the Royal Oak, drunk on grief and ale, to visit the grave of his beloved fiancée? Jamie felt as though he was walking in ancient footsteps, following the same dark and mysterious path. Only Aldus and Rathbone were warriors, in their own way: brawlers and thieves. Had their hearts drummed so quickly in their chests; had their breaths come in such quick, shallow gasps?

"Jamie." Liam's voice, flat and low through the darkness. "We're here. Stop daydreaming."

They were the first words his brother had uttered since leaving the Lodge. Jamie knew Liam was in pain, his left arm damaged by the *draugr's* blow. Even if Liam refused to say anything, his occasional winces of pain told their own story. Keeley's mum had done the best she could, bandaging the arm and giving him some painkillers, but without an X-ray it was impossible to tell whether anything had been broken. Jennifer Marshall had arrived soon after Jamie had brought down George Rathbone's diary. She had taken charge with crisp efficiency, ordering them to take Sarge to Jamie's bedroom, where she had patched up his head wound and examined him for further injuries.

For as long as Jamie could remember he had been scared of his dad, desperate to please him and make him feel proud, but unsure how. But as he looked down at Sarge, now helpless and almost lifeless, Jamie felt an unexpected emotion flooding through his veins like hot water: anger. He didn't care what kind of creature Mathers had turned into – Jamie wanted to find him and hurt him.

He felt a hand on his shoulder.

"I know how you feel, little bro," Liam said solemnly. "Believe me. But first of all let's get Redgrave off our backs – then we'll take care of what needs to be taken care of." He looked across at Jennifer Marshall. "If Jamie and I go out for a bit, is Sarge going to be OK?"

Keeley's mum nodded. "He isn't in any immediate danger," she told them. "He's taken a nasty blow to the head and he's in deep shock but I don't think his injuries are life-threatening."

"What about you?" Liam asked. "Can we leave you here alone?"

"Don't you worry about us," Jennifer replied firmly. "Us Marshalls can take care of ourselves. We'll be fine indoors. It's outside that's dangerous at the moment. You just make sure that you look after each other."

Liam grinned. At that moment Jamie could see where Keeley had got her stubborn streak from. The two brothers went to work immediately. Rifling through Sarge's toolkit, they selected some tools and put them into a rucksack along with a length of rope and a pair of torches. Liam also took a shovel with him – "might come in handy if we run into any more zombies," he said, with grim humour. Keeley demanded that she come with them, but her mum silenced her with a single look. She contented herself with pressing the silver lighter Lawrence had flung at Mathers into a surprised Liam's palm.

"You might need this if you run into any more bad guys," she said. "You didn't have much luck with the shovel."

Liam nodded appreciatively. "Thanks, lov— Keeley," he said, checking himself just in time.

All the while Lawrence remained at the kitchen table, leafing reverently through George Rathbone's diary. He had produced a small notebook from his pocket and was furiously scribbling notes. When Liam tapped him on the shoulder he looked up owlishly.

"We're off," Liam told him, slipping the rucksack over his shoulder. "You learn anything else that might help us?"

"Not yet," murmured Lawrence, with a shake of the head. "But there are a couple of things here I'd like to cross-reference with some of my books. Let me take it back to Withershins now. If I find out anything useful I could call you with it."

"I'm not the one to ask," said Liam. "It's not my diary. Jamie?"

Jamie bit his lip. For reasons he couldn't quite explain, he was reluctant to part with the diary, even for one night. Then again, he wasn't going to need it at Lark Farm, and Lawrence had just saved their lives. He nodded.

"Thank you," Lawrence said meaningfully, wrapping the book back up in the cloth Jamie had found it in. "And don't worry – if there's one thing I know, it's how to take care of an old book."

Lawrence accompanied them as far as Withershins, softly wishing them luck as they parted in the street. Jamie looked up wistfully at the bright light burning in the window of the flat above the bookshop. He wished he could stay indoors, protected from the howling wind and whatever else lurked in the darkness. Every building they passed in Alderston was shut down for the night – the pub had closed early and Roxanne's Cabs was empty, no lights on behind the blinds in the back office. It felt to Jamie like everyone in the town was watching him from behind closed curtains. Waiting.

The ominous atmosphere didn't improve as they

continued down the lane into the countryside. Lark Farm had been forbidding enough in daylight – in the middle of the night, with its buildings cloaked in shadow, it looked like the lair of some kind of murderous creature. Jamie stayed close to his brother as they laboured up the hill and carried on past the farmhouse and the yawning maws of the barns. As he looked out across the field, Jamie shivered at the sight of the shattered scarecrow frame that had held up Mathers's body. Everywhere he went in this town, there seemed to be reminders of death in one form or another.

"Well, we're here," Liam said softly, the wind ruffling his blond hair as he looked around. "Don't suppose that diary of yours left any directions to the barrow, did it? You know, walk twenty paces east as the crow flies and all that?"

Jamie shook his head.

"No," sighed Liam. "I didn't think it would be that easy."

Jamie scanned the horizon, deep in thought. Both George Rathbone's mother and Frank's friend Jack had found their treasures in the woods – which Jamie took to mean the thin line of trees running along their left-hand side. He led his brother across the field and into the small wood, and for half an hour they paced back and forth through the trees examining the ground for any unusual marks or features. It was cold, tiring work, and Jamie could feel Liam growing impatient beside him.

And then, suddenly he saw it. No X marking the spot, no monument or headstone. Just a raised indentation in the ground between two trees, little more than a bump in the ground. Hardly a fitting resting place for a Viking King, the feared and legendary Aldus, the father of Alderston. No wonder generations of treasure hunters had failed to find it. Without George Rathbone's diary to point him in the right direction, Jamie would have walked straight past it every time. But as he approached the small knoll Jamie's skin was alive with goosebumps – he knew what lay beneath it. He could almost feel Aldus's presence.

Liam strode to the top of the mound and stamped down through the snow to the hard ground. "Not going to be easy, digging through that," he said. "Better get started, eh?"

Jamie helped his brother brush the snow away from the mound, piling it up by the trees. When Liam dug down there was a dull thud as the shovel struck something hard. As they cleared the snow and earth away, Jamie's heartbeat quickened at the sight of a layer of wooden planks beneath.

"Jackpot," said Liam.

He raised the shovel above his head and brought it down hard. There was a loud crunch as the metal hit the aged wood. Liam brought the shovel down again and again until the wood splintered and broke off, tumbling into the inky depths of the barrow. Jamie took the coiled rope from the rucksack and tied one end around the nearest tree, fastening it in place with several double knots. The other end of the rope he fed down into the barrow.

When he had cleared a large enough space for them to crawl through, Liam stepped back, panting for breath. The hole looked uncomfortably like a creature's mouth, complete with jagged wooden teeth. Jamie shivered.

"No need for both of us to go down there," said Liam, eyeing his brother carefully. "Why don't you stay up top and keep watch?"

Jamie shook his head. Whatever lay in wait for them down in the barrow, they had to find Aldus's hoard. It was their only chance of escaping from Alderston alive, he knew. Mr Redgrave wouldn't stop until they were all dead. The sight of his dad lying sprawled out in the snow, blood pouring from his head, was imprinted on Jamie's brain. He wouldn't let Sarge down. Not this time.

"If you want a lookout that badly you can stay up here," Jamie told his brother. "I'm going into the barrow."

A smile flitted across Liam's face. "Suit yourself, little bro," he said, dropping the shovel and strapping on his rucksack. "But I go first."

He took hold of the rope and eased himself through the hole in the wooden boards. Jamie watched as the darkness swallowed up his brother, until the rope stopped twitching and he heard Liam's voice waft up from the depths:

"You can come down. It's safe."

Gritting his teeth, Jamie took hold of the rope and climbed down into the barrow. With every new handhold he could feel the earth closing in around him, the ground swallowing him up. The air was cold and musty, the exhalation of an ancient spell that had been brewing for a thousand years. Concentrating on his descent, Jamie was surprised when his feet brushed against a solid surface and he could let go of the rope. Liam had already turned on a torch and was examining their surroundings. They were standing in a small circular chamber with a stone floor. Jamie shuddered when the torch picked out a pile of old bones heaped against the wall. Liam crouched down to inspect them.

"Animal bones," he said. "If this Aldus guy was as important as you said, maybe they buried some of his horses with him. Not much of a hoard, though."

Jamie pulled out his own torch and began shining it around the chamber. The light landed on a small crawlspace at the bottom of the wall.

"What do we have here?" asked Liam. Crouching down by the entrance to the tunnel, he pulled a face.

"It's too small," he said. "I'll never fit through there."

Jamie's heart sank. He could barely squeeze inside the tunnel himself – and there wasn't enough space for him to turn around if he ran into any problems. It was the darkest black he had ever seen. The last thing on earth Jamie wanted to do was get down on his hands and knees and crawl in. This had all started when Aldus had broken into a barrow and been touched by the curse of the *draugr*. What if there was a Viking zombie waiting for Jamie on the other side of this tunnel?

"I'll go," he said finally.

Liam looked at him. "You sure?"

Jamie nodded, not trusting his voice to stay steady if he spoke. As he got down on his hands and knees, Liam glanced uneasily around the chamber.

"Don't hang about, eh? This place is giving me the creeps."

Jamie took a deep breath, and crawled into the darkness. Sharp stones cut into his hands and knees. His breaths came in quick, terrified gasps. In his haste to get through the tunnel he banged his head on the ceiling, and bit back a cry of pain. He felt like a worm slithering through the ground, the weight of the earth pressing in around him. More than that, as he wriggled on, Jamie felt himself travelling deeper through time, moving back through the accumulated centuries that had passed down here in icy solitude since Aldus had passed away, and his remains had been entombed deep beneath the earth.

To his undying relief Jamie saw the tunnel's end. He emerged from the crawlspace, scrambling to his feet and brushing the dirt from the clothes.

"You OK, bro?" Liam's disembodied voice echoed down the tunnel after him.

"I think so!" he called back, rubbing his head. "Just let me. . ."

Flicking on his torch, he found himself standing in another circular chamber, about the same size as the first. But this chamber wasn't empty: there was a stone coffin in the centre of the room. Hesitantly Jamie went forward and ran a hand over the lid, feeling the cool stone against his palm. Within the coffin, he knew, lay the remains of Aldus the Viking. Here, in this small vault hidden underneath the ground, was the real heart of Alderston.

As Jamie slowly circled the coffin, he saw that it wasn't the only object in the chamber. The floor was littered with silver treasure – not just coins but rings, necklaces and arm bracelets. A hoard of precious metal, fit for a Viking king. Dropping to his knees, Jamie picked up a handful of coins and let them trickle through his fingers.

Then he went to work.

There hadn't been enough space in the tunnel to bring a rucksack, so he hurriedly began filling his pockets. As he scooped up a fistful of coins Jamie paused, assailed by a sudden pang of guilt. He had stood watch as Sarge and Liam had stolen from warehouses and railway sidings, but this was the first time he had committed the act himself. The fact that Jamie was stealing from the dead only made it feel even worse. But what choice did he have? He wasn't stealing to make himself rich; he was trying to save his family from Mr Redgrave. Surely people would understand that?

The shadows in the tomb lengthened as the light

from Jamie's torch wobbled and dimmed. He swore softly. Had Liam checked the batteries before they left the Lodge? Jamie couldn't remember. Panicking, he took one final glance at Aldus's coffin before the torch emitted a farewell flicker, and the chamber was plunged into darkness.

CHAPTER TWENTY-THREE

THE MAN UPSTAIRS

Jamie stood frozen to the spot, barely daring to breathe. As an eerie glow cut through the pitch black, he looked across the chamber in horror. Coils of white smoke were seeping out from beneath the lid of Aldus's coffin, stretching out towards him. Jamie backed away, reaching down to the floor in search of a weapon amongst the silver treasures. When his fingers closed around a short metal blade with a handle, he held it fearfully out in front of him.

"Jamie!" he heard Liam shout from the entrance chamber. "What happened to the torch? You OK?"

His brother's voice broke the spell. There was nothing here Jamie could fight – he needed to *run*. Still clutching the blade, he dived back towards the tunnel, coins and rings spilling from his bulging pockets, and began crawling for his life. Ignoring the rocks digging into his elbows and knees, Jamie struggled along the tunnel, desperately trying not to think about the pale tendrils of smoke creeping after him. He kept his eyes firmly fixed ahead, where a narrow beam of light from his brother's torch was flickering in the entrance chamber. Liam was crouched by the tunnel's mouth, frantically calling out Jamie's name and urging him on.

As the white mist swirled around Jamie, his mind no longer felt his own, and his eyes began seeing visions from another time and place. He was a villager in a coastal town, running for his life as Viking raiders descended upon the settlement amid a storm of axe blades. He was Aldus in the chieftain's barrow, doing battle with a lumbering nightmare of the undead. He was looking down over Alderston graveyard in the shocked months after Aldus's death, as a knot of villagers frantically poured pitch over graves writhing with wormlike fingers. As Jamie looked on, the sound of his own ragged breaths in his ear, one of the villagers stepped forward and dipped a flaming torch against the pitch, engulfing the churchyard in a sheet of roaring flame...

"Come on, Jamie!" Liam shouted, his voice cracking. "Nearly there!"

As Jamie scrabbled closer, his brother reached into the tunnel and grabbed him by the jacket, pulling him free. He dragged Jamie over to the dangling rope.

"Get up there now," he ordered.

Tucking the metal blade in his belt, Jamie took hold of the rope between his hands. He couldn't stop his eyes flicking back towards the tunnel. White mist was seeping out of it, taking the shape of a ghostly hand, wraithlike fingers stretching out towards them.

"Hurry, Jamie!" urged Liam.

Jamie's arms had turned to jelly, and he was

struggling to pull himself up the rope. He let out a grunt as he slipped. Beneath him Liam grabbed his body and pushed him upwards with a desperate heave. As the surface neared, Jamie reached out and grabbed hold of one of the shattered planks, ignoring the pain as its jagged teeth bit into his palm. Summoning every last drop of energy, he pulled himself up through the hole and on to solid ground.

Jamie looked back to see the rope twitch wildly, and then Liam's head appeared, grim determination etched on his face. He scrambled clear of the hole and dived on top of Jamie, sending them both rolling through the snow. Behind them a wisp of icy mist in the shape of a giant hand rose up from the barrow and swiped through the air where Jamie had been standing a second earlier. There was a piercing shriek from deep within the barrow, a centuries-old cry of loss, and then the mist melted away to nothing and the noise died.

Liam waited until he sure the coast was clear before gingerly picking himself up and brushing the snow from his clothes.

"You OK?" he panted.

"Yeah. You?"

"Ask me later. What *was* that?"

"Aldus, I think," said Jamie. "His spirit, anyway, trying to protect his treasure."

Liam looked back towards the shattered remains of the barrow. He blew out his cheeks. "This town," he muttered.

234

"Yeah."

"When I saw your torch go out I got worried. How did you get on in there? Did you find anything?"

Wordlessly Jamie reached into his pockets and began tipping coins into his brother's outstretched palm. A ghost of a smile appeared on Liam's face.

"You little beauty," he said.

After the icy terror of the barrow, even the bleak expanse of Lark Farm held few fears for them now. In the shelter of the barn they carefully collected all the treasure Jamie had gathered from Aldus's tomb, transferring it to a pocket in Liam's rucksack.

"Wish Sarge could see this," said Liam, zipping up the pocket. "He'd be proud, you know." His teeth flashed white in a grin. "The crazy old crook."

"You think?" asked Jamie.

"No doubt about it, little bro. You were great back there, absolutely top notch. You wouldn't have got Sarge crawling through that tunnel, not in a million years. Small spaces freak him out."

"Really?"

"Don't tell him I said so, like. He'll do his nut."

They left the farm behind them, heading down the hill and along the lane back towards the orange streetlamps of Alderston. As the town grew closer Jamie sensed Liam become preoccupied, his eyes flicking back towards his rucksack pocket.

"How much do you think they're worth?" Jamie asked.

"Mm?"

"The coins and stuff. How much?"

"Oh, enough," Liam replied. "Enough to buy our freedom out of this place, at any rate." He paused. "Makes me wonder if we should take a little percentage for ourselves. Call it a finder's fee."

"What about Mr Redgrave?"

"How's he going to know? I'm not going to tell him. Are you?"

"I don't know, Liam," Jamie said dubiously. "Taking from that barrow because Mr Redgrave made us is one thing, but taking some for ourselves, it's just. . ." He searched for the right word. "It's wrong, isn't it?"

Liam stopped in his tracks.

"It's *wrong*?" His voice rang with mocking incredulity. "Have you only just figured that out, Einstein? Stealing's wrong. Oh, OK. Let's just forget about the last five years then, because *that's all we've been doing.*" He poked a finger into Jamie's chest. "And don't think you weren't there helping us, little bro. Too late to play Mr Innocent now."

"That's not fair! I didn't have any choice!"

"Neither did I!" Liam's voice with hoarse. "You think it was any easier for me? I didn't have an older brother to do the hard stuff for me. I didn't have the luxury of being a scared, weak little mummy's boy. I just did it. I shut my mouth and got on with it. And now I'm holding a bag full of treasure and just a few pieces could help us start over, make a fresh start. But you want me to hand it all over to another thief, because stealing's wrong."

Jamie flinched as though he had been hit, tears welling in his eyes. Liam waved a hand dismissively.

"For God's sake don't start blubbing," he said. "You're not a baby."

"Remember what happened to the others," pleaded Jamie. "To Jack, to Kitty Hawkins. They died with Aldus's treasure on them and they became *draugr*. Do you want that to happen to other people? Do you want to spread this curse outside of Alderston? Look what it's done here!"

"I don't care about Jack Nobody and Kitty What's-Her-Face," Liam retorted. "And I don't care what happens to anyone else as long as we get some money."

"You don't mean that, Liam!" pleaded Jamie. "I know you don't!"

"Oh, shut up with your whining!"

Liam shoved him, hard, sending Jamie toppling into the snow. Jamie stared at up him in a mixture of shock and amazement. Liam's fists were clenched as though he was ready to follow up with a punch, and he had to physically check himself as Jamie picked himself up from the ground. They stared at each other for a few seconds, and then Jamie turned and fled.

"Hey, I'm sorry!" Liam called out after him. "Come back!"

Jamie didn't reply. He ran blindly along the lane into Alderston, not caring where he was going, or if there were *draugr* waiting in the shadows for him. He ran until his limbs burned and his eyes were dry of tears. Finally, when he couldn't run any more, Jamie staggered to a halt. He leaned against a shopfront, his breaths coming in great shudders. The anger and the humiliation were starting to fade, replaced by a creeping regret that he had run off. This wasn't the night to be alone.

Jamie looked around, trying to get his bearings. He was on the street leading away from the clock tower up towards the church. Above the row of terraced shops, a solitary window was lit up. It was the flat over Withershins – Lawrence must still be up, poring over George Rathbone's diary. The bookshop owner would understand why Jamie didn't want to keep any of Aldus's treasure; maybe he could help him persuade Liam. Taking a deep breath, Jamie walked up the street and went to bang on the door of the bookshop. The door swung open at his touch. He frowned. Had Lawrence forgotten to lock up? It seemed unlikely, especially with the threat of the *draugr* roaming the streets. Jamie crept inside, careful not to disturb the precarious towers of volumes blocking up the aisles. In broad daylight Withershins was a confused jumble; in darkness it was a labyrinth. As Jamie edged deeper into the shop he realized it wasn't only the atmosphere that had changed. There were no incense sticks smouldering in the pot behind the counter, freeing the air of their cloyingly sweet fog. It had been replaced by strains of a different, even more unpleasant odour – a stale, acrid waft of rotten meat. Jamie had come across it before, when he had been attacked in his kitchen and when they had saved Sarge from Mathers. It was the smell of death and decay.

It was the smell of the *draugr*.

"Can I help you?"

Jamie jumped as Lawrence emerged from the shadow of a bookcase by the wall. A moonbeam arrowed in through the window, slanting across the gleaming dome of his bald head. Although the bookshop owner's tone was courteous, the smile on his face hadn't reached his eyes.

"A little late for book shopping, isn't it?" he asked. "Didn't you see the sign in the window? We're closed."

"I'm sorry," Jamie stammered, edging backwards. "I thought you might still be up. I'll go."

Lawrence stepped calmly in front of him, blocking his exit out of the bookshop. "What's wrong, Jamie? You look like you've seen a ghost." He peered closer. "*Have* you seen a ghost, Jamie?"

Jamie shook his head.

"Because ignorant people like to laugh at the occult world, but there are things on this earth that they couldn't begin to explain. Ghosts. Ancient evil. The undead."

"*Draugr*?" Jamie said bravely.

"*Draugr* too," replied Lawrence. "They're all too real – real as a blow to your head, or a hand around your throat. You could ask Sarge about that, but I'm not sure he'd be able to reply."

Jamie tried to dart past him but Lawrence moved like a snake, grabbing hold of his collar and pulling him back. He wasn't a big man but his grip was surprisingly strong, and no matter how much Jamie wriggled and squirmed he couldn't break free. He reached down for the dagger in his belt but Lawrence saw what he was trying, and wrenched it from his grasp.

"Careful," he said firmly. "You might hurt someone with that. Come on – it's time to speak to the man upstairs."

Keeping a hand latched around Jamie's neck, Lawrence marched him behind the counter and through the beaded curtain over the doorway beyond. As they plunged into a dark staircase the smell of rotten flesh thickened, curdling the air. Jamie gagged and tried to run away through the curtain but Lawrence hauled him back, shoving him roughly up the steps. When they reached the door at the top of the staircase, the bookshop owner rapped three times on the wood before entering the room.

It was as though someone had turned over a fresh page in a picture book of Hell. The room resembled an old-fashioned Victorian parlour, with thick drapes over the windows and ornate gas lamps turned down to a sombre orange glow. Two armchairs were positioned by the hearth, which was struggling to contain a fierce fire that threw out waves of crackling heat into the room. In the chair facing Jamie was a corpse in a three-piece suit. Its skin was the dark-blue shade of centuries-old bruises. Bloated flesh burst out through the seams of its clothing. The corpse's eyes were closed, its head tilted back against the headrest. The smell of rotting flesh was as unrelenting as the heat, a noxious cloud of death choking and stifling the room.

"Sit," ordered Lawrence.

Jamie took a seat in the free armchair, desperately trying to stem the rising tide of panic inside his chest. His brain was whirring, thoughts cartwheeling one after the other. All this time, Lawrence had only been pretending to be his friend. Whilst they had been talking in the shop downstairs, this corpse had been sitting here. It was insane. What did Lawrence expect him to do now – pretend to have a conversation with a dead body?

The corpse's mouth let out a long exhalation, like the opening of a sarcophagus. A blackened eyelid flicked open.

Jamie let out a terrified yell and tried to leap out of his seat. Lawrence pushed him back down.

"Manners, Jamie!" he chided him. "You can't leave now – Mr Redgrave's been dying to meet you."

CHAPTER TWENTY-FOUR

MR REDGRAVE

Jamie stared at the creature in horror. Mr Redgrave shifted in his chair with a rattle and rending of flesh, his decaying mouth twisting into a grimacing smile. Jamie felt pinned against the chair, too frightened to run even if he could have moved his legs. The fire writhed in the hearth like an angry creature. Sweat was pouring down Jamie's back, his stomach churning with the stench of decay.

"What's the matter, Jamie?" said Mr Redgrave, in the same gravelly rasp that had assailed Jamie down the phone line. "Never seen a *draugr* before?"

Counting Greg and Mathers, Jamie had seen three. But they had been fresh from the grave, whereas Mr Redgrave's features seemed to be crumbling under the weight of centuries.

"As Lawrence says, my associates know me as Mr Redgrave, although you might know me by another name."

A burning coal fell down in the grate with a fiery thud.

"I think I do," Jamie said cautiously. "I think you're George Rathbone."

It had to be. In life, Rathbone had been a criminal; didn't it make sense that he would carry on in the same vein after his death? Even as he stared at the creature, Jamie could feel hatred and scorn emanating from him.

The *draugr*'s dead eyeballs stared back at Jamie. No one spoke, the only sound in the room the spit and crackle of fire in the grate. Then the creature's mouth opencd and a wheezing chuckle spilled out.

"Nice try," said Mr Redgrave. "But wrong, I'm afraid. Rathbone is where he belongs, burning in Hell."

Jamie frowned. "But if you're not George Rathbone, then who are you?"

The *draugr* proudly adjusted his tie. "My name," he rasped, through parched lips, "is Tom McNally."

Initially the name meant nothing, but as Jamie leafed back through the pages of George Rathbone's diary in his mind, suddenly he remembered where he had come across it before: *As we turned and fled from the hellish scene, Silas stumbled over Tom McNally's body. The farm boy was lying beside the grave, his throat crushed like a stalk of corn. . .*

"The farm boy!" Jamie exclaimed. "You were the one who guarded Kitty's grave!"

Mr Redgrave inclined his head. "That I was. I promised John Hawkins no harm would come to Kitty while I still had breath in my body, and I kept my word. I gave my life in my attempts to keep her safe."

"You thought you were protecting her from George

243

Rathbone and the Resurrection Men," said Jamie. "The town thought they were going to rob Kitty's grave but all George wanted to do was say goodbye to her. They weren't the ones who killed you."

The *draugr* shook his head. "Rathbone wanted to, all right – and he would have tried had our paths crossed that night, but someone else took care of that before he turned up."

Someone else. Some*thing* else. The only thing that it could have been.

"Kitty," said Jamie. "It was Kitty Hawkins. She came back as a *draugr* and killed you."

"I didn't know what a *draugr* was, then," said Mr Redgrave. "How could I have known? How could any man be prepared for the dead to rise behind them? I had been so intent on protecting Kitty it had never occurred to me that I was the one needing protecting from *her*. By the time I realized what had happened, it was too late. She hit me with a shovel, and grabbed me in a grip so tight she squeezed the very life from me. The last thing I saw was the hatred in her eyes."

A series of hacking coughs assailed Mr Redgrave, and it was a minute or so before he was able to continue:

"The first thing I remember . . . afterwards . . . was coming to in the coffin. A sudden jolt of panic, like a needle straight into my heart. Barely room to move, barely room to breathe. I screamed. Flailing blindly, like an animal, I shattered the coffin with my fists and clawed my way to the surface. I still remember the moment when I burst free from the earth, that first deep lungful of night air . . . it was only then that I realized that I had changed. I was consumed by hate, an unspeakable envy gnawing away at my insides. Looking out across the churchyard, I could see a light burning in the Lodge's window, and I was overwhelmed by the urge to go towards it and hunt down the man within. But then I saw lanterns moving along Church Lane, the sound of laughter and voices as a party neared, and I hastened away into the shadows. Had I yet known the full extent of my powers, the night would have had a very different ending.

"As it turned out, I never got the chance to settle my score with George Rathbone. The good people of Alderston took care of that for me. A mob went to the Lodge and pummelled him from this world with their fists and the soles of their boots. I watched from the fringes of the wood as they threw his broken body on to a pyre in the fields behind the Lodge and set it alight. There was no Christian burial for *this* Resurrection Man."

"But that's not fair!" protested Jamie. "George Rathbone loved Kitty! It wasn't his fault that the dead were rising, it was Aldus's!"

Mr Redgrave moved without warning, lunging forward and fastening an icy clench around Jamie's wrist. "It *was* his fault!" he snarled. "He gave Kitty the ring! If he'd left her alone, then she wouldn't have come back!"

Jamie cried out and the *draugr* slowly relinquished his crushing grip, one finger at a time.

"You found Kitty, didn't you?" Jamie said quietly, nursing his wrist. "Afterwards."

Mr Redgrave let out a long, crackling breath and sat back in his chair. "After Rathbone's death I hid out in the woods," he said finally. "I wanted the townspeople to think that they had got their man, and I knew that I could no longer walk forth in the world amongst the living. It was in the woods where I saw her – standing by the edge of Black Maggie's pond, gazing into the waters where she had drowned. The girl with the golden hair and the warm smile I had loved was gone, replaced by something altogether darker, but even then, with my soul blackened and consumed with hatred, with no beating heart to feel love, I felt . . . something."

"So what did you do?"

Mr Redgrave stared levelly at Jamie, his eyes like coals.

"I picked up a rock and brought it down upon her head," he said. "Again and again. I beat her until she couldn't get up and then I set fire to her, right by the pond, until she was destroyed."

Jamie gasped. "But you loved her!"

"I loved *Kitty*," Mr Redgrave said hoarsely. "My Kitty drowned in the pond. The thing that came back afterwards wasn't her. It was a monstrosity, a perversion. Destroying it was the only thing I could do."

The *draugr* sat back in his chair, letting out a long,

stale sigh. "After that I couldn't stay in the wood. I roamed the countryside, feeding on farm animals and the occasional lone traveller. For a long time I considered trying to destroy myself like I had Kitty. But I was filled with too much pride, too much rage. My mother always said that Viking blood ran in my veins – perhaps it was fitting that this is what I became, a creature of the Norse night. From somewhere within me I found the strength to carry on, to thrive even. I may not have been able to walk the streets in daylight, but I could haunt the twilight, the criminal underworld: back alleys and sidestreets, dark cellars and sewers. Near on three centuries of robbing and murdering – not bad for a farm boy." Mr Redgrave laughed, a harsh retching sound that sprayed his waistcoat with flecks of spittle. "Perhaps George Rathbone and I could have been friends after all."

"I doubt it," said Jamie, with sudden boldness. "I don't think George Rathbone had friends. I don't think he liked anyone, apart from Kitty."

"He didn't deserve her!" the *draugr* snarled, slamming his fist on the armrest. "If only Kitty had loved me, everything would have been different. But now, if I can claim the Viking hoard, I can prove to her that I was the best man: better than Rathbone, better than Aldus even. The mortsafes were just about money, and a nice profit they would have made me, too. I may have been poor in life, but in death I have made my fortune many times over. The hoard is different. It's a matter of *pride*."

Lawrence picked up an iron stoker from the fireplace and poked the fire in the hearth, his bald head gleaming red in the light. The bookshop owner had remained silent all this time. Jamie had been so wrapped up in Mr Redgrave's story he had almost forgotten he was there.

"What about you?" he asked. "How do you fit into all this?"

"The same way everyone in Alderston fits in," Lawrence replied calmly. "Family ties. My name is Lawrence Porter. My great-great-great-grandfather was Silas Porter."

Silas Porter. The Resurrection Man who had fled Alderston for his uncle's farm in Yorkshire. Jamie's head slumped back against the headrest in despair. Local history, trapping him again.

"The story of Alderston and George Rathbone was passed down through my family," Lawrence told him. "I always felt there was more going on than the official version allowed, and I was sure Aldus's hoard held the key. During the course of my investigations I stumbled across Mr Redgrave, who persuaded me to move to Alderston and join forces. Believe it or not, I had my suspicions about Lark Farm being the location for the hoard but I couldn't find any proof – and then you turned up. I was astonished when you showed me George Rathbone's diary. That was the key to the whole puzzle. Once you had found it, all we had to do was sit back and let you do the hard work for us."

"Enough history lessons," snapped Mr Redgrave. "Where is it, Jamie? Where's my hoard?"

"We-we didn't find anything," stammered Jamie. "We looked for hours but we couldn't find the barrow. The diary must have been wrong."

Mr Redgrave twisted his neck to look over at the bookshop owner.

"You believe him, Lawrence?"

Lawrence slowly shook his head.

"Me neither."

The bookshop owner stepped forward and handed the *draugr* the metal blade he had taken from Jamie. "He had this on him. I think he was planning to use it on me."

Mr Redgrave held the blade up to the light, inspecting it. "Marvellous," he breathed. "There's no mistaking the period – this is Viking craftsmanship, all right." His ruined face snapped back to Jamie. "Now where's the rest of it?"

"I don't have it," said Jamie, trying to sound more confident than he felt. "Search me if you don't believe me."

"Don't bother," Lawrence murmured. "The brother will have it. He fancies himself the brains of the operation."

"If you try and mess with Liam, you'll be sorry," Jamie said fiercely. "He's not scared of you."

"He hasn't met me yet," rasped Mr Redgrave. "He will be. If I hadn't sent Lawrence to protect you, Mathers would have torn your brother limb from limb. And both the scrap dealer and Greg are under *my* control. They are fresh *draugr*, their minds fogged and their wits dulled in the aftermath of death. But I have been dead for centuries; the afterlife holds no mysteries for me. My mind is clear, and my will is stronger than you can ever imagine."

Jamie shrank back in his chair with a mixture of fear and revulsion. At that moment he would have given anything – anything in the world – for Sarge to come crashing through the study door, demanding his son back. But Sarge was frozen in Jamie's bed in the Lodge, his limbs locked and his eyes staring up at the ceiling.

"I know your father's beyond talking right now," Mr Redgrave told him, as though reading his mind. "But I'm betting if he could he'd say he was proud of you, Jamie. You were the one who pieced it all together, not him or Liam. I'm only sorry that you'll suffer the same fate as both of them."

"What do you mean?"

The *draugr*'s mouth twisted into a blackened smile, his eyes flicking up over Jamie's shoulder. Too late, Jamie tried to twist round, only for Lawrence to clamp a sweet-smelling rag over his face. Jamie fought to tear it away but he couldn't prevent the scent seeping into his mouth and nostrils. His head became dizzy; his limbs turned into lead weights. The last thing he saw was Mr Redgrave rising up from his chair, and then everything went sickeningly black.

CHAPTER TWENTY-FIVE

THE HOLE

Jamie came to slowly, reluctant to leave the safety of his unconscious. At first it was all he could do to get his sluggish mind to remember his name, who he was. The ground was hard beneath his back, the cold ravenous and remorseless – an icy creature gnawing on his flesh and sucking the marrow from his bones. Jamie's head was pounding from the drugged cloth Lawrence had forced over his face, his mouth as dry as sand. Groaning, he opened his eyes and sat up.

A thud of cool earth fell into his lap.

Jamie looked up, dazed, to see the night sky far above his head. He was sitting at the bottom of a rectangular hole, earthern walls surrounding him. A lantern was resting on the ground at the surface, casting a light over the iron bars criss-crossing the top of the hole, trapping him below.

It was a mortsafe.

Jamie's breath caught in his throat, and his stomach gave a sickly lurch of panic. As he struggled to stand up, his head thumping in protest, another clod of earth came down from the surface, hitting his knee. Peering up through the darkness, Jamie could see movement near the lantern on the surface, a figure striding about the edge of the grave. His heart plummeted when their face moved into the light.

Greg Metcalfe was digging into the earth, flinging shovelfuls of dirt and snow into the grave. Having come face to face with both Mathers and Mr Redgrave, Jamie thought nothing could shock him any more, but there was something particularly grim about the sight of a young *draugr*, his lithe frame unnaturally swollen and his smooth skin a sullen, seasick blue. The frozen ground should have been too hard to break but the *draugr* had the unholy strength of the undead in his arms, and he wielded his shovel like a Viking weapon.

"Hey!" shouted Jamie. "What are you doing?"

Greg ignored him, not even bothering to look down. Jamie opened his mouth to shout again, only for a shower of earth to rain down into the grave, stinging his eyes and souring his mouth. He coughed, spitting out the dirt. On the surface Greg's pale blue face was blank, devoid of any emotion, displaying no sign of pleasure or satisfaction, still less of pity or mercy. He just kept digging. The *draugr* was going to fill the grave, burying Jamie alive.

"I'll give you what you want!" Jamie yelled. "Anything! Go and tell Mr Redgrave! Just stop it!"

Another shower of earth.

"Someone HELP ME!" he screamed.

It was useless, he knew. The whole of Alderston knew the *draugr* were abroad tonight and were huddled behind locked doors, their hands clasped in prayer or clutching a bottle of strong alcohol, counting down the seconds to morning. No one could hear him; no one would come to help, even if they did.

The earth was raining down harder now, the sleety dirt freezing Jamie's feet and ankles. Sobbing with terror, he began clawing helplessly at the walls, trying to dig his way free. He had been frightened before, terrified for his life, but he had never imagined it could end like this — a slow, icy suffocation in the middle of the night, alone save for his silent, hateful executioner. Jamie slumped to the ground, defeated, and cradled his head in his hands.

Minutes passed, the time marked off by the murderous thump of damp earth into the grave. Jamie's clothes were wet through and he was shaking with the cold, his teeth chattering inside his skull. He thought longingly about being indoors like the rest of the town, somewhere warm, with the TV on and something cooking in the kitchen. People talking and laughing; a family. Jamie was so lost in his daydream it took him time to realize that the rain had stopped falling. He looked up towards the surface to see that Greg had paused, his shovel in mid-air, and was looking away down the hill. Someone, it seemed, was coming.

"What are you looking at, you big blue idiot?"

Jamie's heart nearly exploded with joy at the sound of Liam's voice. Greg took a step forward, a low growl in his throat, then hesitated. Jamie couldn't see from the bottom of the grave, but something about Liam was making the *draugr* uneasy.

"What's the matter, *Gregory*?" Liam called out mockingly. "Scared of a little flame? Or do you fight as bad as you drive?"

Greg changed his grip on the shovel deliberately and sloped away from the grave in the direction of Liam's voice. How long could Liam hope to keep him occupied? Jamie had to get free. Wiping the tears from his eyes on his sleeve, he stood up in the mire and reexamined his surroundings. The only way out was up. In the distance he heard shouts, and a loud clang – Greg's shovel connecting with a headstone? Urgent adrenaline pumping through his veins, Jamie leapt into the air, reaching up for the sides of the grave. His fingers brushed tantalizingly against the edge of the surface, and then he tumbled back to the bottom. Jamie kicked the earth in frustration.

"Jamie?" a voice whispered. "Are you OK?"

Keeley's pale face appeared through the bars of the mortsafe. She glanced around warily, her voice low.

Jamie swallowed a sob of relief. "Get me out of here, please!"

"Yeah." Keeley examined the lock at the top of the mortsafe. "I'll get right on that."

"You have to tell Liam . . . they're all in it together. Lawrence is working for Mr Redgrave, and he's a *draugr* too!"

"I think Liam's pretty busy right now," Keeley told him, "but when he's got a moment I'll let him know."

"What's happening up there? Where's Greg?"

"Trying to avoid getting fried. Liam's got a flaming torch and he's not very happy."

"How did you know I was here?"

"My mum saw them bring you here from your bedroom window. Liam got tooled up straight away. There was no way him or Mum were going to let me help, but I knew Liam couldn't get you out on his own. So I did what I always do: pretend to go off in a huff, slam a door, and then sneak out of the window when no one was looking."

"That's great, Keeley," Jamie whispered. "What now?"

Keeley dangled a set of keys from her finger, grinning wickedly. "Your brother kept going on about lockpicks but I figured it was easier to take the spare set of mortsafe keys the vicar hides in a pot behind the watch house. *No one* knows this graveyard better than me."

Examining the lock around the top of the cage, Keeley frowned and selected a key. The sounds of battle were growing louder – Jamie heard the *draugr* roar with rage, and his breath caught in his throat as he heard Liam cry out.

"Hurry up!"

"Don't rush me!" she told him crossly. "I'm going as quick as I can!"

Her eyes lit up as the lock opened with a dull clink. Taking hold of the bars, she tried to lift up the mortsafe. From across the cemetery came a soft, deadly whooshing sound, and a strangled howl — a horrible, inhuman sound that made Jamie want to press his hands over his ears to block it out. Keeley redoubled her efforts, straining at the iron cage, but it refused to budge.

"It's too heavy!" she gasped. "I can't lift it."

Then suddenly Liam was standing next to her, gritting his teeth as he lifted the mortsafe up in the air and pushed it to one side, allowing just enough room for Jamie to climb clear. His brother reached down a hand and pulled him up out of the grave. Jamie's feet had barely touched the ground before Liam had wrapped him in a giant bear hug, and suddenly Jamie had to fight very hard to stop himself from crying.

"What happened to Greg?" he asked.

"I took care of him," Liam replied softly. He winced, adjusting the rucksack on his back. "Though if my arm wasn't broken before, I'm pretty sure it is now. Are you OK?"

Jamie nodded.

"Good lad. Listen, about earlier . . . I don't know what I was thinking. This place has been getting to me, and with Sarge the way he is . . . but I should never have pushed you around. I'm sorry, OK? You were right — let's just try and get out of here alive, yeah?"

"Easier said then done," a gravelly voice replied.

256

Jamie whirled round to see Mr Redgrave shuffle out of the shadows behind a large gravestone. Lawrence was at his shoulder, a nasty smile on his face. At the sight of the rotting *draugr* Keeley blanched, and Liam's eyes widened.

"What the hell is that?" he asked Jamie.

Jamie swallowed nervously. "Meet Mr Redgrave."

"Oh, you've got to be kidding me."

"It's no joke, Liam my boy," rasped Mr Redgrave. "No one's laughing, no one's smiling. Did you really think I was just going to leave Jamie here? I *wanted* you to come charging to the rescue. I *wanted* you all together." Mr Redgrave leaned forward. "I *want* Aldus's hoard."

Liam stepped forward, took his rucksack from his shoulders and dropped it on the ground in front of him.

"There you go," he said. "Job done."

"No!" Jamie gasped. "You can't just give it to him! Why did you bring it with you?"

"Why do you think I brought it with me?" Liam retorted. "You were in trouble, dummy! If I have to fight, I will. If I have to give them the hoard, I will. The only thing that matters is getting you back."

"Very touching," said Lawrence, with a sneer.

"What was that, Withershins?" Liam shot back. "Got something to say there?"

"Nothing simple enough for you to understand."

"That a fact? Why don't you stop hiding behind your pal, egghead, and we'll see who's laughing then."

"Enough!" barked Mr Redgrave. "Lawrence, take the bag."

As the bookshop owner darted forward Liam looped his foot through the rucksack strap, dragging it back towards him.

"Not so fast," he said to Mr Redgrave. "You get the hoard – what do we get?"

"What do you want?"

Liam looked the *draugr* straight in the eye. "This ends now," he said. "The three of us get to walk out of here and leave this town without any more ghouls or zombies or Viking nutcases attacking us. Nothing happens to us or Sarge or Keeley's mum. We're free."

"Free?" Mr Redgrave raised a craggy eyebrow. "Free to tell whoever you like about Alderston? About me?"

Liam let out a bitter laugh. "You think anyone's going to believe us if we start talking?"

"Maybe. Maybe not. I haven't survived for two hundred years by taking chances. Or leaving loose ends."

Jamie shivered. Liam might not have looked scared of Mr Redgrave, but Jamie knew what the *draugr* was capable of. He was no lumbering corpse – he had killed Mathers.

"Fair enough," said Liam, with a shrug. "If you don't want to do business, we can always sort this out another way. Ask Greg. He's the pile of ashes behind that grave over there."

"You're your father's son, all right," rasped Mr Redgrave. "All hot air and threats, raging and fighting to the bitter end. Losing Greg was ... regrettable, but the young are so much harder to control, I find. They get impatient, hotheaded. Try living for a couple of centuries. You'll learn how to wait."

As Liam and Mr Redgrave stared at each other there was a loud rustle in the bushes behind the watch house. Keeley turned and peered over towards it.

"There's someone there," she told Liam.

He frowned. "Who?"

Jamie knew. *It had killed Mathers...* "We forgot something," he said quietly. The trees quivered as a deafening bellow rent the night in two. "There's more than one *draugr* left in Alderston."

CHAPTER TWENTY-SIX

FIRELIGHT

Mathers came stalking through the graveyard, a nightmare of charred flesh with ugly scars running down the left-hand side of his face, along his neck, and disappearing into the blackened remnants of his overalls. The smell of damp earth and decay that hung off the *draugr* had been sharpened by the acrid tang of burnt flesh. One eye was shut, lost in the fire-damaged half of his face where the lantern oil had gone up in the flames. The other eye was bulging with nameless, unquenchable rage.

At the sight of the group facing off around the grave, the *draugr* came to a halt. He saw enemies everywhere he looked. Mindful of their previous meeting, Liam and Keeley both slowly backed away, while Lawrence shifted nervously. Mr Redgrave alone seemed unperturbed by Mathers's entrance, the faintest trace of a smile crackling across his swollen lips.

"Welcome," said Mr Redgrave. "I wondered if we would be seeing you again tonight."

Mathers forced open half of his mouth, and a low,

mangled noise came forth. The fire that had ravaged the creature's face had also burned his vocal cords, and Jamie struggled to decipher his meaning. The *draugr* clenched his fist with frustration and repeated the word. With a chill Jamie realized what he was trying to say.

"Smiler," Mathers said again, and took a lurching step towards Liam.

"Wait!" cried Jamie, waving his arms in the air. "You've got it wrong. Sarge didn't kill Smiler – he did!" He pointed a trembling finger straight at Mr Redgrave. "He killed Smiler and buried him in our back garden as a warning to Sarge, then he told you it was us who did it. But it was Mr Redgrave!"

"Don't listen to the boy, Mathers," Mr Redgrave warned. "He's flesh and blood, not like you or I."

Mathers stopped, his deadened brain struggling to unpick the tangled lies and truths laid out before him. Jamie watched, his heart in his mouth, as the *draugr* took one ragged breath after another. Then he pointed a long finger at Lawrence. The bookshop owner paled, and took a pace back.

"You," Mathers growled, in a low voice. His hand reached up slowly to touch the charred flesh on the side of his head, remembering the battle in the field behind the Lodge, the moment when Lawrence's hurled lighter had engulfed him in flames. Lawrence glanced at Mr Redgrave, pushing his glasses nervously up his nose as Mathers took a crunching step towards him.

"Stop him!" he quailed.

Mr Redgrave looked down at his feet.

"What are you waiting for? We had a deal!" cried Lawrence, his voice almost hysterical with indignation.

"The deal was that you'd help me find Aldus's hoard," Mr Redgrave said calmly. He nodded towards the rucksack lying in the snow. "And there it is. Thank you."

Mathers continued to advance on Lawrence, his remaining eye consumed with hatred.

"Please," Lawrence said weakly, holding up his hands. "I was only following orders! He told me to make sure the boy was all right. If I had the choice, I would never have hurt you."

He turned to run away, only to catch his foot in a tree root and go sprawling across the ground. Lawrence looked up and gave Jamie a pleading look, his face drenched in sheer panic. Mathers reached him before he could stand up, the *draugr* swatting him back down into the snow with a shuddering fist. Knocked half senseless, Lawrence lay supine and helpless as Mathers placed a giant knee on his ribcage and began to press down.

"Jamie! Don't look!" Jamie heard Liam's command, but it was somehow impossible to look away, or to block out the sound of bones snapping like so many dead twigs. Mathers seemed to be barely making any effort at all, pressing his knee down with a merciless gentleness. Lawrence's scream died in his throat, and with a cough of red blood he felt abruptly silent.

All the while Mr Redgrave had been silent and

262

still, an impassive onlooker. But as Mathers begin to straighten up, the elder *draugr* reached into his waistcoat. Jamie caught a silver glint in the moonlight, and saw Mr Redgrave pull forth the small dagger he had taken from him back at Withershins. With two or three smart steps he closed the gap to the scrap dealer, raised the dagger high into the sky and drove it between Mathers's shoulder blades.

The bellow of pain was loud enough to stir the dead in their graves, for the ancient remains of decaying bones to shiver and shake. Mr Redgrave made no attempt to follow up his attack, to pull out the knife and drive it again and again into the scrap dealer's back. Jamie had witnessed Mathers shrug off Liam's shovel as though it were straw, yet this slender blade seemed to have pierced the giant's black heart. Mathers clutched futilely at the knife handle but it was just out of reach. With a low, keening groan, Mathers tumbled to the ground beside the corpse of the man he had just killed, joining him in eternal stillness.

A shocked silence fell over the graveyard like fine snow.

"You killed him!" gasped Jamie. "But ... how? Lawrence said only fire or beheading can kill a *draugr* – all you did was stab him with a dagger!"

"You stupid boy," chuckled Mr Redgrave. "Don't you realize what you brought me? It's not a dagger, it's a spearhead. The spearhead Aldus used to cut off the head of the *draugr* he battled in the chieftain's barrow, at the very moment the creature cursed him and all his treasures. This blade has been bestowed with the darkest Viking magic, and even the *draugr* have learned to fear its touch."

He walked over to the fallen oak tree that was Mathers's prone body and pulled the spearhead from his back, wiping the sickly dark blood from the blade with a handkerchief.

"Wouldn't want this falling into the wrong hands, would we?" Mr Redgrave rasped.

The carnage of the last few minutes had left Jamie reeling. With every fallen body – first Greg, then Lawrence and Mathers – the odds should have shifted in their favour, but as the *draugr* walked slowly towards them Jamie realized that they were in greater peril than ever. With all the loose ends tied up, they were the only thing left standing between Redgrave and Aldus's hoard.

"Do something!" Jamie urged Liam.

"Like what?"

"I don't know! Use the lighter!"

"And what, singe his eyebrows?" Liam snapped back. "I used up my last torch getting rid of Greg. Unless you've got a oilcan in your pocket we're in trouble."

The wind had dropped, leaving the graveyard utterly still. Then Keeley darted in front of Liam, grabbed the rucksack off the ground and started running. Before Jamie could call her back, she was flying away through the graves, her ponytail bobbing against her back.

"You want this?" she called out to Mr Redgrave over her shoulder. "Come and get it, then!"

"What is she doing?" Jamie asked Liam.

"Thinking on her feet," he replied. "The Lodge, little bro – now!"

Jamie turned and ran through the graveyard, his feet slipping and sliding in the treacherous snow. The one advantage he had over the *draugr* was speed – Mr Redgrave could only follow after them in halting, lumbering steps. Liam quickly closed the distance to Keeley, who had already dropped down through the gap in the railings and was running towards the Lodge. If they could lock themselves inside the house, perhaps they could keep Mr Redgrave at bay until dawn. Maybe daylight would force him back into hiding. Anything had to be better than this graveyard. Jamie could feel the dead watching him as he stumbled past their resting places. At any moment he expected pale hands to come scrabbling out of the soil, reaching out hungrily towards him.

At the bottom of the hill, the cemetery railings rose up to greet him. Liam was already crossing Church Lane, his athlete's stride having outstripped his brother's. Jamie plunged through the gap after him, only for his foot to go out from under him. Then he was falling.

He hit the pavement hard, the landing punching the air from his lungs. For several seconds it was all he could do to lie there, despite the shrill voice in his head urging him to get up. Winded, he rolled on to his front and tried to crawl away on his hands and knees. There was a loud thump in the snow behind him as Mr Redgrave dropped down on to the lane from the graveyard, followed by the slow, deliberate crunch of footsteps, until Jamie found himself staring at a pair of gleaming black shoes. From back near the Lodge he heard Keeley scream, and then a hand fastened itself around his throat and hoisted him into the air.

"Enough running," Mr Redgrave hissed.

The *draugr* slammed Jamie into the graveyard wall so hard he felt his teeth rattle. The rotting stench made his eyes water, and he flinched at the peeling flesh on the creature's fingertips.

"How long will it take you to learn?" snarled Mr Redgrave. "You can't escape from me!"

Jamie shook his head. Through blurring eyes he saw a shadow flit across the driveway of the Lodge, climbing up into the removal van.

"Please—" he croaked. "Can't . . . breathe. . ."

"There's nothing to fear, Jamie my lad," Mr Redgrave told him. "Death won't be the end for you, it will be the beginning. You'll live for centuries, be the master of all you survey. No one will ever dare to push you round again. Isn't that what you want, deep down? After all these years of trailing around after Sarge, sleeping in the van, being ignored, dancing to whatever tune he plays?"

The pressure on Jamie's windpipe was unrelenting. From the Lodge driveway came the sound of an engine's hacking cough as Liam tried to start the van. Mr Redgrave didn't seem to notice, so intent was his dead glare on Jamie. The van had been sitting dormant in the driveway for over a week now and the engine was refusing to start. *Another victim of the cold*, Jamie thought.

"Admit it," Mr Redgrave hissed, his breath like a grave. "I'm doing you a favour."

Jamie was too dizzy to reply. He felt himself teetering on the edge of a very dark, very deep hole. His limbs were going limp, his eyes drooping shut.

The roar of an engine brought him back from the brink; then there was a squeal of tyres as Liam stamped down on the accelerator. The removal van came bumping out of the driveway, its headlights flicking into glorious life. At last Mr Redgrave turned round, only to find himself bathed in a white glow as the van came barrelling towards him. The *draugr*'s grip went slack with surprise. Tearing himself free, Jamie threw himself to one side. The van hit seconds later, burying Mr Redgrave into the cemetery wall.

Jamie lay wheezing on the ground, his lungs burning as air poured back into them. The lane was suddenly eerily quiet, the only sound the indignant hiss of steam as it rose from the engine. Although the van hadn't had time to reach top speed, it had been moving fast enough to embed the front bumper into the brickwork. There was no sign of Mr Redgrave amid the debris. As Jamie crawled away from the van its passenger door banged open, and Liam stumbled clear of the vehicle. Blood was pouring from an ugly gash on his forehead and his arm was hanging by his side but he was alive.

As Liam walked away, he looked down at the black liquid oozing out from beneath the van across the tarmac. A strange look passed across his face – a flicker of amusement. Reaching into his pocket, Liam flicked open the silver lighter and struck up a flame. Then he tossed it casually into the dark liquid pooling beneath the van's engine.

"Get down, Jamie!" he shouted.

The oil caught immediately, a sheet of flame following a deadly trail back to the van. For a while the flames seemed content to gnaw away at the van's chassis, but then the fire reached the engine and the removal van exploded in a thunderous ball of fire, enveloping the graveyard railings and clawing at the nearest gravestones. Amid the billowing smoke, a burning figure tore itself away from the flames, and Jamie caught a horrified glance of Mr Redgrave as the *draugr* staggered away from the van towards him, arms outstretched. He managed a handful of agonized paces in Jamie's direction before collapsing in a charred heap in the middle of the road.

Every joint in Jamie's body was aching, and his skull was pounding. He sat back against the base of the cemetery wall, resting his head on the cool brickwork. The air was thick with the smell of smoke and burnt flesh. Keeley was watching from the driveway, her face bathed in the red shadow of the flames. As Liam hobbled over towards him, Jamie saw, to his amazement, that his brother was laughing.

"What's so funny?"

"Nothing," said Liam, with a shake of his head. "Everything. I don't know. This town." There was a catch in his voice, as though any second his laughter could topple over into tears. He sat down next to Jamie. "This bloody town."

PART THREE

THAW

CHAPTER TWENTY-SEVEN

SCARS

In the aftermath of the battle in the churchyard, the cold hurriedly withdrew its spindly fingers from around Alderston's throat, as though scalded by the flames that had engulfed the removal van. The destruction of the *draugr* had lifted the pall that had hung over the town like a bleak fog, the sun reappearing for the first time in days to burn through the maddening grey blanket of sky.

With the lifting of winter's icy siege, the roads around Alderston became passable once more. The first vehicle to make it over the Moss was an ambulance, urged into the still-treacherous journey by a phone call from Jennifer Marshall. Liam and Jamie looked on as Sarge was strapped on to a trolley and lifted carefully into the back of the ambulance. The patient made no sound, only the occasional blinking of his eyelids indicating that there was any life in him at all. At Caxton General, Sarge was wheeled away for a battery of tests.

Reassured by the doctors that their dad's life wasn't in immediate danger, Jamie and Liam returned to the

Lodge later that afternoon. Jamie had been reluctant to return to the scene of their desperate fight against the *draugr*, but as Liam had pointed out, they were tired and dirty and running low on money. Where else could they go? As the taxi pulled up outside the Lodge, Jamie's heart had sunk at the sight of a police car parked on Church Lane, and two officers inspecting the burnt wreckage of the van. Liam immediately bundled Jamie inside the house, and they raced up to the bedroom to watch through the window. The police were not alone – the vicar was standing with them, with Don at his side. After a few minutes the men all shook hands and the policemen headed back to their car.

Liam laughed incredulously.

"What is it?" Jamie asked his brother.

"Call me crazy," said Liam, a note of wonder in his voice, "but I think we've just seen the end of the police investigation."

"But what about all the bodies?"

"What bodies?" said Liam. "When we left here Redgrave's remains were in the middle of the road. You see them now?"

Puzzled, Jamie looked in vain down the empty lane for the *draugr*'s corpse. "It can't have just disappeared," he said. "Someone had to move it."

"Someone did," Liam replied. "Are you really that surprised? You know how people here feel about outsiders, especially the police. I'm guessing Don and his pals have cleaned up for us. All that's left is a wrecked van, and they can talk their way out of that."

"But what about Lawrence?" said Jamie, struck by an urgent thought. "He was killed by a *draugr*, remember? That means he'll turn into one too!"

"I wouldn't worry about that either," his brother said, turning away from the window. "I think we can trust the locals to take it from here."

Jamie wasn't so sure, and that night he lay shivering in bed, listening out for the tread of a *draugr* on the stairs. But when the police didn't ring at their house the next day, or the day after that, he began to realize that Liam was right. Jamie never did learn for certain what had happened to the bodies they had left littering the churchyard, but that weekend he saw a procession of 4×4s rattle out across the fields behind the Lodge, and as dusk fell he could have sworn he heard a distant crackle of flames, and caught a faint tang of burnt flesh upon the breeze.

The next morning, Jamie opened the door to find a small metal object lying on the doorstep for him. He picked up Aldus's spearhead and carefully added it to the rest of the Viking treasures stashed in Liam's rucksack in the shed.

Though Alderston's residents had stayed in their houses during the night of the *draugr*, their curtains drawn and doors locked shut, it soon became clear that everyone knew what had happened. No one spoke about it, of course – Alderston guarded its secrets jealously. But when Jamie walked down the street he was aware of eyes swivelling in his direction, nudges and respectful nods singling him out. Shopkeepers refused to take Liam's money, pressing groceries into their hands with a smile or a wink. Even Keeley claimed that people had stopped talking about her behind her back – though whether or not she was happy about that wasn't entirely clear.

"I'm not going to fall for it," she warned Jamie, as they perched on the steps by the war memorial. "Just because a couple of people have been nice to me, don't think I'm going to start wearing pink dresses and dreaming about getting a boyfriend."

"I wouldn't dare," Jamie said hastily.

"Good."

No matter what happened to Keeley, he knew, a little part of her would always be Black Maggie. You couldn't escape the past that easily – Jamie had learned that the hard way. He was reminded of it every time he passed the whitewashed windows of Withershins. The bookshop had been closed down, its collection of occult books shipped out of Alderston like a consignment of toxic waste. No one ever mentioned its owner; Lawrence had become a ghost in his own right.

One morning Jamie was walking along the main road into town when a black Mini tooted its horn and pulled up alongside him. Jennifer Marshall wound down her window.

"I'm going to the hospital to drop something off," she told him. "Do you want to come with me?"

Jamie nodded and climbed into the passenger seat. He took every opportunity he could to see Sarge, as getting back and forth from the hospital was becoming a bit of a problem. The charred wreck of the removal van had been towed away the day after Sarge had been taken to Caxton General and neither of them felt comfortable calling Roxanne's Cabs – even if a guilty and apologetic Don had told Liam they could use their cars for free.

It was warm inside the Mini, the car's heater purring smoothly. A jangly pop song was playing on the radio. Jennifer Marshall smiled at him as she drove away.

"It's a good job this snow is starting to clear," she said chattily. "At one point I thought I was going to have to try and ski to get to work!"

"Yeah."

Adults amazed Jamie sometimes. After all they had been through, all Keeley's mum could think about was the weather! She said nothing about the night Mathers's *draugr* had attacked Sarge, and the fiery destruction that had ensued afterwards. But it hung in the air between them, like the dusting of ashy snow still covering the rooftops.

As they left Alderston behind in the rear-view mirror and the Mini entered the wood on the Moss, Jamie suppressed a shiver. Even the passing of the *draugr* couldn't completely strip the trees of their menace.

There remained something about the place that had hold of him – a tangle of tree roots and damp pondweeds around Jamie's heart that he didn't think he'd ever be able to shake off. He was glad when the car passed through the other side and out on to the Moss. The road was covered in grit, snow piled up on either side. Keeley's mum drove slowly, waiting in the lay-bys to let the vehicles heading in the other direction pass first.

"I heard that they've put the deeds to the Lodge in your dad's name," she said to Jamie. "After what your family's done for this town, it's the least they can do."

Jamie shrugged. "I guess."

"Do you think you'll be stopping in Alderston for long?"

"I don't know. I think so."

"Keeley will be pleased."

"Really?"

Jennifer laughed. "She's not very good at showing at it, but Keeley likes you a lot. She'd be devastated if you left. Though for God's sake don't tell her I said that," she added hurriedly. "She'll kill me."

Jamie sat quietly as Keeley's mum chatted away, looking out through the window over the Moss. It was funny how quickly things changed. Sitting in the passenger seat used to be second nature to Jamie, but after his time in Alderston, snowbound and shipwrecked, it felt odd being in a moving vehicle again. All those years in the removal van, the thousands of miles they had travelled up and down the country, the endless service stations and scrapyards, the ever-present fear of being caught: it all felt like a lifetime ago. The van was wreckage now. Scrap metal.

It took another twenty minutes of driving along gritted roads to reach the hospital, a large complex of buildings on the outskirts of Caxton. A plastic bag danced in the wind blowing across the car park. Jamie followed Keeley's mum as she hurried up to the automatic doors and through into reception. He was already familiar with the route up the staircase and through the long corridors to Sarge's ward. When they reached the double doors outside the ward, Keeley's mum squeezed Jamie's arm and left him alone, heading off towards the nurses' station.

Sarge was lying in a bed at the end of the ward, surrounded by bleeping machines. He didn't turn his head when Jamie approached, his blue eyes dim and blank. A catatonic state, the doctors called it. Something to do with post-traumatic stress disorder. There had been a lot of long words when they'd explained it to Jamie and Liam, and Jamie hadn't been able to follow it all. He got all he needed to know from Liam's grim expression.

"Will he come out of it?" Liam had asked the doctor.

"It's hard to say," the doctor had replied. "The brain is a remarkably complex piece of machinery, and has its own methods of coping with sudden shock or trauma. Your father might be like this for years, or he could wake up tomorrow. We can't make any promises."

Liam had nodded slowly. There wasn't much else he could do. Now Jamie pulled up a chair beside Sarge's bed and sat down. He stared at the floor.

"Um, hi, Sarge," he said awkwardly. The doctor had told them it was important to keep talking to Sarge, but Jamie couldn't help feeling self-conscious mumbling away with no hope of a reply. "Things are all right, I guess. I think we're going to hang around Alderston for a while. The van's a wreck but we can stay in the Lodge for as long as we like, and Liam's got some work at that gym in Caxton. We thought his arm was broken but it's not too bad and healing pretty quickly. So that's good."

He trailed off guiltily. Of course it wasn't good. How could anything be good, how could he be happy, with his dad like this? Throughout his life Sarge had sworn to stay out of prison, only to find himself trapped in a cell of even smaller dimensions. Inside his mind was he furiously pacing up and down, banging on the bars and raging for someone to free him? Jamie shook his head, banishing the thought from his mind. He got up and gave his dad a fierce hug. Sarge's cheek bristled like the striking surface of a matchbox against his face.

"We'll be waiting for you when you come back," Jamie whispered. "I promise."

He talked for another ten minutes or so, until he had run out of things to say. As he walked away from his dad's bedside he saw Keeley's mum waiting for him in the ward doorway.

"Ready to go?" she asked brightly.

Jamie nodded.

"Come on, then," she said. "Let's get you home before your brother starts wondering where you are."

She put her arm around Jamie's shoulder and gave him a little hug. He was surprised how comforting he found it. As they walked out of the ward into the corridor, a door opened and a nurse with a blonde ponytail popped her head around it.

"Ooo, Jen, I was hoping I'd catch you," she said. "Have you got a sec?"

"Of course, Rachel." Keeley's mum glanced down at Jamie. "Stay here, love. I won't be long."

She disappeared inside the room, leaving Jamie alone in the corridor. He walked over to the window, his trainers squeaking loudly on the floor. The afternoon was melting away before his eyes, the streetlights in the car park already shining brightly in the gloom. Visitors hurried back to their vehicles, struggling against the growing wind. Jamie leaned his forehead against the window, feeling the cool kiss of glass on his skin.

"Leave me alone!"

Jamie jumped at the shout, a girl's cry that had erupted from one of the private rooms down the corridor. A low voice murmured something in reply, only for the girl to let out a loud, choked sob. Jamie pulled away from the window and began walking along the corridor towards the room. The door had been left ajar, allowing him a glimpse inside. The blinds had been drawn over the windows, plunging the room into darkness. A blonde-haired girl in a hospital gown was sitting bolt upright in bed, being comforted by an older, heavyset woman. With a jolt Jamie recognized her: it was Roxanne.

"It's all right, Donna!" she said soothingly, stroking the girl's cheek. "Nothing can hurt you now, I promise."

"You don't understand!" Donna retorted, through clenched teeth. "Every time I close my eyes I keep seeing it, over and over again. I can't stop seeing it!"

"Give it time, sweetheart," said Roxanne. "You'll get better."

"I'm just so *tired*!" Donna told her, with a catch in her throat. "At night I lie there trying to think about anything but the accident, but just as I'm about to fall asleep, I'm back in Greg's car on the Moss. The radio's on loud and he's laughing. There's a van up ahead and he swerves past it ... I tell him he's driving too fast but all he does is grin and push down harder on the accelerator. Then we're in the woods."

"Hush now, Donna," Roxanne told her. "Don't go back there again."

"Go back?" Donna let out a bitter laugh. "I haven't left. I'm still in that car, Mum – don't you get it?"

Her eyes glazed over, and Jamie knew that she was back in the front seat of Greg's car.

"*Look out, Greg!*" screamed Donna. "*You're going to hit her!*"

She threw her hands over her face, and collapsed sobbing into her mum's arms. As they hugged each other Jamie felt a hand on his shoulder gently pulling him away from the door.

"Come on, love," said Jennifer Marshall, closing the door softly. "Let them have their privacy."

"Sorry."

Jamie walked away down the corridor, the sound of Donna's sobs echoing in his ears. Outside, tall trees bent and sashayed in the wind. The sky darkened.

CHAPTER TWENTY-EIGHT

OVER

When he returned home, Jamie was greeted by an unexpected sensation as he walked through the front door – warm air, enveloping him in a soft hug. The radiator in the hallway was ticking happily, and when Jamie pressed his hand against the surface it was gloriously hot to the touch. The stale tang that had soured the air inside the Lodge had melted away, and there was an unexpected waft of cooking smells coming from the kitchen. As Jamie unzipped his coat and kicked off his shoes Liam came padding barefoot into the hallway.

"Warm enough for you?" he asked.

"You fixed the heating!" Jamie exclaimed.

Liam's eyes crinkled with amusement. "I can't take all the credit," he said. "A guy came round this afternoon and sorted out the boiler. Wouldn't even take any money for it – said it had all been taken care of."

"By who?"

"Who knows?" Liam shrugged. "Thanks to you, everyone in this town is trying to give us free stuff. Make the most of while you can – you earned it." He beckoned him into the kitchen. "Come and have a look at this."

Jamie followed his brother through the doorway to find the worktop strewn with half-opened tins and vegetable peelings, and dirty saucepans piled up in the sink. A murky stew was bubbling fiercely on the stove.

"Thought I'd have a go at this home-cooking lark," Liam said, stirring the stew with a wooden spoon. "Here, try a bit."

Jamie cautiously tasted a drop of stew from the end of the spoon.

"Well?" said Liam. "What's the verdict?"

Jamie pulled a face.

"Yeah, I thought so too." Liam tossed the spoon back in the stew. "OK, so the cooking might take a bit of practice. Got to start somewhere though, eh?"

"If I were you, I'd start with the takeaway menu."

"Cheeky monkey!" Liam gave Jamie's arm a dig. He grinned. "Come on, let's go see what's on the telly."

They ate takeaway pizza in front of the TV, watching a football match together. Jamie barely followed the game, relishing the warmth as it melted months of tension from his shoulders. Liam chatted non-stop about the football, falling about laughing when one of the players missed an open goal. When the game had finished, he fished out the remote from down the side of the settee and turned the TV off.

"Early night tonight," he told Jamie. "I'm starting at the gym tomorrow morning. And we're going to have to see about enrolling you in a school. Can't have you sitting around on your bum all day while I'm out doing a honest day's work."

"OK," said Jamie, getting to his feet. Even though he was tired, he could have happily stayed where he was for hours. He looked around at the warm, brightly lit room. "Do you think Sarge would have liked this?"

"Course he would," Liam said quickly – maybe a bit too quickly. Jamie wasn't sure he believed him. The people of Alderston might have given them a house, but Sarge had long since forgotten how to sit still. If he had been well, they would have probably been back on the road by now, navigating midnight motorways with cargos of illicit treasure. More than ever, that thought seemed like a terrible prospect to Jamie.

He had reached the bottom of the stairs when he heard his brother call out his name.

"It's over, little bro," Liam told him softly. "All of it. Time for a fresh start, eh?"

Jamie nodded, and climbed the stairs to his bedroom. He closed the curtains quickly, preferring not to look at the graveyard. Would it always be this way, he wondered – a constant reminder of the terrors he had been through? Would he ever be able to look out at Alderston church and not think about Lawrence being crushed to death, or Mr Redgrave staggering down the road as the flames engulfed him? Jamie could feel the tiredness in his bones as he climbed into bed, but despite the lifting of the chill from his room, sleep proved elusive. He spent a restless night tossing and turning, nagged by an inexplicable doubt. It was nearly dawn before he finally tumbled into an exhausted, dreamless sleep.

Jamie woke up feeling wearier than before he had gone to bed. As he brushed his teeth he saw the dark circles beneath his eyes in the bathroom mirror. Liam had already left for work: he'd left a note on the kitchen table calling Jamie a rude name, and a twenty-pound note in case of emergencies. Jamie poured some cereal into a bowl and ate breakfast slowly, staring out through the blinds over the window. When he had finished eating, he washed up the bowl and left it to dry on the rack. Then he put on his coat and shoes and went out to the back garden. It was mid-morning, a pale, defiant sun hanging low in the sky. Although it was still cold, the wind had lost its mean edge. Jamie pushed through the hedges at the back of the garden and leaned on the fence, looking out across the fields towards the wood at the edge of the Moss.

It's over, Liam had said.

Jamie opened the door and walked over to the shed, threading his way through the rusty jumble of tools. His brother's rucksack was where they had left it, stuffed inside a lawnmower. It gave off a guilty jangle as Jamie picked it up and slung it over his shoulder. Aldus's hoard was all there, every ring and coin he had taken from the barrow, every bracelet. Every spearhead. Jamie and Liam had been at a loss for what to do with it. They could have sold it through one of Sarge's contacts, but neither of them wanted to return to that world. They could have handed it in to a police station or a museum, but there would have been too many awkward questions. And more importantly, by taking the hoard out of Alderston, weren't they risking taking the curse out of the small town and into the wider world? Who else might die with a ring on their finger, or a coin in their pocket, only to rise as a *draugr* afterwards? Jamie didn't know, and neither did his brother. So they had left the cursed treasure in the shed. Jamie half-believed that Liam was hoping someone would come and steal it from them, removing the responsibility from their shoulders.

It's over, Liam had said. But it wasn't, not with this still here.

Adjusting the rucksack on his shoulder, Jamie hopped over the fence and started walking. The snow had lost its crisp certainty, squelching beneath his feet as he tramped across the field. In the distance, a flock of birds banked and wheeled as one, drawing out a wavering shadow across the sky. Instinctively Jamie knew he was following the same trail that Kitty Hawkins had taken two hundred years earlier, with a cold silver ring on her finger and her heart fluttering like a small bird.

The past doesn't go away here, Keeley had told him in the wood.

Jamie moved like a sleepwalker, so wrapped in thought that he barely noticed his feet were already soaking wet. With every step the wood on the Moss grew larger before his eyes, tangled branches clawing their way up into the air. As the field petered out at the trees' edge, Jamie stopped and looked back at Alderston, the comforting outline of the Lodge masking the graveyard on the other side. It felt as though he was standing on a kind of threshold, with the way ahead shrouded in darkness. Jamie took a deep breath, and entered the wood.

The draugr are Viking undead, Lawrence had said, *condemned to forever haunt the location of their death like guard dogs of Hell. . .*

The unnatural winter might have released Alderston from its grip but there was still a chill amongst the ageless trees. Branches shivered and dripped with melting snow in the wan sunlight. The ground was wet and slippery – once more Jamie thought of Kitty, dancing merrily through the trees, her mind lost in romantic dreams, her laughter echoing the empty wood.

My Kitty drowned in the pond, Mr Redgrave had told him. *The thing that came back afterwards wasn't her. I killed it.*

Echoes from the past, all floating around inside of Jamie's head. He was so engrossed that he almost walked past the bank; it was the sound of water streaming down the slope that made him stop. Only a week had passed since he had ignored Keeley's warning and scrambled to the top of the bank, but it felt like a lifetime ago. The going was harder this time, Jamie's feet slipping and sliding in the mush as he struggled over the top. He was out of breath by the time he had reached the top and looked down the other side.

The thawing snow had not stripped the pond of its brooding atmosphere, even if the cradle of silence in which it rested had been disturbed by the loud trickle of running water. The water was still black as ink, a blank wasteland drained of light and warmth. As Jamie stood and watched, a chunk of snow fell away from the bank and slipped into the water.

Look out, Greg! Donna had screamed. *You're going to hit her!*

Puzzle pieces, slowly sliding into place. Jamie had the eerie sensation of his mind becoming loose, like a hot-air balloon that had slipped its mooring rope. It felt as though he was looking down at a different Jamie, a Jamie he had no control over. From up in the air he watched as this Jamie edged down the slope to the pond's edge, and then stepped into it.

The water was so cold it made him gasp, so cold that it burned. Jamie gritted his teeth and waded on until the icy water lapped at his knees. His feet had gone numb. Somewhere in the corner of his mind, a voice was screaming at him to stop this craziness and get out of the pond, only to be drowned out by an eerie calm, a certainty that he was doing the right thing. Jamie needed to get to the heart of the pool, where he could leave the hoard so no one would ever stumble across it. The bottom of the rucksack was wet but it didn't matter. He took it off his shoulder and opened all the pockets. Then he tipped the rucksack upside down. Coins and jewellery came tumbling out in a priceless silver waterfall, splashing into the pond and sinking slowly to its depths. Jamie waited until the bag was completely empty, checking the bottom to make sure no stray coins had become stuck in a nook or cranny. He let out a deep sigh, feeling a heavy weight lift from his shoulders. *Now* it was over.

He turned to wade out of the pond, and the world exploded.

A creature erupted from the water with a roar that ripped through the wood like a bush fire; a bloated monster with a sickly blue tinge to its skin and lank hair matted with twigs. Its eyes festered with sullen hatred like two open wounds. A grotesque parody of the beautiful girl it had been two hundreds years before.

Too late, Jamie understood. Mr Redgrave had lied. He hadn't killed Kitty. Loyal beyond death, he had covered for her, protected her. It was Kitty who had stepped out in front of Greg's car and killed him; it had been Kitty who'd stood beneath Jamie's window and gazed up with hungry hatred. It was to Kitty that Mr Redgrave wanted to show Aldus's hoard, to prove that he was the best man. For two centuries she had dwelt at the bottom of this pool, a *draugr* tethered to her watery grave, only occasionally venturing forth to satisfy her terrible hunger. And now Jamie had walked straight into her lair.

Kitty lunged at him with her arms outstretched; long, wicked fingernails slashed Jamie's face. As Jamie stumbled backwards, he lost his footing and splashed down into the water. Kitty let out a triumphant screech and leapt on top of him, forcing him beneath the water with her bloated weight. The world was a confusion of bubbles and roaring water. It was a hopeless struggle – the *draugr* was far stronger than Jamie, slamming him against the bottom of the pond with ferocious force. Fighting for his life, Jamie managed to wriggle free, just enough to get his head above the surface and snatch a desperate gasp of air. Then Kitty dragged him back down again, her hands fastening around his throat and beginning to squeeze. Through the tears of pain Jamie could see Kitty's mouth twist into a smile. He could feel the coins he had strewn across the pond bed beneath his back. For the first time Jamie felt a flicker of fear – not that he would die, but that the last thing he would ever see would be the *draugr's* malicious smile. He was dizzyingly light-headed, dark blotches raining down in front of his eyes. Then his hands brushed against an object tangled up in the weeds. A blade. With the last remaining vestiges of his strength, the final bubbles of air in his lungs, Jamie snatched Aldus's spearhead and drove it into Kitty's belly.

The creature let out an ear-splitting scream that deepened in pitch as it grew in volume, until a bestial, inhuman snarl rang around the wood. As Kitty released him Jamie broke the surface of the water with a splash, coughing and retching. The *draugr* was writhing in pain in the middle of the pond, clutching forlornly at her punctured stomach. Dark liquid was oozing from the hole where the arrowhead remained lodged – Aldus's final strike against the dark curse the Viking chieftain had brought with him when he had first stepped foot upon the northern shores a thousand years earlier.

As the *draugr* sagged, the hatred drained from her eyes, and for a brief second Jamie thought he caught a glimpse of the girl she had once been as her head bowed into the water. Then Kitty's carcass sank slowly beneath the surface of the pond, and the wood toppled into an astonished silence.

CHAPTER TWENTY-NINE

THE AFTERWALKER

Jamie walked home.

It was getting dark now, the road and the hedgerows melting into the shadowy horizon. Jamie wasn't sure how much time had passed since the struggle in the pond. Hours, he guessed. He was very cold, and very tired, and it was hard to think straight. Every step required concentration. He had fallen over several times, and each time it was harder to get up again. Escaping the pond had used up his last reserves of strength; he'd clawed his way to the bank as Kitty's lifeless husk sank to the bottom of the pond like a shipwreck. Jamie didn't dare look behind him as he crawled away, forcing himself to his feet and stumbling away through the trees. He had no idea which way he was going. All he knew was that he didn't dare stop. Then, without warning, the trees came to an end, and he found himself standing at the spot where, a lifetime ago, Greg's car had ploughed into the wall. The road was empty. Soft birdcalls rang out in the fading light.

Jamie's sodden clothes had stuck to his skin, trapping

him in a freezing embrace. Ice had set into the marrow of his bones and the chambers of his heart. His teeth were chattering so violently his jaws ached – whether because of the cold or the shock, Jamie couldn't say. Probably both. His ribs were aching and his throat hurt, whilst his face was covered in long red marks where Kitty's rotten nails had marked him. Although it hadn't really been Kitty, Jamie told himself. She had died two hundred years earlier. It hadn't been Kitty who had choked him with such dreadful strength, and tried to drag him to the depths of her watery hell. Surely she would be grateful to Jamie for ending her body's torment. Even if he didn't feel elation at having slain a monster, Jamie should have been relieved that he had somehow survived. But he didn't feel anything except the numbing cold. Maybe feelings would come later.

Streetlamps were flickering into life ahead of him, beckoning Alderston out of the darkness. On the hilltop, the church stood solemn and proud, as it had for nearly a thousand years – Aldus's gift to the town that took his name, even as his hoard became its curse. But it was over now, finally. Was it? It was hard to be sure. Jamie really was very cold. It was tempting to stop walking and to curl up beneath one of the hedgerows out of the wind. Then Jamie thought about his brother waiting for him back at the house, and Keeley, and – unexpectedly – Sarge, watching on from the prison of his hospital bed and his shattered mind.

Cresting the hill, he looked down Church Lane and saw the Lodge, its windows bright rectangles of light. The front door was open and Liam was standing outside by the front gate, anxiously scanning the horizon. He straightened up at the sight of his brother, folding his arms, his expression a mixture of anger, relief, and a little amusement. Then Jamie passed under a streetlamp, revealing his drenched clothes and the cuts on his face, his shivering, shaking body. Crying out with alarm, Liam flung open the front gate and came running up the road.

Almost there now. Jamie walked towards his brother, each step taking him further beyond the reach of a cold, unforgiving past, and closer to where light and warmth, and the promise of tomorrow, lay waiting to claim him.